WITCH FAITH

WITCH FAITH

NARRELLE M. HARRIS

FIVE STAR

An imprint of Thomson Gale, a part of The Thomson Corporation

THOMSON

GALE

Detroit • New York • San Francisco • New Haven, Conn. • Waterville, Maine • London

THOMSON

GALE

ALL RIGHTS RESERVED

LIBRARY OF CONGRESS CATALOGING-IN-PUBLICATION DATA

Witch faith / Narrelle M. Harris.—1st ed.
  p. cm.
  ISBN-13: 978-1-59414-468-4 (alk. paper)
  ISBN-10: 1-59414-468-0 (alk. paper)
  1. Witches—Fiction.
PR9619.4.H365W57 2007
823'.92—dc22

2006035414

First Edition. First Printing: February 2007.

Published in 2007 in conjunction with Tekno Books and Ed Gorman.

Printed in the United States of America on permanent paper
10 9 8 7 6 5 4 3 2 1

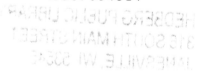

For my brothers: Richard, Stephen, Bryce, and Jason.

ACKNOWLEDGMENTS

I would like to thank Jehni, for constructive criticism and the threat of toe-screws (since thumb-screws would hamper my typing); Yvon for inspiration and the lyrics of "The Sword of Stamford"; and Tim for his ceaseless support. Without the three of you, I'd just be a woman with a lot of unfinished manuscripts stacked up in boxes under my bed.

My thanks also to John Helfers of Tekno Books and Pat Estrada, who has edited *Witch Honour* and *Witch Faith* and brought me to account on some very important points! Without the two of you, I'd just be a woman with a lot of finished manuscripts filled with continuity errors, stacked up in boxes under my bed.

PROLOGUE

Leenan Ni Breshtan flapped her leathery wings once, then stretched them taut in order to glide on the air currents back towards Tyne Castle. She felt heavy and sluggish and rather pleased with herself. It had been a good morning's hunting, between the birds, a rabbit, and the fat karadil she had killed. The karadil was the best kill of the lot—good meat, and she had prevented the river carnivore from taking any of the King's sheep or harming the young shepherd who tended the flock.

The sheep had been a temptation, but her human mind was still stronger than the dragon instinct that led her to hunt. Occasionally she worried about that dragon instinct. When she had first changed shape and then found herself unable to change back, the hunting had sickened her. It was simply dragon nature—there was nothing evil or cruel in it—but her own human nature was revolted by the need to kill, the instinctive pleasure in the hunt and the taste of hot blood. Now, the speed and skill and power of it were a joy. She lost herself in the dragon nature of it, for a time.

Leenan banked and flapped her great wings again, summer light gleaming from her bronze scales. A chorus of high calls greeted her and four darts of bright colour swooped up to join her. Four dragons, a third her size as was normal for the creatures, fell into formation around her. From the start they had accepted her as their pack leader, which she found alternately amusing and alarming.

Leenan circled high over the castle, catching scents and sounds from within its walls and from the city of Tyne which it protected. She was aware of some of those below watching her and her colourful entourage, though whether in curiosity or fear did not reach her. In recent weeks, Witch Leenan had become a familiar sight, wheeling above the towers or perched on the highest spires, and she liked to think that the fear had dissipated. Her sharp sight scoured the courtyard for a sign of her fellow witches, but they must have been busy elsewhere.

She swooped down towards the tower above the western gate to the city, catching the spire with her front paws. Her back claws scrabbled inelegantly for a moment until she could wrap her tail around the spire for anchorage and her wings spread and shifted until she regained her balance. Her small pack found purchase nearby on the archway over the gate.

A woman passing below with a basket full of fruit on her back looked up, startled, and made the warding sign with her right hand at the giant witch-dragon above. Then she nervously stuffed that hand into her pocket, afraid that she had caused offence.

Leenan sighed. Lords, people could be so stupid. And ungrateful.

Well, she supposed they weren't obliged to feel grateful. It was a witch, in league with the King's cousin, who had usurped the throne and driven King Armand into exile, leaving them under the reign of a power-hungry woman and a sadist for a year while Armand Bakar-Tyne recovered from his wounds and his scattered court regrouped.

It was in Berrinsland, a long way from Tyne, where the court jester, the Captain of the Castle Guard, and one of the King's agents had stumbled across the small group of witches living in a large village. Sylvia, on hearing the tale of a witch's intervention in ordinary human affairs, had decided to see that side of things neutralised. The four of them—Sylvia, Magda, Tephee, and herself—had followed, and at times it seemed their presence was more of a hindrance than a help in finding the King and reclaiming his throne.

Leenan supposed that Tephee's behaviour was enough to cause residual suspicion, even considering that most ordinary folk were uneasy enough with witches. The young girl had been enamoured by the Witch Zuleika's power and what Tephee perceived to be her invulnerability—to fear, to pain, to rejection. In an attempt to protect herself, Tephee had become a danger to others and only at the last did she realise mere power was not enough. She had saved them all, then, draining Zuleika's power, allowing the King's army to fight, unimpeded by magic.

That was why this woman's apprehension irked Leenan so. Tephee had nearly died to fight for a King to whom she owed no fealty and had lost her magic for a time. Sylvia, likewise, in trying to defeat the witch had come close to death and even now was unable to perform more than the most feeble of magic. Leenan herself had found the strength to change her shape to make her own contribution during the battle, only to find herself later trapped in the reptilian body. Magda—her strange friend Magda—was the only one to emerge largely unscathed. Perhaps it was the peculiar connection she had with the Arc priesthood and the First King and His Lords who had brought life to this world a millennium past. Perhaps it was just dumb luck.

Whatever it was, even Magda knew their welcome was wearing thin. Four witches—even with three of them near crippled in the service of this foreign King—were too many for comfort, even in the most witch-tolerant of nations. They were guests of King Armand, not subjects, with no role at court they either wanted or were suited for. Soon it would be time to return home to Berrinsland.

There was a subdued sense of activity at the gate below and Leenan craned her neck to see Captain Evenahn emerge in his training leathers, accompanied by a shorter, stockier man. Like the Captain he was lean and fit, with the stance and step of a soldier. His skin was paler than the olive tones of most inhabitants of Tyne, and there was something odd about his accent. She could hear them discussing one of the new guardsmen. There had been a lot of recruitment in the last few weeks, many from the ranks of those Tynean farmers and townsfolk who had joined the King's ragged army along the way.

Captain Evenahn glanced up at her and gave her a half salute. There was one man who was not intimidated by her, whichever body she wore. The other man followed the Captain's gaze and acknowledged her presence with a respectful nod. As they turned to walk along the wall, Leenan heard Evenahn say dryly:

"I'd have thought you'd bow and offer up a prayer."

"Only during Mother's Moon, Captain," he replied lightly. "You Arc folk have some funny ideas about Leylites."

Evenahn paused, then muttered an apology, which made Leenan pause. Kiedrych Evenahn was not generally sorry for anything. The other man murmured a reassurance that he was not offended and gripped the Captain's shoulder briefly in a comforting gesture.

So, thought Leenan, *Kiedrych has a friend. And a Leylite at that. Wonders never cease.*

CHAPTER ONE

"Your Highness, you have to let me see to him." Magda stood her ground, glaring at the King across the floor of his study. The table behind which he sat was laden with books and scrolls; the wall behind him covered with a rug woven with a map of Tyne and the surrounding lands. More maps, books, and scrolls were scattered on the floor around him, part of his work to fulfil his promises of trading rights to his allies and some form of representational government to his subjects.

King Armand Bakar-Tyne had agreed to this audience, knowing what it would be like, knowing that he would have to face it sooner or later. Perhaps this witch would help him to resolve the issue of what to do at last with his traitorous cousin.

"To what end?" he demanded. "So that he can go to trial and then his execution as a fit and healthy man?"

"If it's such a certainty he'll be executed, why bother with a trial?" she snapped, and the King winced. "For God's sake, Your Highness, the man is suffering. He's *dying.*"

A scowl darkened his brow, and his brown eyes were bright with anger. "He plotted against his King and kinsman; he slaughtered my council; he robbed from my people and turned good men into traitors with lies and threats. He did everything it was possible to do to destroy this land for his own ambition and he got nothing less than he deserved. Am I now meant to feel sorry for him, for *his* pain, after he caused so much?"

"Letting him die like this is cruel and stupid and makes you as bad as he ever was."

The King gave her such a look then that, had she not been a doctor, and a witch, she might have turned tail and run. But she didn't run, and the murderous anger in him faltered and fled.

"It seems . . . so pointless. A trial must surely lead to his conviction, you see that. The evidence is irrefutable. Healed, he is a threat. Convicted and exiled, he is a threat. This way, he is alive and cared for, and can't hurt anyone further. It's the only compassion I can spare him."

"He is in agony. Let me at least try to reduce that pain." She spread her hands helplessly. "His body and mind are both so shattered it would take weeks—months—to even enable him to walk without aid. Let me see him. Please."

King Armand looked like he might deny her once more, but he frowned and sighed. "Go then."

She took her leave of him and left. She didn't waste time going back to her own rooms for any equipment, but hurried downstairs to the small courtyard and crossed to the tower. She was a little breathless when she got to the prisoner's quarters, so she merely nodded sharply at the door. It had a marvelously imperious effect and the guardsmen, dressed in the livery of the Palace Guard, stepped aside and held the door for her without question.

The tower cell was not large but it was clean and dry, with kindling in the fireplace in case the night became too cool, as it sometimes did in summer. It was sparsely furnished, having once been used as a study for the treasury accountant, then left bare when King Graym died and his son Armand took the throne. It was also the room in which Saebert Bakar-Cadron had cut Zuleika's throat to save himself and been in turn mortally wounded by her last desperate surge of magic. It had been scrubbed clean of her blood. It was light and well aired.

Its long, narrow windows opened onto blue sky and birdsong. King Armand had done his best for his undeserving cousin, but it was still a prison.

Saebert, thin and broken, was lying on his bed—more unwarranted kindness, it was a proper bed, clean and firm with light, soft bedding to put the least pressure on his smashed body. Saebert's gaze drifted around the room and rarely focussed on anything for long. He saw her and smiled feebly before turning his head to look at the ceiling.

Magda stifled a sudden urge to cry at the sight of him. Some behaviour for a doctor. Her friends had paid a price for Saebert's betrayals, too. She had her medical duty to tend to him; her humanity asked compassion for him; but he wasn't worth *crying* for, for God's sake.

With an effort, she composed herself and went to kneel at his side.

"Saebert," she said quietly, "I've come to help you, if I can."

His eyes brightened again and he looked straight at her. "Can you?"

"I want to try, if you'll let me."

"Yes . . . of course . . . it hurts . . . so much, you know."

"Yes." That urge to cry welled up again, and Magda quelled it sternly. "But you understand what will happen if I heal you?"

But his gaze had drifted off again, and he was humming to himself.

Magda hesitated to begin while he was so unaware of what it would mean. Perhaps he would understand better later on. She couldn't heal him completely in one day in any case. Swallowing hard against her pity for him, Magda leaned over Saebert's broken body and closed her eyes.

He hadn't been lucky enough to break his back entirely when the Witch Zuleika had pitched him across her chamber into the hard stone walls in her last surge of vicious defiance as he had cut her throat to save himself. He might have died then, or at least become quadriplegic, and there would have been less pain. Under the circumstances, such a horrible ending might have been better.

Carefully, she found the worst of the injuries—badly healed and yet unhealed bones; damaged tissue—and gently, slowly, induced changes. Not a perfect healing, but a start.

She drew out of him and, blinking dizzily, she smiled. Saebert was gazing at the ceiling still, but his eyes were bright with unshed tears.

"Saebert?"

"Why are you doing this?" he whispered.

"Because it's what I do. I'm a healer. I can't let you suffer pain like that if I can stop it."

"Once I'm well . . . Armand will have to kill me."

Magda looked away, the tears threatening again. "I know. I'm sorry."

"Oh, nothing for you to be sorry for," he said, and his eyes closed, squeezing out a tear from each dark eye. "At least the pain has gone. Whatever comes next, it won't hurt as much."

Magda didn't know what to say.

"I have to go now," were the words that she was finally able to get past her lips. "I'll come back tomorrow . . . if you like."

Saebert's eyes were open again, and he was staring at the sky through the tower window. Bright, stunning blue, not a cloud to be seen through that narrow opening in the stone of his prison. A beautiful day.

Knowing that he had gone again, Magda stood slowly, careful not to lose her balance in her weakened state, and walked to the door. She knocked faintly and the guards opened it for her to let her out again.

As the door was closing, she heard Saebert's voice say, "Thank you," followed by a sigh.

Damn. She farewelled the guardsmen and began her descent downstairs with dignity, only giving in to the tears once she was out of sight. Saebert Bakar-Cadron was a liar, a thief, a killer, and a traitor. He wasn't even repentant. But he didn't deserve the death he was suffering. No one did.

Before emerging in the courtyard she dried her face on her skirt. She felt weak still, and ravenously hungry. The scent of fresh-baked bread made her salivate and she looked around quickly to identify the source. Loman, Baker Dhug's youngest, was carrying a tray of bread across the courtyard and into the King's Hall.

"Loman!"

The boy stopped at her call and turned to find her, smiling as he did so. Holding the tray carefully balanced on his head, he changed direction and went to her.

"Morning, Witch Magda."

"Good morning, Loman. Hold still a minute . . ." She reached up to take a loaf of Dhug's fruit loaf and wobbled uncertainly on shaky legs. "Bend down a bit . . ."

"You shouldn't, ma'am," Loman said dubiously. "That's the King's loaf."

Magda's stomach rumbled. "What, this one in particular?"

He giggled. "No ma'am, they're all the King's loaves. For his lunch today."

If I don't eat something soon I'm going to faint. "And I'm the King's guest. I don't think he'd mind, really. Do you?"

"Yes, Witch Magda. I mean, no, ma'am. I don't think so." Loman appeared torn between his duty to deliver the goods and Magda's pale features. "There's always plenty," he decided at last, shifting the tray to help her to a small fruit loaf and a savoury bun. "Is that all, ma'am? Only, I'm supposed to go back for another tray in a minute, and Dad'll be wondering where I am."

17

"Off you go," she shooed him through an inelegant mouthful of bread. "And thanks."

"Pleasure, ma'am," he assured her, and scooted off.

Magda ate some more of the bread before moving away from the support of the door frame. She didn't want to go back into the castle and risk seeing King Armand just yet. Instead, she kept close to the wall and skirted around the edges of the courtyard, looking for a place to sit. Across the yard, a number of the Castle Guard, Kiedrych in their ranks, were being put through their paces by a rugged and serious man who moved with natural precision. The guards were partnered and were going through a series of stylised movements with wooden practice swords, and while most of them were very good, only a very few came close to the economical grace of their Sergeant.

"They look good, don't they?" said a familiar voice close by. Magda drew her eyes away from the men to smile at Sylvia, sitting on a bench with a sheaf of papers in her lap and a stick of charcoal in one hand. She had black smudges on her nose and at the corner of her mouth.

"I didn't see you there."

"I know you didn't," Sylvia smiled, then she gazed away, at the soldiers, and Magda was reminded painfully of the way Saebert drifted away in the middle of conversations. She studied Sylvia for a moment, noting for the first time how her upswept cheekbones and almond-shaped eyes had hollowed and darkened recently. Her features, always exotically elfin, were pale and ethereal now. For the first time since they'd met, she was looking something like her forty years.

"What are you doing there?" Magda asked, sitting down beside her friend.

Sylvia looked at her, then down at the pictures in her lap. "Oh, just some drawings. I used to draw a lot, when I was younger." She allowed Magda to take some of the completed ones. "It helps me to focus," she said simply. She rubbed her nose again, leaving a fresh smudge.

She's using it as therapy, Magda thought. She had been uncertain in her own attempts to heal the injuries Sylvia had suffered at the Battle of Tyne. Magda didn't know enough about the brain, she didn't know why Sylvia's memory had suffered, or her ability to concentrate, and was wary of doing further damage by meddling in such a delicate area. Better to leave it and see how well Sylvia fared on her own.

She looked at the pictures. The first few were of the courtyard, quick and simple sketches of the shape of the buildings around it, the well in the centre, birds wheeling overhead. Magda realised with fascination that the first picture had been drawn early in the morning, and the second some hours later. The shadows were different. So much in so few lines.

"These are good," she said. Sylvia, head down over a new picture, didn't appear to hear her.

The next picture was of a dragon perched on a watch-tower, tail wrapped around it for anchorage and wings slightly spread for balance as the long neck poised elegantly—the dragon was listening to something. Leenan, she realised, and glanced up into the sky to see where she was. No sign.

The fourth picture was a study of faces spread across the page—on one side, Loman grinning cheerfully under the tray of loaves he had taken across for breakfast; another showed the tall figure of a bored guardsman at the gate—his face unseen but the slump of his shoulders and lopsided posture indicative of his state of mind; several pictures of Sylvia's cat, Pywych, who was asleep under the bench; some faces deliberately smudged out in a fit of dissatisfaction, others only half drawn, as though the artist had lost interest. One was of Kiedrych in one of his sterner moods. Sylvia had spent some time on that one. There was another of the Sergeant and Magda was surprised to see that for all the roughness of the man, his eyes were very gentle.

Magda leaned across to see what Sylvia was drawing now, and shook her head with embarrassment to see it was herself. Her long, bony frame was only hinted at while her face with its high cheeks, long nose and chin, and clear blue eyes were more detailed. Sylvia had drawn her long, dark hair in its habitual loose waves. She looked tense and worried in the drawing.

"Do I really look like that?"

Sylvia looked up at her, then back down at the drawing. "At the moment." She grinned at Magda, bent to add a few more strategic lines, and when she came away, Magda's charcoal-drawn face had lines of dismay on it as well. Her grin widened, then her expression became suddenly solemn. "What's wrong?"

Magda shrugged and looked away, back at the soldiers. The Sergeant was demonstrating a defence technique with Kiedrych. From nowhere, Tamalan came running up—he tripped and tumbled over himself before landing back on his feet in front of the two of them—and grinned, sweeping into an extravagant, courtly bow.

Magda's heart thudded, as usual, at the sight of him. It was so typical that of all the men she had met, she had to fall for the court jester. Who was only interested in being good friends. Damn him. If she hadn't been a witch, would he have been so respectful?

"I may have lost my memory and my concentration span," Sylvia said quietly next to her, "but it hasn't made me stupid."

"Of course not," said Magda resignedly. "I just . . . I just don't want to talk about it."

"Is it Tam?" Sylvia indicated the jester, speaking animatedly with Kiedrych before taking to his heels to disappear in the King's Hall.

"No." Magda managed a wan smile. "But he isn't helping much."

A figure appeared at the castle gates, running straight for them. "Sylvia! Magda!" The girl skidded to a halt in front of them and panted, grinning, for a moment. Pywych, disturbed, glared disapprovingly at her and stretched fussily before sauntering off to find a quieter place to nap.

Magda laughed. "What's the rush, Tephee?"

Tephee pressed a hand into her diaphragm to try to get her breathing back to normal. Then she waved her hand towards the gate where a tall, cloaked man was entering, leading a brown horse. "It's Sebastian!" she finally gasped out. "From the Temple."

Kiedrych had gone to meet him and the traveler had removed his riding cloak to reveal the silver hair and the Arc priest robes beneath. They spoke a moment before Sebastian waved to them across the yard, his lined face lighting up in that wonderful smile Magda remembered so well. She waved back. She liked Sebastian, although he made her a little uncomfortable as well. The few days their group had spent sheltering at the Arc Temple in the mountains, before moving on to find the King, had been both educational and worrying.

The three witches walked across the courtyard to greet him. A shadow flickered over them and a faint reptilian trill high above told them that Leenan had also seen their visitor and was swooping in to join in the reunion.

The trill changed pitch halfway down, however, becoming a warning shriek. There was another sound, a human cry of triumph, then of protest. The wind whistled over leather wings, scales rattled, and there was a thud, heavy and disturbingly wet.

Leenan's dragon form twisted aside and up, then spiraled down to land beside the thing that had fallen from the tower. She rattled her scales, distressed and winded, and spread her wings so that she wouldn't have to see the mangled body beside her on the stone.

Magda knew there was nothing to be done, but she reached out anyway. Dead. Of course. She couldn't get the sound of that triumphant cry from her mind.

She couldn't believe that after one session, Saebert had found the strength and the will to drag himself to the window, let alone lever himself over the ledge. She had seen bodies retrieved from space after implosion accidents; radiation burns, torn limbs, the shattered remains of worse deaths than his. Not once had she felt a horror as deep and as repellent as this.

Her reunion with Sebastian consisted of him holding her shoulders as she sank to her knees and vomited.

Chapter Two

There were celebrations at the Guardsman's Inn early that evening. The inn's actual name was The Hogshead, but it was a favourite among the Castle Guard and was irrevocably stuck with the name by which it was more commonly known. It stood not far from the west gate, a modest two storey stone building, sturdy enough to withstand the occasionally destructive revels of the King's elite. The doors opened onto a large front room, filled with tables and stools. A door at the back of this room, beside the bar, led to a smaller chamber, usually employed by army officers for gambling sessions. Another door at the side led to the alley which ran alongside the inn and down to the privy.

Off duty guardsmen themselves took up most of the front room, barring one table in the corner. This was occupied by their Captain and his two friends.

It was hard being Captain of the Castle Guard. Almost as hard as it was being the Sergeant, responsible for training and a good deal of the discipline. Kiedrych and Cadogan Ho had fallen into one another's company almost by accident as a result, two years ago, and were now irregular drinking companions. The others tended to give them plenty of elbow room, but Tamalan cheerfully joined them in their isolated corner on this occasion, drinking to the general public relief at Saebert's suicide.

Tamalan was, in fact, less cheerful and considerably more frustrated than when he'd first joined them. Kiedrych was being difficult this evening—his first big marital row with his new wife had put him into a dark mood these last two days—and Cadogan didn't seem to get the idea.

"No, no, no," he was saying, wagging his head emphatically and almost falling off his stool, "S'gotta have a beat before the last word. It's part of the joke, y'see?"

Kiedrych was frowning sullenly. "But it doesn't rhyme," he insisted.

"It's called a half rhyme. It's fine. Ask anyone. Ask Kay . . ." Or maybe not. At least until she started talking to him again. "For the Lords' sake, Rych . . ."

"Son of a blood-worm couldn't sing, anyway," Kiedrych muttered on regardless. "Sounded like a scalded cat."

"We're not singing about his singing," Tamalan explained impatiently. "We're singing about his very tiny d . . ."

"Sang like a fart," Kiedrych overrode him. "Rode like a sack of wheat. Armand may look like a farmer, but he can ride."

"That's the second verse," Tam interjected, "when he rides the black snake."

Cadogan shook his head, his brows drawn down over his blue eyes, hiding the unexpected mildness in them. "That's an ananol . . ." He frowned harder, producing the kind of expression that had been known to terrify both new recruits and enemies on the field alike. "An an-al-o-gy," he said with great care. "Means somethin' else."

" 'Course it means somethin' else! The black snake is . . ."

"Repr'sents his . . . his . . . seducshion . . . by power. Riding the power of ambition and self-interest . . ." He warmed to his subject, an earnest look settling over his rugged features. Tamalan groaned and clasped his hands over his face in despair.

"Couldn't ride for shit," asserted Kiedrych sullenly. Then he smiled unpleasantly. "Fell like a rock, though."

"Hit like a bag of bread dough," Tamalan added, then looked

queasy at the memory.

Cadogan had been thinking about it very seriously, and he leaned forward to talk to Tam. "You mustn't forget to incorporate his downfall at the hands of his colleague . . . it has a rightness, a circularity of moral implications . . ."

"It's a dirty song, for crying out loud!" Tamalan slammed a fist down on the table, upsetting his tankard which skittered over the edge. Cadogan, with hardly a thought, caught it and set it back on the table. Tamalan scooped it up again, muttering about humourless drunks. "Is this something about Leylites," he demanded of the Sergeant, "or is it just you?"

Cadogan pursed his lips and appeared to give the question due consideration. Kiedrych punched his one-time foster brother roughly on the shoulder with a black look of warning, eliciting an exaggerated howl of pain.

"I think," said Cadogan, before the two men could take the row further, "it's just me."

"I don' have anything against Leylites," Tamalan mumbled, rubbing his shoulder and giving Kiedrych a wounded look. Kiedrych arched his eyebrow at him, an acid and quelling expression. Tamalan ducked his head and muttered an apology to Cadogan.

Cadogan, who had not been in the slightest bit offended, filled up the jester's cup once more, then Kiedrych's. He found it both amusing and touching that his friend felt this need to defend him against religious insult, even when the Captain indulged in it himself. The comments he received here in Tyne were few and mild and of little consequence. Cadogan had been born in a country where being a Leylite was to invite death. Tyne was a tolerant place, on the whole.

Soon after, Tamalan gave up trying to teach either of them his new song and had drifted over to the other tables. When he had ten men bawling it out at the top of their lungs he jumped onto the bar to conduct. Kiedrych, wincing at the noise, decided it was time to leave. Cadogan placed three coins on the bar and followed Kiedrych out into the street.

Seeing Kiedrych standing still as stone in the middle of the street, Cadogan paused at the doorway, searching the shadows for trouble. It materialised in the form of Kayla Brittane, the Captain's wife, as she took another step towards her husband.

"I've been looking for you since I heard about Saebert. Are you all right?"

Cadogan saw Kiedrych shake his head, slowly. He couldn't see the Captain's expression, but Kayla reacted to it by launching herself into his arms. The Captain's tense posture melted as he wound his arms around her and buried his face in her long black hair.

"I'm sorry," she was saying. "It was stupid. It was a stupid fight. I'm sorry."

"No . . . my fault . . . my fault . . ."

The Captain never admitted to being at fault, Cadogan thought with a wry smile, only ever to have "made a decision without all of the facts to hand."

"I've been so worried about the council this week, about what will happen . . ."

"Don't worry. The King will see to everything. The Lordship will come to me, the estate, everything. Don't worry . . ." Words were lost in a deep kiss—long, increasingly passionate, and right out there in the middle of the road.

Cadogan wasn't sure if the pang he felt was relief that he didn't indulge in such public displays, or envy. It wasn't only being the company Sergeant that made him a loner. He was different, too. Born and raised in other lands, adopted by Tyne but still an outsider, after all these years. He'd found a place for himself, but he was still too much a soldier for a gentlewoman, too much a philosopher for a farmer's daughter.

And too much of a thinker for his own good. Cadogan grimaced, annoyed at his unworthy envy. It was good that young Kiedrych had finally found a soulmate. A worthy match for him, too, as the last month had borne out.

"It's about time," he said to them suddenly, and smiled warmly. Kayla, previously unaware of his presence, jumped and blushed, though Kiedrych, still mildly inebriated, only nodded solemnly. "Get him home," Cadogan advised her.

"I can get myself home," said Kiedrych, and with his arm around Kayla's shoulders he left steadily enough.

Cadogan could see them as they paused in the shadow of the castle wall, sharing another long kiss before disappearing through the gate and towards their quarters above the barracks.

With a sigh, Cadogan raked his fingers through his dark hair. The alcohol was singing melancholy in his blood; the muffled sound of raucous laughter behind him added glum harmony to his mood. He felt lonely.

Then the inn door opened and Tamalan tapped him on the shoulder.

"Where's Rych?"

"Gone home. With Kayla," he shouted back, over the noise.

"Bugger. Well, do you sing high, middle, or low?"

"Low," he replied quizzically. "Why?"

"Need another voice." Tamalan beckoned him back inside. "Just follow the others. Don't start analysing the bloody thing."

Grinning, Cadogan returned to the inn, surrounded by warmth, sound, and his brothers in arms.

Magda could still not face food, despite feeling dizzy from the afternoon's efforts. Sebastian sat with her in the witches' chambers and coaxed her to take some spiced wine while he watched with concern. She drank some, for his sake, but it felt sour in her stomach.

She kept thinking: *I didn't mean to heal him so he could kill himself.*

King Armand had come in to see her, once, but his expression had been one of guilt mixed with relief and one sharp, accusing look from her was enough to make him leave again.

Leenan had curled up by the fireplace and regarded her friend with unblinking green eyes, refusing to think about how Saebert had fought against her as she tried, instinctively, to catch him as he fell. The dragon part of her thought of him as *bad meat,* but her human mind saw the distress his death had caused her friend and was sorry for it. Tephee sat on the floor beside her, absently stroking Leenan's dog, Alard, lying alongside his changed mistress and looking equally mournful.

Tephee kept wondering if she could have stopped Saebert from falling, if she'd wanted to enough. She hadn't tested the limits of her returned power yet. Perhaps she might have been able to save him. If she'd wanted to.

Sylvia sat on her bed, her bare feet tucked up under her skirts, frowning slightly. She had in fact tried to reach out, but her power was so scattered now she hadn't been able to focus except for an instant. Leenan had almost caught him then, but he'd fought her, and had fallen, leaving Sylvia momentarily disoriented and then with a blinding headache for the remainder of the day.

Sebastian sighed and gave up trying to get Magda to eat. "It wasn't your fault," he told her.

"If I hadn't gone to him . . ." she began, then bit her lip. She would *not* cry again.

"If you hadn't gone to him, he would have been lying in that prison in pain and despair," Sylvia said brusquely. "And you would be here feeling guilty for his pain."

Magda raised her head to look at the older witch. "He'd still be alive, at least."

He didn't want to be alive, Leenan mind-spoke with them. *He actually tried to* bite *me, did you know? To keep me from catching him?* Leenan tilted her head to one side quizzically, still trying to comprehend the desperation of anyone who would try to bite a dragon.

"I don't say it to be cruel," Sylvia said, her tone softening, "but it's the truth. At least this way it is over. For him, for the King, for everyone. If Saebert hadn't wanted this, he could never have pulled himself to the window."

"And I gave him the strength to do it." Magda closed her eyes, frowning at her own bitterness.

What is it you feel bad about? came Leenan's voice in her head alone. *That he killed himself, or that he used you to do it?*

Tephee wondered at the ferocious glare Magda directed suddenly at the dragon on the hearth, and the rattle of scales that followed. Magda shook her head.

"I don't want to know," said Magda at last, leaving all but Leenan puzzled. Magda scrubbed a hand across her tear-puffed face and composed herself to meet Sebastian's gaze.

"I'm sorry," she said. "You came such a long way and you haven't even had a chance to speak to the King."

"I didn't come to see the King," Sebastian said, glad of the change of subject, "though I am pleased to see him returned to health and house. Word had reached the Temple of your success, praise the First King."

"You didn't come all this way just to see us?" Tephee asked, delighted and doubtful at once.

Sebastian smiled at her, immensely pleased to see how the child had matured since he'd last seen her. Her often surly expression had vanished, making her hazel eyes bright and lovely. Her brown hair had grown longer; she had grown taller, too, he thought, and looked both leaner and prettier than she had in the spring.

"Of course I did," he replied, "though I must admit to an ulterior motive." At Tephee's questioning look, he smiled at Magda. "I was hoping that Witch Magda might advise me about a matter that arose recently. A messenger from one of the western temples has come with stories of an Arc vessel on Marin Kuta."

"Marin Kuta?" Magda tried to remember the tapestry King Armand had hanging in his study, a map of the explored world. The large island west of this continent. Unusual oriental-looking symbols had delineated it as a country quite different to Tyne. "Oh." Then she realised what he had said. "A vessel?"

Sebastian nodded. "And visitors from the True World."

Magda's second "Oh" was heavy with a dozen realisations at once. That she finally had someone from her own world to talk to. That she wasn't sure she wanted to. That they might have showers and chocolate and music rods of Beethoven and Nova-Jak's last recording. That they might not be friendly. That even a freighter might have enough medical facilities to find out what was wrong with Sylvia.

"Oh," a third time, and she breathed out slowly.

CHAPTER THREE

King Armand leaned back in the large, ornately carved chair in his audience hall, looking very regal until he began to gnaw absent-mindedly at his knuckle.

Kiedrych, standing to attention to the left of him, glanced down to watch his King considering the matter, then raised his eyes to meet Kayla's. She stood with the witch who had come at the King's request, and she smiled at him. He almost smiled back, before remembering himself and coming to attention again. Queen Jailan, sitting in the chair on Armand's right, noticed the exchange and suppressed the urge to roll her eyes. Perhaps the Captain would not be quite so acid, for a few days at least. Then she caught Tamalan's eye as he slouched against the wall at the back of the audience room. He grinned and mopped his brow in a parody of relief. She did smile then, but quickly hid it.

Before the King and Queen stood Magda, looking annoyed.

Armand rubbed his temple and shook his head. "I'm not sure you should go. Marin Kuta isn't a very welcoming place for your kind, Witch Magda."

"I'm not sure," said Magda coolly, "that it is your place to decide if we go or not."

King Armand grimaced. "I am not forbidding the journey. As you are so fond of pointing out to me, you are not a subject of mine, and I have no power over you at all." He shifted forward in his chair and held his arms out beseechingly to her. "But can't I be permitted to worry? To advise, at least?"

Kiedrych observed that King Armand was very good at that earnest gaze, which he used very effectively in the new council as well. The most unusual thing about it was its absolute sincerity. The King actually meant what he said. Most of the time, Kiedrych didn't know if he should admire it or scorn it, but he had to admit that it was, for the most part, effective.

The earnest gaze worked as well on this occasion too. Magda sighed, and glanced away, then back to meet his eyes. "It's good of you to worry. But I have to go."

"At least let me send someone with you."

"But I don't even understand what the problem is," she said. "I'm a witch, damnit, I can look after myself. Your Highness."

"I know you can. But Marin Kuta isn't like Tyne. Or Berrinsland, or even the Southern Kingdoms. Witches aren't welcome."

"What, they have a sign on the port saying 'Witches Go Home!'?" Magda was finding this hard to take seriously. What in the First King's name could possibly be the danger?

Kayla stepped forward and Armand, grateful, surrendered the floor to her.

"The problem, Witch Magda," said Kayla, "is that they believe that witches are evil, agents of the Red Lord. Magic poisons those it touches. It is a corruption of humankind's role, which is to work and sweat and bleed to the glory of the First King and his Lords."

"But I . . ."

"The troupe went through there only once . . . about six years ago. There had been rumours of a naval buildup there, and King Graym had sent my father and I to find out what we could . . ."

That's right, thought Magda with a little surprise, *she was the King's Agent before the Battle of Tyne.*

". . . we found a fleet and defensive battlements in place

along the coast—not planning for invasion though. They just wanted to keep the . . . heathen nations . . . out. When we stopped at the port, we found a crowd in the square." Kayla shifted uncomfortably, unhappy with the memory. "There were . . . fires." She shook her head, knowing the others were waiting, and regained control. She looked directly at Magda and spoke abruptly, forcing the memory out. "There were half a dozen fires in the square, each built around a stone pillar. Tied to each pillar was a witch, burning. They weren't all dead yet."

"And . . . none of them . . . fought back?"

"I expect most of them had, to start with. I remember one of them, about Tephee's age, had arrows through her thighs and chest."

Magda swallowed and looked at Armand. "You weren't kidding when you said it wasn't welcoming to my kind."

"It wasn't always so bad. There was also a witch cult there at one time—how such a small island came to have two such extreme views I don't know, but about thirty years ago there was a civil war—the witch worshippers were defeated—the details are uncertain, but it seems that most of them were slaughtered—and these people remained."

"Armand, I have to go. Sebastian says that a ship landed there . . ."

"A ship . . . ?"

"An Arc vessel," Magda amended hastily. She hated trying to explain this part. "Only it isn't from the First King, or the True World. It's . . . oh, for God's sake, it's just a kind of sky ship, all right? With people from my world. I have to go. If it makes you feel better, I don't particularly want to. But they might have a cure for Sylvia. I can't pass up a chance to do what I can. And Sebastian intends to go anyway. He needs someone with him."

Armand didn't fully understand what was meant by a sky ship, or Magda's world, but he understood that it was not something she wanted to discuss. He also understood very clearly that despite what she knew, she would go anyway. He sighed.

"It is your decision, Magda . . . but please . . . let me send someone with you. You will get safe passage as far as the coast, and perhaps he may be of assistance in Marin Kuta. I can do that much for you."

Magda regarded him silently. She was still angry with him over Saebert's death, and he knew it. He still wanted to help her . . . protect her, even, which she found both disconcerting and touching. "All right, Your Highness. I would appreciate an escort. Thank you."

The King stifled a sigh. "You're welcome." Then he did sigh, heavily, and spent a moment studying the back of his large hands. Kayla glanced at Magda, then Armand, and stepped forward to bow slightly.

"By your leave, Your Highness . . ."

"Hmm . . . ? Oh, yes, of course. Thank you Kayla—I know it was distasteful for you. And I'm glad to note you've come back home."

She glanced up at Kiedrych again, who was steadfastly watching the back wall, and grinned. "So am I, Your Highness." She bobbed in a courtly farewell and left, Tamalan following her out. As the door closed they heard the last of his low-voiced: ". . . you're both *impossible* . . ."

There was another long silence. Finally, Armand raised his eyes to meet Magda's gaze again. "I have given him . . . the best burial I could."

Magda's lips pursed. She had hoped to avoid talking about this.

"I know it's not much . . ."—here he shrugged—"there was nothing else I could do for him. You were right. I was cruel." A shadow passed over his features, and he looked disturbed.

"You did what you thought was best, Your Highness—for the kingdom, and for your subjects."

"I did what was expedient," said Armand harshly.

"Armand . . ." Magda laid a hand on his arm. "Even if I had acted sooner . . . he would still have killed himself. He didn't have the courage to face those he'd hurt, to accept their judgement. He died so that he wouldn't have to confront you. He was a weak, selfish, cruel man."

"Was I any better?"

"Infinitely," she assured him, and she found she was no longer angry with him. "It's over, Armand. We don't have to forgive him. Just forget him and move on."

He sighed. "Yes."

"I should go now. I have a lot to prepare."

"Of course . . . I will speak to Captain Evenahn about who should go with you."

The witch left and Jailan rose to follow. She kissed Armand on the cheek. "Ask him about the Sergeant," she suggested before sweeping gracefully out.

Armand turned to Kiedrych. "The Sergeant?"

"Sergeant Cadogan Ho, Your Highness. He's responsible for training. He comes from Marin Kuta, originally."

"Oh, yes . . . the pale one. I wondered where his family came from."

"They were refugees from the war you mentioned. He doesn't talk about it; I don't ask. But he knows something of the area."

"Would he object to going back?"

Kiedrych shrugged. "He's a soldier. He'll go where he's told."

"Yes. Well. I'll talk to him first."

"Shall I send him in now?"

"Yes . . . a private audience." Armand produced a wicked grin. "I wouldn't want your presence to scare him into agreeing to do anything he doesn't want to do."

Kiedrych met the grin with a mild look under an arched eyebrow. "Regrettably, he's the one soldier under my command I've never been able to terrify."

"Lords!" said Armand, his grin growing wider, "he must be a dragon-hearted fellow."

Kiedrych merely shrugged. "I dare say. Though he once told me his aim was to be more . . . tree-like." He finally smiled at Armand's puzzled look. "No, I didn't understand it either. By your leave . . . I'll call him in now."

"Thank you, Captain." Armand rubbed his nose thoughtfully as Kiedrych departed. *Tree-like?* he wondered.

Sergeant Ho had time for only a brief cleanup before reporting to the King's audience room. He was wearing the Guard's standard training outfit—black trousers and tunic with a leather overshirt bearing the Royal Knot in red over the left breast. He had been admitted by the two guardsmen on duty at the door who had looked questioningly at him. He had given them an impenetrable gaze in return and strode in, hair still damp from the water he'd thrown over his face to cool down before answering the summons.

Cadogan stood to attention before the King's chair. The King was not in it currently, though the door at the back of the room, leading to another chamber, was ajar. The sounds of paper rustling could be heard there.

Cadogan tried not to frown. He had sweated out his hangover in a vigorous morning training session for which the old guard and new recruits had both roundly cursed him. He had remained unaffected by their muttered complaints—he could see that they were improving, and that they knew it as well. He was quite clear-headed now, and that, unfortunately, was the problem. He had heard the rumours brought by the Arc priest; he knew why King Armand wanted to see him. What he didn't yet know was how he really felt about it.

"Ah. There you are. My apologies for keeping you waiting." Armand strode into the audience room, a bound folio of reports in his arms.

"Not for long, Your Highness," Cadogan assured him. His accent retained some of the lilt of his ancestors, despite having lived in this kingdom for most of his life.

"Captain Evenahn tells me that you are originally from Marin Kuta."

"Yes, My Lord."

"I have no doubt you have already heard the stories going around about Sebastian and Witch Magda."

"Yes, My Lord."

Armand paused and looked up at the Sergeant, studying him for a moment. What he saw was a soldier, compact and hardy. He was clean-shaven and wore his hair in the short style that was standard for the Guard. He had a high forehead, a strong chin and, Armand was surprised to note, very few worry lines. Ho stood at attention, heels together, arms by his sides. He looked to Armand as stiff and unyielding as a marbletree. *But I doubt that's what he meant by tree-like,* mused the King. Marbletrees did not usually exude such an air of equanimity.

Armand tossed the folio onto a desk and dragged out a stool. "Come sit with me—I can't discuss this with you all the way over there." There was a hint of humour in his tone, and a cautious welcome. After a moment, Sergeant Ho took the other stool.

"How may I be of service, My Lord?"

"I have been studying old reports from Marin Kuta . . . the last reliable one came from Ayman Brittane, some six years ago, and nothing since. They've become isolationist to an almost paranoid degree, although they still trade with the western coastal nations. I suppose you know all of this."

Cadogan gave a slight shrug. "I hear things."

"What do you hear lately?"

"That the persecutions continue." His tone was very even and his steady gaze looked past the King's shoulder to the tapestries on the wall behind. "It hasn't been much better since my family fled during the war."

Armand nodded. The Marin Kutan Purge was thirty years ago. Sergeant Ho had been a boy of ten, according to the brief entry in the enlistment journal, when he, his parents, and siblings had stowed away on an outgoing trading vessel. The information was scanty, but it appeared that several family members had died during the escape, and eventually Dae Ho brought what remained of his family to the court of Tyne and swore allegiance to the King that had given them sanctuary. He had joined the army, and within a few years his son had followed him into Tyne's forces.

Dae Ho had brought an unusual fighting style with him and had taught some of his techniques to his unit. He had died during the Tyne Rout, when Saebert Bakar-Cadron had slaughtered the old council and driven the King into exile. Cadogan Ho knew those same exotic moves and had, for five years, been instructing the Castle Guard, barring that same year of exile. He practiced his religion discreetly. He performed his duties diligently. He had few friends.

That was the sum of what Armand had been able to discover, reading through old records and talking to those at court who knew old Ho and his son.

Armand frowned and pulled at his lower lip. Sergeant Ho waited patiently. Finally, the King braced his arms against his thighs and sat straighter in his chair.

"I have a problem, Sergeant Ho. I think you might be able to help, but I'm not at all certain you will want to."

Cadogan raised an eyebrow. "I have sworn myself to your

38

service, Your Highness. You have the right to ask me whatever you wish."

"To ask, perhaps. But not to order. And I won't."

"The Arc priest and the Witch Magda," said Cadogan solemnly, taking his eyes from the wall and meeting the King's gaze at last. "They insist on going to Marin Kuta, don't they?"

"I'm concerned, but I can't stop them."

Cadogan's blue eyes had darkened. "It isn't safe."

"She knows that. She insists all the same."

Cadogan frowned. "She won't be reasoned with?"

"Have you ever tried to reason with a witch?" asked Armand, laughing ruefully.

Cadogan's expression changed again before resuming an impassive stare. "Not for a long time."

"It isn't easy."

"No. It's not."

"I want to send a guide with them. Someone who knows the country. Perhaps someone who can keep them out of trouble until they find what they're after."

"I can do that."

"I know. But you're no safer than they are, are you?"

Cadogan was still for a moment, then shook his head, slightly. "Not much. But safer. And I know the situation."

"You don't have to go, if you would rather not."

Cadogan looked surprised at this. "You ask me to go. I will go."

"*Asked*, Sergeant Ho. You have a choice."

The Sergeant considered this for a moment, then smiled crookedly. "If you say I do, My Lord. I'll take them."

"Are you sure?"

"Yes, Your Highness. I am double-bound to the duty, by my oath to you and by my faith." Before Armand could question him further, Cadogan bowed. "It is a great honour, to serve both my King and the Mother in this way." He straightened and smiled reassuringly. "I want to go."

Armand wanted him to go, too. Too much to argue against it further, though he knew it would not be an easy journey, for many reasons. "I'll prepare a Letter of Protection. It should give you safe passage to the coast at least, and passage on a Tyne ship to Marin Kuta. It might afford some protection there, as well, though I can't guarantee it will be much. Anything you need, give a list to Supply and you'll have it."

"Thank you, Your Highness."

"Don't thank me, Sergeant. I've no doubt that in a few weeks you'll be cursing me. But thank *you*."

Sergeant Ho simply saluted and, at the King's dismissal, left the audience room.

He strode down to the courtyard and stared across it, at the stones of the training yard, the walls, the gate which had only recently been fully repaired after the Battle of Tyne. For a moment they felt distant, alien almost.

After thirty years, he was still, in some ways, a stranger here. Now he was to return to Marin Kuta. To the homeland he had barely known, where his faith was reviled, where his brother had died a martyr protecting the Witch Akiko, in vain. Where he might do the same for the sake of the Mother Incarnate in the form of the Witch Magda. And gladly, too.

Surely I'm too old for this, Cadogan thought, a little light-headed. *Surely I'm not worthy.* He closed his eyes and reached out with his relatively blunt senses, seeking the Mother. *But I have been chosen, and I'll accept the task with a glad heart.*

It was twilight before the Sergeant had finished his duties and took leave to go into the city. He walked steadily, hardly noticed despite his pale skin and Guard colours—he had a way of moving with the city folk, of gliding among them like a cat. But when he stopped to buy some bread, and later to bargain for an elegant perfumed fan and a brightly coloured scarf, he knew how to draw attention.

Kynwyn was playing with a kitten outside the house when he arrived. She looked up and jumped to her feet with a grin. "Cadogan!" She ran at him with childish glee and leapt into his open arms.

Cadogan swung the six-year-old around and laughed when she planted a kiss on his rough cheek. "How's my baby sister today?"

"I'm very well, thank you, sir," she answered primly, then spoiled the effect by glaring at him. "I'm not a baby. I'm nearly seven. Did you bring me a present?"

"Don't I always? Here." He deposited her gently on the ground and pulled out the scarf for her. Her brown eyes grew large and she could barely bring herself to touch it.

"Oooh. Cadogan. It's like Mama's, only better."

"Try it on," he said, and helped to wind it around her shoulders and over her blonde hair.

"Do I look as beautiful as Mama?"

"Every bit as beautiful," he assured her.

"You spoil that child," said a woman emerging from the front of the house. Cadogan smiled at her and kissed her cheek, then presented her with the fan. Lyria exclaimed with delight and shook her head. "You spoil the both of us."

You're all the family I have left. Who else am I going to spoil? he thought, but he only shrugged. Lyria NiDaggio was some years younger than him and he'd never been able to think of her as his new mother as such. He was grateful to Lyria for the happiness she had given his too-much bereaved father before he too was finally left to bleed his last into the Mother's soil at the Tyne Rout. Sometimes he wondered if his family had been cursed by the Red Lord—Rudig murdered at Marin Kuta; baby

Koto drowned during their escape; his mother Mariko dead soon after and then finally, Arika taken by the Fever. His father had at least been able to die for a reason, though that was precious little comfort. Cadogan had been desperate with worry for Lyria and his half sister during that awful year of exile. He'd once tried to get back into Tyne to find them, but the Usurper's troops had recognised him long before he ever reached the city and he had nearly sent his own flesh back to the Mother before he had escaped. The Mother clearly hadn't wanted him yet, however, and he finally struggled back to Jailan Kesma's lands and spent an uncomfortable month in the infirmary there.

He absently rubbed at his ribs—the scar was only a fine line and didn't bother him much now—and he smiled ruefully at Lyria's questioning look.

"Let's go inside," he suggested. Lyria arched an eyebrow at him but led the way through the door without a comment. Kynwyn, wrapped in her scarf and swaying back and forth in what she imagined to be graceful courtly movements, skipped nimbly between the adults so that she could curtsey to them as they crossed the threshold. Cadogan bowed in return and the girl giggled.

Lyria poured cider for them both while Kynwyn arranged herself prettily on a stool. She offered to hold her mother's new fan and then sat there, the picture of six-year-old poise, fanning herself with perfume and pretending she was Queen Jailan.

"What's wrong, Cadogan?" Lyria asked, sitting at the table with him.

Cadogan unhitched a heavy pouch from his belt and placed it on the table between them. "This month's pay, plus a few bonuses. It should keep you both for a good while."

"How long is a good while?" Lyria swept an errant lock of dark-blonde hair out of her eyes and regarded him steadily. "Where are you going?"

"The Captain will look out for you while I'm gone. He'll make sure you're all right."

"No doubt. But where are you going?"

"Marin Kuta."

Lyria's eyes widened, then she glared at him. "Why? You're mad to go back. I know what that place did to you. I know what it did to your father. You can't . . ."

"I must," he said simply, and her anger gave way suddenly to the fear that was behind it.

"Why?"

"The Witch Magda has business there. King Armand has asked me to go with her, to try to keep her safe. I'm double-bound to the duty."

Lyria bit her lower lip and glanced towards her daughter, who was watching them both with solemn interest.

"Are you leaving, Cadogan?"

"Yes, Kynwyn. I have to go away for a while."

"Back to Kuta?"

"That's right."

"That's a bad place," the girl pronounced slowly, warning him, the way he warned her against wandering down into the city.

Cadogan's expression changed briefly to a melancholic wistfulness. "Not always, Kynwyn. It was beautiful once. I lived there when I was small. Our father was born there."

Kynwyn chewed on her bottom lip, a childish version of her mother's anxious expression. Cadogan returned his gaze to Lyria.

"Before I go . . . I want . . . would you allow me . . . to carry some of his ashes back to Marin Kuta with me?"

Her face set stiffly against the suggestion, but Cadogan just sat there, looking at her with entreaty, trying not to pressure her with how important this was to him. And she knew it was important. Dae had told her once, that this might be asked one day. Of course, at the time he thought he still might live to die of old age. When you died, some of your remains should go back to the place where the Mother first recognised you in the world—a lock of hair, or a cutting from a plant that had grown on your grave. It was not the Leylite way to burn their dead, but ashes were as suitable as anything. Of course, the Mother would still find you, but it was proper to complete the Wheel, if you could.

Strange notions, but they were what Dae had believed, and Lyria respected that, even if she didn't understand it.

The early evening meal they shared was subdued, and afterwards the three of them went to the small strip of garden behind the house, to the shrine where the small urn nestled in its alcove in the outer wall of the house. The shrine still held some withered flowers and a lock of hair from the last Lords' Day offerings.

Reverently, carefully, Cadogan took the heavy lid from the urn and shook some of his father's ashes into the jade-green-enameled vessel he had brought for the purpose. He gently replaced the urn and went to seal the container. Kynwyn was watching him, large eyed, and before he could replace the lid she cried out:

"No! Wait!"

Cadogan paused and looked at his little sister, worrying that he had upset her with this. But she had reached for the knife that was kept in the alcove beside the urn for such rituals, to saw off a lock of pale-blonde hair. When she'd done this, she passed the knife to her mother. Solemnly, Lyria cut off a lock of her own hair and gave it to her daughter, her eyes bright with tears. Kynwyn, equally solemn, turned to sprinkle the hair into the jar.

"I don't want Daddy to forget us," she explained simply.

That was not one of the Mother's traditions, Cadogan thought, but it's one of theirs. He put his hand out for the knife and added a few of his own dark hairs to the vessel. "He would never forget you, Kynwyn."

He sealed the jar and inside, at the table, he used a brush and a small bottle of paint he had brought to decorate the lid with a circle surrounding a stylised flame.

It was getting late, and time for the Sergeant to be back at his post. He kissed Lyria's cheek, knowing that it was a farewell.

"When are you leaving?"

"I'm not sure. Tomorrow or the day after."

"When will you be back?" asked Kynwyn. The question her mother had not wanted to ask.

"I'm not sure, Kynwyn."

"Will you bring me back a present?"

"If I can."

He left their home, feeling guilty, like he was abandoning them. But the Captain had promised to look to them. His father's ashes were safe in their vessel, sealed with the Mother's protection, wrapped in soft cloth and tucked under his shirt. Now he was thrice duty-bound to go.

Mother, be with me. Give me strength. I have a terrible feeling I will need it.

Chapter Four

The sun had already burned away the morning's coolness and the day's burgeoning heat was promising a ferocious summer. It was cooler inside the Guards' stables, built with thick wood and whitewashed to give proper shelter to the fine animals that carried the King's own soldiers into battle. The stables were half empty now—some mounted guardsmen were patrolling outside the castle walls; other horses had been taken out by the stable-boy to graze by the river; others had died in the Battle of Tyne and had not yet been replaced.

The centre of the covered stable was taken up with a caravan. It had once been a riot of colour, bright swirls of blue and red announcing that it belonged to Ayman's Players. The sign still showed up under the new layer of paint that was being applied. Kayla had offered it for Magda's use now that she no longer required it herself.

Cadogan dipped the bundle of tightly wrapped reeds into the paint pot and slapped more pale blue over the wood. He could see Kayla Brittane sitting on a bale of hay near the door where she could watch the gateway that joined the main courtyard to the Guardsman's Square. Her expression was pensive.

"They won't be long, ma'am," said Ho.

She raised an eyebrow in surprise, but he was busy on the other side of the caravan. "Do you think the council will agree?" she asked after a pause. Kiedrych's father and family had disowned him as a child, because his mother could not bear to live with a brute. The old King had known it was unfair; King Armand had come to see it too. No one else had a claim to the title and lands of Lord Evenahn. No one else deserved it. Surely the council would find in his favour. Surely.

"No doubt of it, My Lady," Cadogan said firmly. "The new council are sympathetic to the King's ideas." Especially since most had lent him their full support against Saebert and Witch Zuleika, and owed their current position to him. "I understand that there are precedents, particularly since the previous Lord Evenahn was a traitor. Even if there was another to challenge his claim, the King chooses the Captain's claim. Few would argue against it."

"I suppose so." Kayla grimaced at herself. "Really, I know so. It's just so important to him. I couldn't bear to see him disappointed now."

"He won't be." A pause. "Will you?"

Kayla regarded him warily. "You notice entirely too much, Sergeant Ho."

He remained silent.

She shrugged. "I love him. I don't want to . . . embarrass him. I'm a dancer, not nobility."

"The Captain is a soldier," he pointed out.

"But at least he has some idea. I don't know where to start. What do court ladies do?"

"They walk with dignity and speak with grace. They smile and are charming and beautiful. You'll be fine." He spoke solemnly, as though his words were a promise.

That surprised a laugh out of her. "You're a charmer yourself. What else? I'm used to practical things."

"The estate will need someone to manage it." Cadogan was pleased to see her spirits rallying.

Kayla nodded. "I've seen the account ledgers. I fail to see why the Evenahn estate is in such poor condition with the assets it has—except of course that the previous Lord Evenahn was a profligate spender and a tax cheat."

"As you say, ma'am."

"I do say." She glanced outside again—still no sign of Kiedrych—then returned her gaze to Cadogan as he appeared at the far end of the caravan. There was a splash of blue on his cheek. He shifted the large clay pot of paint around to where he could reach it more easily and began to attack the backboards.

Movement caught her eye and she looked up to see Kiedrych coming through the gate, King Armand walking beside him. Armand was grinning broadly and the Captain looked both relieved and pleased.

Kayla jumped to her feet then hesitated, plucking hay from her skirt and nervously arranging her hair, her blouse.

Cadogan took her hand, stilling the trembling, and bowed deeply. When he straightened he looked her in the eye. "You have all the courage and dignity of any Lady of this court, Lady Evenahn," he said gently.

"I don't want to disgrace myself."

"You won't," he assured her, then stood aside. Kayla took a deep breath, smiled, and stepped out into the yard.

Cadogan nodded briefly at the Captain's look in his direction, part reassurance, part congratulation, then watched Kayla approach her husband and the King with her fluid dancer's stride. She curtseyed to the King, then Kiedrych caught her hands in his and kissed her fingers, speaking to her in a low voice. Kayla, in a delightfully un-Lady-like gesture, flung her arms about his neck and hugged him fiercely. He, grinning, hugged her back and King Armand looked very pleased with himself.

Cadogan turned with a smile to take the bunch of paint-smeared reeds back to the clay pot to finish the job on the caravan. There would be plenty of room inside for supplies as well as providing a comfortable place for Witch Magda to sleep. He and the priest would have to make do with sleeping in the open, always a pleasure at this time of year when the nights were neither too hot nor too cold. A bedroll to sleep on and the stars for a blanket—a kind of peace, he'd always found.

Excited voices in the courtyard caught his attention again and he looked up to see a large bronze dragon and several smaller dragons of various colours wheeling overhead and a gaggle of witches come into view. Queen Jailan was among them, golden hair shining in the bright summer sun, and something indefinable in her expression that both softened and illuminated her. Greetings were exchanged and then Captain Evenahn took his leave of the King and departed with his wife, already planning their move to the long vacant Evenahn House in the city.

Sylvia looked across the courtyard and caught Cadogan's eye within the shadows of the stables. They had exchanged a few words in the last few weeks as she sat sketching in the main courtyard most mornings and had a nodding acquaintance. She waved and he gave a half salute back. A few words were exchanged between the witches, and a conspiratorial smile. They said farewell to the royal couple and headed towards the stable.

Over their heads, Cadogan could see King Armand's puzzled look and Queen Jailan's smile broaden with a hint of smugness. She leaned close to him and spoke quietly.

The result was astonishing. The King stood back, looking stunned, then he grabbed her in a bear hug, and almost as quickly let go and hovered, wanting to touch her and clearly unsure whether or not he should. Jailan was laughing, and so was Armand and he clasped her hands in his and kissed them. Then he walked with her, an arm protectively around her shoulders and the other holding her hand as though she were suddenly a tender invalid. Jailan, normally proud and independent, submitted to this with grace.

The clatter of claws on the roof announced Witch Leenan's landing with her dragon escort, and the other witches arrived shortly after. Cadogan raised an eyebrow at Sylvia, although he already suspected the news.

"There's an heir apparent," she quipped.

Magda rolled her eyes at her, but she was smiling. "I examined her this morning—she's about five weeks along and the foetus is fighting fit."

"Armand looked like he was going to explode with pride," said Tephee with a giggle. "Anyone would think he'd done something clever."

"It's good news," Cadogan said, salvaging some dignity from the laughter which greeted that comment. "The line must be continued."

There was a thump as a dragon dropped from the roof and landed in the open doorway. Cadogan saluted welcome to her.

"I'm told you'll be guiding us to Marin Kuta," said Magda, claiming his attention.

"Yes, Witch Magda," he replied respectfully, "I'm making preparations already." He motioned towards the half-painted caravan.

"We won't all fit in that, will we, Maggie?" asked Tephee. She glanced from the caravan to Magda and her expression became very still. "I . . . are we all going, Magda? I mean . . ." She bit her lip. "If you want me to stay behind," she said timidly, "that's all right."

Magda regarded the young woman with affection. The poor girl had become very quiet lately; such a contrast to the troubled child who had caused so much anxiety in recent months. Magda wondered if she had been that unpredictable as a teenager. "We've all learned a lot since we left Swiftfort," she said. "I imagine this will be dangerous, maybe more dangerous than last time. The decision's yours. But if you want to come, I'll be glad of the company."

Tephee grinned and they hugged, oblivious to the stiff and slightly shocked expression that had come over Cadogan's face.

"Ah . . . Witch Magda . . . how many of you are coming?"

"Myself and Sylvia of course," she said. She had discussed this with Sylvia and the older witch had insisted on joining her. If medical facilities were available on this ship, it would be better if they could treat Sylvia immediately.

"Of course," echoed Cadogan faintly.

"And Tephee," she said, smiling at the girl, who beamed back.

"I see."

"Mreeeeeeeeeeeeee," came a dragon's trill from outside.

"Oh."

"It'll be fun!" asserted Tephee.

It'll be a nightmare, thought Cadogan. *I will never be able to protect them all. Mother, is this a test?*

"This is . . . too much honour for one man," he managed to choke out.

Sylvia smiled kindly and patted his arm. "I'm sure you'll cope."

Cadogan couldn't escape the thought that she was somehow laughing benignly at him.

Great Mother, I'm sure You have a plan in all of this. At least, he *hoped* she had a plan.

CHAPTER FIVE

There was bustle and noise throughout the main yard as supplies and bags were carried down and arranged in the pale-blue caravan, and when it was realised that more luggage than space existed for everything the witches and the priest insisted on carrying, another cart and a horse were found and the packing was rearranged. Alard ran around, barking and getting underfoot while the cat complained and the four little dragons dived among the workers and spooked the horses. It was all taking much, much longer than anticipated and their early morning start looked more and more like an afternoon adventure.

In a quiet part of the yard, Sergeant Ho had found it expedient to let the witches see to their own packing. Which was to say that he had been told testily and in no uncertain terms to get out of the way while they saw to things. It was easier to give in gracefully, he'd decided, and easier to conceal how frustrated he was by the delay if he took himself off somewhere.

Unnoticed, he put aside his sword and leather tunic and for a moment he stood in shirt and trousers, eyes closed. A stillness came over him that was both relaxed and alert as his breathing steadied.

Slowly, he began to move. His hands made delicate shapes and his arms swept up in elegant, dynamic curves. One knee bent, a leg extended, his weight shifted and he flowed into another movement—slow, gentle, powerful.

The creak of wings above did not distract him, nor the long

shadow that passed over him. He followed the ancient pattern and shifted in this quiet corner with economical grace. When the pattern was complete he came to rest, a perfectly still place in the midst of activity.

He opened his eyes to see the dragon standing before him, her head cocked quizzically and her green cat's-eyes unblinking.

"Good morning, Witch Leenan."

"Rrrrrrrooooooooo," she replied aloud. *Were you dancing?* she mind-spoke.

"No, Witch Leenan. I was . . . meditating."

It's a funny way to meditate. It's not how Sylvia does it. Why do you move like that?

The rugged-looking soldier was strangely deferential in replying to her. "It's a way of moving with the world, Witch Leenan." He made an expressive gesture with his hands, as though he were pulling something from the earth into himself. "A way of connecting with the Mother."

Leenan tilted her head the other way. *The Mother?*

"The . . . spirit of the world. The heart and soul of the soil and the sky and all between. The . . . Mother," he finished, his expression oddly plaintive.

Oh. It was a peculiar Leylite concept, Leenan thought, but an attractive one. She rattled her wings and stretched her neck up to see how things were progressing with the carts. *They're nearly ready,* she reported. *It's astonishing how long it can take witches to get ready to travel anywhere.*

Cadogan merely nodded then retrieved his tunic and pulled it on over his shirt. His own pack consisted of one change of travelling clothes, a formal Guard uniform, and a simple, white hopper-skin robe wrapped around the enamel jar. It had taken him exactly four minutes to prepare his personal items for the journey. It had taken him exactly eighteen minutes to have the supplies he had organised to be loaded by the storeman into the caravan. Then the witches had arrived and proceeded to unload the supplies, reload the caravan with sealed metallic boxes and devices belonging to Witch Magda, stow bags, make room for the dog, rearrange things not once but twice and generally take a long and talkative time of it. He suppressed a sigh, belted his sword in place, and strode out to join the others.

Sebastian was riding on the cart and looked out of place in his robes. Tephee sat with Magda under the canopy at the front of the caravan with Alard curled up on the floorboard between them. Pywych had found a place to sleep inside the caravan. Tephee's cat Cauldron had flatly refused to have anything to do with this further adventuring and had made himself at home in the Castle kitchens, where Ma Fingal fed, pampered, and spoiled him as much as he liked.

A stableboy resettled the pack on Cadogan's horse, which had been waiting patiently for an hour or more, and led the animal into the yard. Cadogan greeted the grey gelding with affection and swung lightly into the saddle.

As he led the way into the main courtyard and to the city gate he saw the new Lady Evenahn directing the loading of carts and he wished he'd had her in charge of this morning's organisation. She saw him and waved and he gave her a casual salute in return. The Captain emerged from the barracks in conversation with one of the men. The soldier strode away to carry out instructions and the Captain paused, apparently to admire his wife's ability to issue clear, efficient instructions and have them obeyed with such good humour, then he saw Cadogan and crossed the courtyard to intercept him.

Cadogan reigned his horse aside, signaling for the others to continue, and met the Captain.

"Sir," he saluted.

Kiedrych returned the salute crisply then relaxed slightly. "I'd appreciate it if you'd stay out of trouble," he said.

"I'll do my best, sir."

"I don't want to be left with just Tamalan for a drinking companion. Besides, I still want you to explain this tree-thing to me." A lopsided grin softened his features and Cadogan laughed gently.

"The tree-thing is a question of being," he said, knowing that Kiedrych still didn't get it. He drew his attention back to Kayla. "Your Lady wants to do well by you, Kiedrych."

Kiedrych glanced across, and as always his eyes gentled when he looked at her. "How could she not?"

"Tell her so."

The Captain gave his Sergeant a dark look, but after a moment replied: "I will."

Cadogan nodded. "Sir," he said in farewell.

"Good luck. First King be with you."

"And the Mother with you, sir."

That made Kiedrych laugh and he stood back to allow Cadogan to turn his horse around and trot after the others.

They made slow progress through the city square and down the avenue leading to the main gates that led out of the city, due to the number of people who had filled up the spaces since the early morning. Many stopped to wave and wish them luck—some with genuine friendliness, a good many without real animosity but a sense of relief nonetheless. Leenan could dimly sense the release of tension as they passed.

Finally they left the city and took the wide road leading west. It passed through the fields where the Battle of Tyne had taken place. Cadogan noted that the field was lush with grass and flowers, even the place where Witch Zuleika's pyre had burned to the ground and gone cold without a soul to mourn her passing. Cadogan had said a prayer for a part of the Mother gone mad and wild, and like all others, the blood and flesh she gave to the earth was given back in beauty and life. The Mother took everyone to her bosom.

When Leenan tired of flying, she swooped down and found purchase on the back of the cart, startling both the horse and Sebastian. The priest brought the horse quickly under control and laughed at his own surprise. "You shouldn't sneak up on people like that," he admonished her.

I wouldn't have thought a dragon could sneak up on anyone, let alone a dragon of my size, she replied laconically.

"You're surprisingly silent until you land," Sebastian told her.

That brought a definite dragon-hiss of amusement which startled the horse again.

They stopped a short while before dark and Cadogan built a fire, upon which Sylvia and Tephee cooked a simple vegetable stew flavoured with dried beef strips. Leenan and the little dragons went fishing in the river before joining the others, and Alard, after a moment, went to curl up with her by the fire. For a time they sat in companionable silence until Sebastian waved towards the road.

"How long do you think it will take for us to reach the coast?" he asked Cadogan.

"That will depend on the storm that's coming."

"Storm?" Magda looked at him in surprise. "What storm? The sky is clear right to the horizon."

"There's a storm brewing west of here, Witch Magda."

"How can you tell?" asked Tephee.

Cadogan cast a glance at the Arc priest then looked back to the witch. "I can feel it, Witch Tephee."

"I suppose an old soldier like yourself must be used to the weather patterns around here," Magda said.

"Yes, Witch Magda," he replied noncommitally.

"Cadogan . . . it's just Magda, all right?"

Cadogan struggled with this for a moment. "Yes, ma'am."

Sylvia, who had been drawing patterns in the fire's turned soil with a stick, paused and cocked her head to regard him with a faint smile. He smiled quizzically back, and she went back to her doodles. Tephee yawned and stretched and announced it was her bedtime and Sylvia joined her in the caravan after affectionate good-nights. Leenan was drowsing in the warmth and watched Magda talk with Sebastian and the Sergeant through heavily lidded eyes.

Magda peered westward, trying to see some sign of activity. "So when do you think the storm will get here?"

"Tomorrow or the day after, Witch Magda."

She sighed. "You can't do it, can you?"

"No, Witch Magda," he agreed.

"Could you at least try?"

"Yes. Ma'am."

"You can be very frustrating, Sergeant Ho."

"So I'm told, ma'am."

"What is it with this . . . this terminal reverence?"

When the Sergeant did not answer immediately—he was nonplussed for a moment—Sebastian said quietly: "It's his religion, Magda."

"Religion?" Magda looked at Cadogan with curiosity. "What religion is this?"

"He worships witches," said Sebastian, and although he said it kindly, Cadogan thought he could detect a faint undercurrent of humour.

"Leylites honour the Mother," he corrected carefully. "Witches are Her manifestation."

Magda leaned forward, interested. "Tell me about Her."

Cadogan met her gaze and spoke quietly. "The Mother . . . is the soul of our world."

"Oh!" A light of understanding made her blue eyes sparkle. "Like an earth mother. Gaea, that sort of thing."

"I've never heard Her given that name before," Cadogan said, "although some call Her 'Leyla.' "

Magda leaned further forward, smiling. She had never heard of any faith other than the worship of the First King and His Lords. As far as she had been able to work out, the First King had probably been Captain of the colony ship that had crashed on this world about a thousand years ago, bringing humanity and earth animals to a mainly reptilian world. This sounded more like one of the religions that had existed in her own universe.

"Where does the First King fit into the scheme of things?" asked Sebastian.

Once more, his tone was nearly neutral but Cadogan thought he detected a note of challenge. *Or perhaps I'm just getting paranoid.* "The Mother called Him to Her, to populate Her lands and to share the essence of Her self with humankind."

"A few generations ago," said Sebastian gently, "you might have been imprisoned for heresy."

"Not even one generation ago," responded Cadogan sharply, "my brother was killed for it." *Koto and my mother died for it. We were exiled for it.* He looked away and took a breath, seeking calm. It was foolish that anyone could still make him so angry and hurt, with so few words, after all this time. It was because he was going back, he knew. It made all those losses fresh and raw again. Thirty years, and deep down it still hurt. He closed his eyes and felt for Her quiet pulse with his senses, found it, and let peace come with the sensation. Let the Arc priest believe what he will—the Mother didn't mind. She didn't have to be worshipped to be real.

He opened his eyes to see Magda casting a reproachful look at the priest, and Sebastian looking contrite. Leenan was looking at him quizzically, the firelight glinting on her green eyes.

"My apologies, Sebastian. I'm tired." That and the storm he

could sense were making him over-sensitive and irritable. "I would get some sleep if I were you, Wi . . . er . . . ma'am. We should start early tomorrow."

"All right, Sergeant," she agreed readily. "I'll see you in the morning."

The priest watched her go into the caravan before turning back to smile ruefully at Cadogan. "I should apologise myself," he said. "I don't get out of the Temple often. I am not always as tactful as I ought to be among others, especially with those of different faiths."

Cadogan inclined his head in tacit acceptance. For a moment he regarded Sebastian's introspective expression. "You don't know what you expect to find in Marin Kuta, do you?" he said at length.

Sebastian frowned. "No. But it worries me." He met Cadogan's gaze. "I expect it worries you too."

"I am . . . concerned about Marin Kuta, and the witches' safety. And about some other things," he admitted, "but probably not for the reasons you think."

"They say it's an Arc vessel."

"It may be." Cadogan shrugged slightly. "We have never denied the existence of the First King."

"No. No, you haven't." Sebastian rose and brushed down his robes. "Well, good night Sergeant Ho."

"Good night, Sebastian."

The priest left to bed down in the back of the cart, and Cadogan turned to meet Leenan's large cat-like gaze. "And what do you think, Witch Leenan?"

Her mouth curled in a reptilian echo of a human smile. *I thought you'd forgotten I was here. A lot of people do.*

"A dragon is very difficult to forget, Witch Leenan."

She laughed at that. *But they forget that I can understand. They think it's no different to talking in front of Alard.* The smaller dragons around her moved restlessly and lifted their heads, sniffing the night air. Leenan's wings shivered.

"You must hear some interesting things that way, Witch Leenan."

I don't suppose you could just make it "Leenan," could you?

". . . No, ma'am."

Oh well. She stretched her neck and shook her wings again. Plum and Greedy hissed at one another and Captain tried to bite them both. Buttercup squawked. Leenan's tail thumped on the ground and frightened them all into silence, but their restlessness continued.

"Is anything wrong, ma'am?"

Just restless. Probably this storm coming. Leenan sat on her haunches, stretched her wings out to full span then shook herself all over, making her scales rattle and startling Alard from his sleep. *Might fly a bit. Wear the jangles out.* The others sensed her intention and flapped impatiently by her side, Captain launching herself skyward ahead of them. Leenan leaned back a moment then pushed off from the ground, extending her leathery wings and then pulling them down mightily against the night air. The remaining dragons took off after her within moments and Alard whined at being left behind.

Don't wait up! her mind called down to him, before they all disappeared into the darkness.

Cadogan peered into the sky, still hearing the creak of her wings. He went to his bedroll by the caravan still carrying that image of her, fluid and powerful as she dove into the sky.

CHAPTER SIX

It took considerably less time to get started in the morning than Cadogan had feared, but there had still been time enough for him to shave, harness the horses, saddle his own mount, and go through his exercises while the witches had breakfast and brushed their hair. He could hear Sebastian reassuring them that he hadn't been cold, mostly because Alard, feeling lonely, had jumped into the cart and slept beside him all night.

The dragons had been flying again that morning, hunting in the distance, though Leenan had returned early enough to watch the Sergeant's graceful steps. When he had finished, he half bowed in her direction. Tephee called out to him then, as she climbed into the caravan with Magda, declaring their readiness to get moving, so he whistled to his horse and swung into the saddle, light as air. Sylvia, seated with Sebastian in the cart, guided their horse onto the road behind the caravan. Leenan flapped her wings hard as though shaking off the earth as she rose into the sky.

It was a fine, clear day, the summer scent of fields and flowers sharp. Alard sat on the cart behind Sebastian and Sylvia and pushed his nose against their faces and arms, seeking head-scratches and ear-pulls and whuffed with pleasure when they, laughing, surrendered to his demands. Pywych had made himself at home on the buckboard between Tephee and Magda and took great interest in the world as it passed by.

They had been travelling for some hours when Magda heard

the thump on the caravan's roof. She glanced up to see Leenan taking grip with her forepaws before she hung her head over the end. She looked straight ahead and seemed very tired.

"Are you okay, Lee?" asked Magda.

The dragon snorted slightly and put her head on one side. *Tired.*

"You've been out a lot lately," said Tephee.

Yes.

"Flying with the pack," Magda observed, and there was a tone to her voice that made Tephee aware that something was wrong. She looked inquiringly at Leenan.

Yes, replied Leenan. Perhaps she could have hidden the underlying tension with the spoken word, but Tephee knew that minds couldn't lie like that. Motives might be hidden, but the feelings were always true. Something was very wrong.

"What's going on?" she demanded, her voice low.

Leenan's head only hung further and Magda reached up to run her long hands reassuringly over her friend's bronze cheek. "It might just be the storm," the healer said.

I wish it was.

"Would one of you tell me what's going on?"

Dragon and healer both glanced at her, then Leenan sighed. *There's something wrong with the dragons. They're restless.*

"Oh," Tephee sighed, relaxing, "that's probably just the storm, like Maggie says."

It's been going on for a week or so now. Long before the storm.

"Well, it's probably just the summer weather . . ."

"How old are the dragons now?" Magda asked suddenly.

"They were hatchlings when I called them up last autumn," Tephee replied. "Sylvia said I'd probably called them up from a nest in the southern mountains. That must mean they were laid earlier . . . oh!" Realisation struck: she paused and raised her eyebrows then aimed a grin at Leenan. "Poor little things are in mating season, aren't they?" When no one laughed, her smile faltered. "But that only affects the dragons, surely."

I'm mostly dragon these days, Tephee. In case you hadn't noticed.

"Oh . . . Lords . . ." Tephee bit her lip, her hazel eyes round and large. "We have to find a way to change you back."

It's not as bad as all that, Leenan assured her, *I just keep getting this . . . pull to fly south. Seems to be in the blood. I can fight it, but I'm keeping the others here too, and it's getting harder.*

"Can't you just let them fly off?"

It doesn't work that way. I have the strongest mind. They think I'm the pack leader. It's very weird.

"We'll ask Sylvia," Tephee said firmly. "She'll have some ideas."

It feels strange, Maggie, Leenan "spoke" plaintively to her.

"We'll think of something," Magda promised. "Don't worry."

Summer skies and scents surrounded their journey—a cloudless blue canopy overhead and the scent of crops and flowers nearby. The landscape changed slightly as they passed farms and villages, becoming more hilly as they went. Whenever the roads got crowded, Leenan and the dragons took to the air and flew on ahead to wait for them in a quieter place. The static electricity in the air was palpable now even to the least sensitive of them and Sebastian, Tephee, and Magda kept watching the horizon, expecting to see black clouds, darkened skies, *something* to reflect this restless foreboding. When they stopped to lunch on bread and cheese, Pywych took to hiding in the caravan and Alard slumped in the cart and whined occasionally. The carthorses swished their tails as though chasing flies and stamped their feet impatiently. Sylvia rubbed the bridge of her nose from time to time but was otherwise unaffected. Cadogan spoke quietly to his mount, quelling its restlessness with a touch and a word.

They made camp before sunset, fed and hobbled the horses,

built a fire, made a meal, made small talk, watched the west while the sun melted into the horizon. Sebastian glanced around at the trees a little nervously.

"Will we be safe here?"

Cadogan nodded, indicating the taller trees nearby and the low hills which surrounded their camping ground. "You might want to sleep under the cart, just in case," he added thoughtfully.

In the night sky, the pack of dragons wheeled and called to one another. They hunted, though game was scarce. From time to time they would head south, but Leenan would turn and circle the travelers and the others would return, trailing her. With a worried look skyward, the witches went to bed in the caravan and Sebastian took shelter under the cart, Alard crawling in beside him.

The Sergeant took his blanket and found a tree to lean against. Despite gnawing storm-bred anxiety, he managed to fall asleep for a time.

The call was stronger this time. The wind howled way up here, high above the trees and hills and the winding river, and it brought out something wild in her. She felt she could fly forever, that she *must* fly, beat her wings until she could no longer feel them, but they would stretch and fold, beating against the sky without her conscious effort required. It ached to be here, to stay here, when all she was called her south.

South . . . to the mountains . . . to the pack . . . what am I doing? Leenan banked and wheeled back towards the camp, and she could feel the disappointment in her mind, radiated by the pack at her heels. *Go, then!* she exhorted them, trying to force them away. *Go and leave me! I can't come with you. I'm not really a dragon!*

Images crowded her mind, of herself as they saw her. Strong

and beautiful and as the lightning flared in the distance her bronze was gilded eerily with blue light. You are pack leader, the images said to her, we go with you.

She shrieked, frustration and fear combined, and giving in to the two took her a little further from her humanity for a moment. Pulled by her blood, she turned south again, fought it, gave in . . . she thought she was flying in circles, but she was being tugged southward ever so slightly each time. It ached less when she gave in. Sometimes, when it became too much, she would let it take her and she flew like a spear, straight and true, before finding herself and balking against it. It was like falling parallel with the earth, exhilarating and terrifying.

I can't go with you! I can't . . . oh, Lords help me!

Then the lightning began in earnest, great fiery bolts that leapt out of the stars and shattered sight and sound in their wake.

Not lightning making the noise, she told herself, trying to keep reason foremost, fighting the instincts. *That's the thunder. Lightning's just light. Just fire. Like witchfire . . . but moreso.* The analogy wasn't a good one, she knew, but it kept her thinking. *Look at it . . . like someone cut the sky in half. So much power in it . . . so much . . .*

Then she realised what she could do.

Cadogan woke when the wind whipped his blanket aside, and opened his eyes to a night oppressive in its sense of anticipation. The wind was just starting to blow and clouds gathered overhead, obscuring the moon. A faint blue crackle in the distance heralded the lightning to come and a faint rumble rolled far above.

Cadogan retrieved the blanket, pulled on his boots and leather tunic and strode over to the cart. He found Sebastian, only half asleep, and woke him.

"You'd best get in the caravan. You'll get soaked when the rain starts," he said.

Sebastian thought of arguing—it would be crowded in that van, and the ladies might not appreciate his presence—but a sheet of lightning illuminated the western sky again, and the following rumble was louder this time, so he took his bedding and Alard and went to knock on the door at the rear of the caravan. Sylvia answered before long—she was obviously having trouble sleeping herself—and let both priest and dog inside.

Cadogan led the horses around to what he expected would be the leeward side of the caravan, petted the animals and tried to reassure them, but they stamped nervously and snorted.

Another sheet of lightning. Cadogan looked up to see the silhouettes of five dragons circling above. He blinked, the afterimage burned into his retina. Four small shapes led by a great dark shadow, spiraling across the sky, heading south.

The rumble became a growl of thunder, through which Cadogan distinctly heard a dragon shriek. He stepped out into the campsite, took ten more strides to reach the road and searched skyward. There was nothing for long moments—no lightning, no thunder, no sound but the wind rushing by and tugging at his hair and clothes. He thought for a moment that this would be the worst the storm had to offer, and now it would just rain . . . and as he thought it, a great jagged line of blinding white split the sky in two, the air boomed and the ground shook.

The horses whinnied in fright and Cadogan heard Alard barking within the caravan, along with human exhortations to be calm, it's just a storm, hush . . .

Another jagged line, a crash of thunder . . . Alard howled. The Mother was in a rare mood tonight. Cadogan continued to scan the sky, looking for the dark shapes there, and found them. The great dragon was flying as though mad, diving and climbing in tight circles, wings pounding against the wind. She shrieked again, a high and alien sound and suddenly flew, straight as an arrow towards the south, four shadows in her wake.

She banked again, plummeted, pulled out of the dive mere metres above the ground, climbed again, shot like an arrow again, but northwest this time, towards the river. Lightning crackled across the sky there, illuminating the river like a ribbon of steel.

And she dove into the arcs and spears of light, wheeling and spinning through the spider's web of fire like a demented thing. Cadogan was running, pushing hard against the grass and soil, shouldering past trees and shrubs. Shot like an arrow along the earth, making for the river where he saw her swooping, tumbling, falling from the sky as her wings fell and vanished.

First King be with me . . . This is suicide. I'm going to die. Die or become dragon to the core . . . let it work, please First King, let it work. I'm counting on You. I never ask You for anything. Let me . . . Aaaaaiiiiiiiiiiiiiiiiiiiiiiiiiiii!

Leenan flew into the bolt of fire, and tried to accept its power—the way Magda had done, when she borrowed from Kayla to save Kiedrych's life; the way Tephee had taken Zuleika's power at Tyne; the way Tephee had given that power to her, pushed it into her so that she could change from human to dragon and have the strength to carry the seriously wounded Sylvia from the field.

She hadn't counted on it hurting so much. She fell, stunned. She tried to move her wings and found she no longer had them.

He'd watched her fall, seen where she would land, and was stripping off his tunic as he ran. She hit the water before he reached the river bank, but in scant seconds he had dived into the dark waters. He'd seen exactly where the river, wide and deep, had swallowed her whole and he cleaved into the depths, unable to see, feeling blindly for her. His hand touched something soft, and he could make out a pale shape . . . seized upon her, pulled her to the surface.

Cadogan let the current help him carry her, thanking the Mother for Her aid, and dragged the unconscious witch onto the shore. Efficiently he turned her onto her stomach, pushed hard upwards to force the water from her lungs; turned her again to help her sit as she coughed and gasped, barely conscious. She had burns on her right side and was starting to shiver.

When he was sure she was breathing, he gathered her naked body in his arms and held her close against his chest for warmth, but he was soaking wet and the wind was picking up. He carried her back to where he'd left his tunic, wrapped her carefully in its worn leather and cradled her cocooned body against his own.

"Don't worry. You'll be all right. The Mother looks after Her own," he murmured to her. Water squelched in his boots, but he was more concerned with keeping her away from branches that scratched at her pale skin.

Above them, the skies grew quiet. The winds blew still, but the rain did not come.

"Open the door!" Cadogan shouted, stumbling out from among the trees into the campsite. The horses were still there, noses flaring and flanks flecked with sweat. Alard had stopped howling at last. The door opened in the darkness and Magda peered out.

"Oh my god."

"She flew into the lightning," Cadogan told her. Bodies tumbled out of the van—Sebastian dragging a reluctant Alard, Tephee and Sylvia pushing the animal from behind. Cadogan ducked and squeezed inside long enough to lay his charge gently on the mound of bedding there, then withdrew to allow Magda room to work. The healer witch was tightlipped and business-like, taking a pulse, inspecting the wounds. Cadogan shut the door on the witchlight and stood in the darkness.

There was a shrill cry, then another, from the sky, and he saw the four dragons chasing one another in circles overhead. They called again, then straightened in their path and flew—due south.

As the first drop of rain fell against his upturned face, Cadogan sighed. *I'm definitely too old for this.*

CHAPTER SEVEN

Sylvia suggested moving the cart alongside the caravan and stringing, between the two, the oiled wool blanket that covered the goods in the cart. She and Tephee held witchfire aloft while Sebastian and Cadogan pulled the cart into place. The discomfort of being wet through concentrated Sylvia's attention long enough for her to fix the tarpaulin, sloping from the roof of the caravan, to the side of the cart, but it exhausted her and brought on another headache.

Cadogan was already wet through from his dive into the river, and it struck him that getting rained on further wasn't going to much detract from the situation. At least it was summer rain—heavy and hard, but not cold. He volunteered to gather some wood, and while Tephee used magic to dry out the branches and twigs so that a fire would hold, he found a log and dragged it back to the shelter for the witches to sit on. The priest looked so bedraggled, although he did not complain, that Cadogan found a large flat stone and brought it back for him.

"What about you?"

"Things to do," Cadogan replied. He went into the cart then, holding a leather bag carefully so that he could take things out without getting everything else wet, and brought some supplies back.

They ate the last of the bread and cheese along with some dried fruit and nuts. Sebastian chewed carefully, savouring the simple pleasure of the meal. He felt slightly guilty that Cadogan was the only one of them still standing, but the soldier looked comfortable enough leaning against the side of the caravan and looking out into the darkness. He was a good ten years older than the Sergeant, and not so used to the discomforts of outdoor life. His joints ached and his back hurt and he was having to pray hard for fortitude, when all he really wanted to do was find a nice soft bed and sleep for a few days. Ironic considering he had been elected as one of those to make the journey to Marin Kuta because he was thought best able to cope with it.

Well, cope with it he would. And more. If the rumours were true, this strange occurrence in Marin Kuta was a visitation from the First King. Perhaps His Return, as prophesied by one of the more extreme branches of the faith. Whatever he found, he had his theological training, his common sense, and his certainty that the First King's emissary among them would help him to determine what was happening and what it meant for the Arc priests.

Sebastian's reverie was interrupted when Tephee jumped to her feet and said through a mouthful of bread: "Hell! I forgot Maggie! Back in a minute." She swallowed hastily, grabbed some food and ran out briefly into the rain.

She tapped on the rear door of the caravan before letting herself in. Magda was kneeling by Leenan's side, looking pale and exhausted. Her patient was also very pale, with dark shadows under her closed eyes and her hair spilled untidy and wet across the pillows.

"Sorry, Maggie, you must be starving," Tephee said, helping Magda to eat some fruit at first, then the more fortifying cheese. A flask of water kept inside the van washed it down and the healer ate and drank thankfully. Tephee kept glancing back to Leenan. "Her hair has grown."

"Yes. I suppose she'll want it cut again."

"She's going to be all right, then?" Plain relief showed itself.

Magda nodded weakly. "Don't think she was right under the bolt," she said, "and she converted some of the electricity to change, I think. Burn should have been much worse."

Tephee frowned worriedly. "Is she burnt?"

"Not anymore." It had burned right through, entering at Leenan's right shoulder and emerging above her right hip, but the burns had been mostly internal, in the nature of lightning strikes on flesh—the bolt just kept on going until it earthed, right through whatever was in the way. The bruises would take a few days to come out, from the strike and from Leenan's graceless plummet into the river. They could be dealt with later. Now, she was out of danger and in a natural sleep. Magda felt like she might pass out, herself.

"Maggie?"

Magda opened her bleary eyes to Tephee's timid inquiry. "Be nice if we could go somewhere without having to patch my friends up all the time," she said with a half smile.

"Are all witches as trouble prone as us, do you think?"

"Better ask Cadogan." Magda's voice was dissolving into a mumble.

"I'll do that. Here, you should eat some more. You've worn yourself out. I . . ." Tephee trailed off, then very gently, very quietly, drew some blankets over her sleeping friend and slipped out into the night again.

The rain had slowed to a spasmodic patter. The air was pleasantly cool and the trees on the hills to the east were dark shapes against the first faint blush of sunrise. Under the tarpaulin Sebastian was rubbing Alard's head and trying to distract the animal as it stared anxiously at the caravan. On the log, Sylvia was leaning, half asleep, against Cadogan, who had his arm protectively around the witch. He seemed calm, but there was concern in his eyes as he looked up at Tephee.

"Are they all right?"

"They're both asleep. Maggie says Lee will be fine. A bit bruised."

"There's a town a few hours down this road. There's a good inn there, if you wish to stop."

Tephee was flustered by his deference. "If you think we should," she replied, passing the decision back to him. She saw that Sylvia had woken up again and was giving her a speculative look. "Whatever you think," she continued.

Sylvia drew away from Cadogan and tugged at her untidy hair. Cadogan raised an enquiring eyebrow at her but she only blinked owlishly.

"Oh, for the Lords' sake," said Sebastian testily, "let's stop at the inn. The ladies need some rest and these old bones of mine need a hot tub."

Sylvia patted Cadogan's knee in a motherly fashion. "You don't need to ask permission for everything," she said.

"I would not wish to impose my will on you, Witch Sylvia."

This brought a light laugh and a quick grin. "Do you think you could?"

Cadogan's embarrassment was quashed by the look on her face—conspiratorial, impish. He smiled back at her. "Indeed not, Witch Sylvia."

"I would like you to call me Sylvia."

He breathed a faint sigh. "Is this some kind of campaign against me, ma'am?"

"Whatever your faith says we are," she said gently, "we are just people."

"People, yes, and something more," Cadogan replied stolidly.

"I prefer not to have a title. I am just Sylvia."

Cadogan shifted uncomfortably. "It does not sound . . . respectful, ma'am."

"You would be respecting my wishes." Sylvia's tone was kind. "Could you at least try?"

"I will try. Sylvia." A pause while he digested that. "Ma'am."

"It's stopped raining," announced Tephee.

The sun was finally making a bolder appearance on the eastern horizon and the blurred shadow-shapes were defining themselves. The rain had indeed stopped and when they looked out from under their makeshift cover the clouds were dissipating. While Cadogan walked around to fetch the horses, Sebastian doused the fire and the witches took down the tarpaulin.

Tephee used a little magic to detach the cover from the cart and caravan, forgetting that the concave-hanging cloth was not merely loose but filled with water. The cover collapsed on the three of them, spilling water all around them and effectively smothering the fire. They struggled out from under the heavy material, Sebastian pulling out an alarmed-looking Alard. Tephee was mortified and embarrassed but before she could stammer an apology, Sylvia popped out, her hair looking like a hopper nest, her clothes askew, and burst into gales of laughter. Sebastian, who had looked very cross, glanced at her, a smile growing, then began to chuckle. A sheepish grin crept across Tephee's face. When Cadogan appeared briefly, his puzzled look transforming to surprise as he saw the mess, she waved. "Don't worry. It's all under control."

He nodded, as though to say, "Of course it is," which just reduced the threesome to more helpless laughter, and he sensibly took himself back to the horses.

He managed to get the caravan hitched up without too much disturbance to those still sleeping inside, then the cart, and finally saddled his own mount. Just before they were ready to go, he took his saddlebag into the woods and emerged a short while later in Guard uniform, complete with black boots. The black pants and jacket in combination with the deep red shirt was striking, as always, and the plumes in his hat flounced as he got into the saddle. Sylvia wondered briefly how Cadogan managed to keep his things looking so tidy inside a saddlebag.

"You look rather fine," Sebastian called out from the cart as they moved onto the road.

"We're going into a town, and I am the King's representative," Cadogan told him, riding alongside. It was also true that his travelling boots and clothes were soaked through and he could not have worn his dress boots with his dry set of travelling clothes, so it was either the uniform or clean clothes with soggy boots. All his wet apparel was laid out in the back of the cart to dry, and the day, after the night's storm, promised to be hot.

By the time they reached the town of Jubilee, Magda was awake and had joined Sylvia on the seat of the caravan while Tephee had once more gone to sit with Sebastian in the cart. Cadogan led them down to the one of the minor squares off the main market square and dismounted at the Half Moon Inn. It was a large stone haybarn that had been converted into lodgings twenty-odd years before and the building took up almost one whole side of the square. A path down one side led to the remnant of an orchard and the stables. It was disproportionately large for the relatively small town it was set in, but Jubilee was right on the east-west trade route and there was plenty of call for short-term accommodation.

A large, friendly woman with her dark, grey-streaked hair tied back in an untidy bun and dressed in a brightly coloured skirt and vest over her linen shirt, came out to meet them, wiping her hands on her apron.

The Sergeant bowed deeply and spoke a few words to her. She raised a speculative eyebrow at his companions and then laughed. "I suppose this means you expect free lodgings," she said.

"It means we expect fair prices," Sergeant Ho told her in his best firm-but-fair parade-ground voice. "And a hot tub for the priest," he added in the same tone. The woman chuckled and waved at a young boy who was skulking around the side of the building. The boy emerged shyly.

"Help Sergeant Ho stable the horses, Tyler. Make sure they get the good feed. Then I'll want you to help Gilly draw a bath."

The boy looked anxiously at the Sergeant in his finery. "Are you here to arrest someone, Sergeant Ho?"

"I'm here to ensure safe passage for some travelers going to Marin Kuta," Cadogan explained with a smile. "I have four witches and an Arc priest with me."

Tyler's eyes went very round and he peered past Cadogan to the people waiting on the carriages behind. He caught Tephee's curious gaze and he gulped, awestruck, before he bowed deeply to her. He didn't see her blush.

"Four witches," he murmured. "Wow."

"Off you go now, Tyler," the boy's mother told him firmly.

"Yes'm." Tyler's expression was infused with a mixture of delight and the grave responsibility that was now his.

Sebastian and Tephee climbed down from the cart and watched the young boy lead the horse and its burden around the side of the building to the stableyard at the rear. Sylvia joined them while Magda went around to check on her patient.

"This is Madam Imber," Cadogan said by way of introduction. "We can lodge here until Witch Leenan is well enough to go on."

Magda reappeared beside the caravan. "I'd like to get her into a warm bed as soon as possible," she said. "And I'll need some light broth for her when she wakes up."

Lina Imber swept a brief, respectful bow towards her, then addressed Cadogan. "The apple room would be best. I'll get the quilt turned down, then I thought the two upper rooms at the back for the others. You can keep an eye on your things from back there." Madam Imber bowed again then bustled back into the inn.

Leenan moaned slightly in her sleep as Cadogan scooped her into his arms and carried her, swaddled in blankets, into the inn and up the stairs to the third floor of the building. Magda followed at his heels as they passed two large and well-appointed rooms and on to a smaller room at the end of the corridor. Though half the size of the others, it was well furnished and allowed the cheerful summer light to spill across the foot of the down-stuffed bed. The room also smelled deliciously of apple, a scent that wafted in from the ancient apple tree just outside the window. Cadogan laid the witch gently on the soft mattress and withdrew with Madam Imber to allow Magda time and privacy with her charge.

They met Sebastian, Sylvia, and Tephee coming up the stairs after them. Their hostess ushered them into their rooms with pride. The women had the centre room, closest to Leenan's, which held a bed large enough for three to sleep in, along with a second bed against one wall. There was a fireplace, a great copper tub set over its own hearth, and a table setting for four below the large window that overlooked the back yard and the stables. Through the window they could see young Tyler not only feeding the draught horses and Cadogan's mount, but also in the midst of giving them, turn by turn, a vigorous rubdown and combing.

Sylvia smiled her thanks for the attention. "I hope we're not putting you to too much trouble."

"You do my house honour by your coming," Madam Imber replied warmly. "It is no trouble at all."

She showed Cadogan and Sebastian next door and went downstairs to prepare some broth. The men strode into the room, interrupting a teenaged girl as she tended a fire under the bathing copper. "Shan't be long, Sergeant Ho," she promised him, blushing fiercely, "only I need to fetch the water up."

Sebastian looked aghast from the window down. "Dear child, I couldn't possibly ask you to bring water up three flights to fill a copper for me!"

"But the Sergeant said you wanted a bath!" Gilly managed to sound both dismayed and a little outraged.

"I neither want nor need one enough to make you carry all that water . . ."

"Oh, I don't carry it, sir," she told him with a sudden broad grin. "Papa built a pump." To demonstrate, she picked up the hook-ended poker from the fireplace and went over to the window. Sebastian followed her and leaned out to see a long leather hose going up the length of the building, looped through a metal circlet jutting out from the roof. Gilly caught the dangling end of the hose with the poker and pulled it carefully until she could bring the copper head through the window.

"Tyyyyleeeeerr!" she bawled out in an entirely unladylike fashion. "Get the puuuuuump!"

Young Tyler patted the horse he was combing then ran outside, waving up at the window. Sebastian saw the boy stop at a well pump, set close to the inn, to which the hose—with plenty of slack remaining—was attached. He grabbed the handle and worked it up and down ferociously for a few moments before Gilly, satisfied, pulled the hose over to the bath and waited. It took several minutes, but finally water spurted out of the hose and into the tub. It hissed as it hit the warming copper, steam curling elegantly within. When the copper was a third full, Gilly looked over her shoulder and bellowed: "STOP!" She held the hose over the tub until the stream of water trickled away then took the whole thing back to the window and let it go.

Returning to the tub, she poked at the fire in the little depression under the copper, making sure that it wasn't too hot then took a folded piece of sheepskin and settled it onto the bottom of the tub, protection against the heat of the base. "Leave it for about ten minutes, sir," she said to Sebastian. "It should be hot enough for a summer tub by then. I'll come back and ember the fire before you get in. Will the witches be wanting a bath too, Sergeant Ho?" she turned to ask.

"Probably. Why don't you ask them?"

All her confidence at showing off her father's invention drained away instantly, and she blushed and stammered. "Oh . . . I couldn't . . . I . . . it's not . . ." She swallowed hard and covered her face in her hands.

"They don't bite, child," Sebastian told her gently. She took her hands away long enough to stare at him as though he were mad.

Cadogan patted her on the shoulder. "You would honour them by asking," he said quietly.

She peeked up at him. "Do you think so?"

"Yes."

She chewed her lip uncertainly, then walked hesitantly down to their room. Cadogan listened at the door, but heard nothing until Gilly appeared, walking backwards out of the other room, nodding. "Shan't take long. I'll just fetch some wood." She grinned up at him as she ran past and down the stairs.

The sun was just setting as Magda helped Leenan to sit up against the pillows, the golden light spilling into the room, dappled with the shadow of the top of the apple tree. Leenan had woken up only a few hours before, and had been sleeping fitfully since. So far, she hadn't spoken a word.

"Here," Magda said, sitting on the edge of the bed, "I've brought you some soup."

Leenan looked without interest at the bowl Magda proffered.

"You need to eat something, Lee."

Leenan leaned slightly forward to sniff at the bowl. Her nose wrinkled up and she frowned. "Sssss . . ." she tried, then with more concentration, "ssssmells wrong."

Magda felt a knot of tension loosen a little. At least she was speaking now. She took a sip herself. "It's good soup, Lee. Eat some, please."

Leenan submitted to being fed a few spoonfuls of the broth, and by the third mouthful she was enjoying the taste of it again. There wasn't much meat in it, and no blood at all, but it was savoury, and warm like blood, and she felt stronger.

She ate half the broth then slumped back into the pillows. Magda put the bowl aside and took Leenan's hand, turning it so she could take her pulse. Leenan's fingers kept flexing, and occasionally her shoulders would shiver. The way they would when, as a dragon, she would shake down her wings.

"How are you feeling now?" Magda looked into her friend's face as a studied, intense look came over it, followed by a definite look of exasperation. Puzzlement gave way to a sudden realisation. "Lee, are you trying to mind-speak with me?"

Leenan's brows creased, then cleared with her own realisation. She nodded weakly.

"I don't think you can do that now."

" 'Sss . . . how . . . dragons talk," Leenan said with difficulty. Her mouth felt strangely malleable and heavy, hard to shape the way she wanted.

Magda closed her hand over Leenan's, which was still moving spasmodically. "Lee, your fingers . . ."

"Wings . . ." Leenan correctly dozily.

Magda laid Leenan's hand back on the covers. "You liked being a dragon, didn't you?"

"Strong," Leenan said, "safe."

"You get some more sleep. I'll check on you in the morning."

Leenan was already asleep. She was dreaming of flying.

Magda joined the others in the kitchens where Madam Imber had invited them to share a meal with the family. The regular dining hall on the ground floor was filled with other travelers and local drinkers at this time of night, and the sounds of their revelry drifted through the open door.

When all the men went off to the war
The women stayed at home
They filled the night with a woeful roar—
Why are we all alone?
Oh woe! Oh woe!
Who will answer our prayers?
Oh woe! Oh woe!
Who will fix our cares?
Who will come
To our heartfelt call?
Who'll spread his favour
Over all?

Madam Imber excused herself and shut the door, reducing the sound, though it was still audible. "My apologies," she said. "Some of the men get a little rambunctious at night."

"What are they singing?" asked Magda as she sat down. Cadogan looked distinctly uncomfortable, an expression not helped when Madam Imber laughed at it.

"It's an old army song," she said helpfully.

"It's not often the army sings about those left behind," said Magda.

Then Stamford came
And he made a name
For himself and he earned

Their trust.

Tyler, sitting at the end of the table, snorted with a half-swallowed laugh. Gilly kicked his ankle under the table. Magda got the distinct sense she was missing the point.

The whisper ran throughout
The land of the power
Of his lightning thrust.

Oh.

The door burst open again and a tall, muscular man appeared with an empty beer barrel in one hand.

"Sorry ladies," Innkeeper Imber said, passing through the kitchen to the cool store out the back. The rest of the song came clearly through the open door.

For
The long strong sword of Stamford
Was a mighty weapon indeed
Oh yes.
He put it to service rightly
He put it to service knightly
He put it to service sprightly
Of maidens in sore need.

Cadogan's face had passed from extreme discomfort to a hard, unreadable parade-ground expression. Gilly and Tyler were trying hard to keep straight faces and Tephee was looking mildly shocked. Sylvia asked for someone to pass the potatoes, which Sebastian did.

"That's more like the army songs I've heard," said Magda. "This lamb looks delicious, Madam Imber."

"Ladies," the innkeeper excused himself politely on his way

back through, a keg on each shoulder, and his wife closed the door after him.

"It sounds busy out there," remarked Sebastian and their hostess returned to her seat.

"Yes, business is unusually brisk at the moment. That lot are from Derry, and a good number of them fought with the King at Tyne."

"Where are they going?"

Madam Imber busied herself dishing up meat and vegetables before answering, and Tephee wondered if she hadn't been heard. Gilly and Tyler had become oddly still for a moment as well.

"There are rumours coming from the coast," Madam Imber said, slowly meeting Cadogan's gaze. "There has been some kind of miracle."

"The Arc vessel," Sebastian concurred. "I suppose I couldn't have expected the news not to spread."

"Is that where you're going?" Madame Imber's tone was stern.

"I am from the Temple," said Sebastian. "I have to learn the truth. Magda agreed to join me." He turned and smiled at her. "I thought the First King's emissary would like to come, whatever the truth is."

Magda returned his gaze with surprise. *You think I'm an emissary from god?*

"Do you really intend to go back?" This was aimed at Cadogan.

He nodded sombrely at Madam Imber's incredulous demand. "The King asked me to guide Witch Magda."

Madam Imber looked as though she might argue with that, or cry, but after a moment she just shook her head. "Be careful, Sergeant. We aren't much welcome along the coast either. Or the witches."

"Along the coast too now?"

"And it'll be getting worse. That lot are the third we've had here in the last week. More will be going. The rumours are saying it's the First King's Return."

"If that is true," said Sebastian, placing his hand over hers reassuringly, "don't fear. The First King is wise and just."

"Pity you can't say the same for all His followers," she snapped, then bit her lip and looked away. "I'm sorry. That wasn't called for."

The Arc priest frowned slightly and withdrew his hand. "Humanity is flawed," he said. "That is how we get people like Saebert Bakar-Cadron and the Witch Zuleika."

Madam Imber's sharp gaze fell on him again. "Yes," she said coolly, "not all of the Mother's vessels are strong enough for Her gift." She pushed back from the table. "I must go and help Thomlin at the bar. Clean up will you, Gilly, and you help her then get to bed, Tyler. Good night, Witch Magda, Witch Sylvia, Witch Tephee. Sergeant." She departed, allowing a snatch of another bawdy song to swell into the room before the door shut on it.

"I'm sorry," said Sebastian quietly.

Cadogan shook his head. "Lina and Thomlin both lost family in the Purge." He cast a glance towards the Imber children, who rose quickly to clear the table. He rose with them and, at the washtub, had a quiet word. Tyler nodded, and Gilly gave him a brief, shy hug. He returned to the table.

"I thought I had best sleep out at the stable tonight. We have too much gear still loaded out there, and with so many people about it would be safest. I'll see you in the morning. Good night, Witch Tephee. Witch Magda . . . ma'am." The last to Sylvia, who had given him a stern look. "Good night, Sebastian," he said, then left through the back door and walked to the stable. Alard barked a greeting before that door, too, was closed on the sound.

Tephee excused herself and took the rest of her meal upstairs, Sylvia close behind. Magda offered to help the children tidy up, but they wouldn't hear of it, so she and Sebastian climbed the stairs in silence to the third floor.

Alone in his room, Sebastian stood at the window looking down at the stableyards. He could still hear the singing from below and he saw a shadow moving about as Cadogan, carrying a lamp, settled bedding in the hay between the vehicles and Alard slumped down beside him with a satisfied huff. The lamp went out.

Sebastian undressed, blew out his own lamp, and got into bed. When he finally slept, he dreamt of Magda, bright as a star, emerging from an Arc vessel with the First King by her side.

CHAPTER EIGHT

Sergeant Ho woke up with the warm summer dawn. He'd slept well, bedded down on a blanket thrown over straw, and only mildly regretted having passed up the delights of a real bed. The night had been mostly undisturbed, though Alard had sprung up at some hour to growl and snap at someone curious enough to investigate the stables. The would-be thief had cursed then yelped and run off. Cadogan would have to keep an eye out for someone with a bite mark today.

Alard licked his face then trotted out to relieve himself and explore the yard. Cadogan stood up and dusted the straw from his travelling clothes in which he'd slept. He would change into his uniform again later, if necessary. The scent of the apple trees wafted into the stable and he inhaled deeply before picking up his sword and walking over to their shade to complete his morning exercises. The ground was free of stones and the grass soft underfoot, so he pulled off his boots and lay his sword beside them.

He began with his feet braced slightly apart, his eyes closed, his hands by his side, as he breathed deeply and found his centre, a pull from inside, connecting him to the ground below. The scent of the tree was all around him, and the cool air, rushing and curling into his lungs, a morning breeze lifting the hair from his brow and neck. The sound of birds in the trees above, the sounds of the town waking up around him, a part of the world but not intrusive. Everything he sensed was separate,

86

distinct, and at the same time part of him. He was even aware of a window opening above him, of eyes watching, but being part of him too he paid no regard to the observer.

Leenan rubbed her eyes sleepily and drew the bedding closer around her before leaning on the sill to look out on the world. It looked different without dragon eyes and ears. Deeper, perhaps, but not as colourful. She couldn't hear all the things she'd heard with her reptile ears; the texture of scent that had informed her of so much was reduced to the overwhelming scent of apple blossom.

She glanced down and saw Sergeant Ho standing perfectly still. Statue-still, she might have thought, but there was something about him that was intensely aware . . . and then he moved. A slow and graceful shifting forward, a gentle lunge and his arms swept forward then up. *Dancing again,* she thought, then smiled, remembering their conversation back at Tyne Castle. Meditation, he called it. He had that same peaceful, distant look Sylvia got when she was meditating, combined with the underlying dynamic of the movement. *It's a way of moving with the world,* he'd said. It looked beautiful, whatever it was.

He reacted before she noticed the two men appear under the trees, pausing at the end of one set of movements. He straightened up and greeted the men briefly. Their voices drifted up to her clearly.

"Can't find anyone to dance with, huh?" asked one of them, a tall young man with a mop of dark hair. He didn't sound kind.

"I'm exercising," Cadogan replied in a measured voice.

"Yeah, we can see you were working up a sweat, eh Poul?" said the young man to his shorter companion. "Still, I expect you need all the exercise you can get at your age."

"Yes," agreed Cadogan simply. This annoyed his visitors.

"Don't think I don't know what you are."

Cadogan raised an eyebrow.

"You're a witch worshipper. A lousy mother-lover."

Leenan flinched at the ugliness of the tone and looked to Cadogan, wondering how he would react to the insult.

"I worship the Mother, yes." His tone was polite, neutral, but his stance had stiffened slightly.

"First King curse you all."

"We honour the First King as well."

The two men took a step towards him at that, then Alard appeared, growling, his lip curled back in warning.

"Bez, that's the bastard mutt that bit me last night," Poul complained.

"So you're the one," Cadogan said with some surprise. Now he knew, he could see the cloth wrapped around his shin, bulking out the leg of his pants a little.

"Who cares if a mother-lover loses anything?"

"I'm also travelling with four witches and an Arc priest." Cadogan sounded like he was suppressing laughter. "You really should choose your targets more carefully."

"You threatening us?" Bez took a step towards him. Alard snarled loudly and Poul flinched. Cadogan stood his ground.

"I'm telling you," Leenan heard a steely note of warning in his voice, "leave it and go. Now."

"Why you . . ." Bez launched himself at Cadogan and Leenan watched in amazement as the young man suddenly sprawled. The Sergeant had hardly moved, but when Bez's punch arrived where the Sergeant had been, he was simply . . . not there anymore. He turned, unruffled, to look down on the ungainly heap of his attacker.

"I don't want to fight you. Go home."

"Son of a bitch!" Bez scrambled up and grabbed at Cadogan's shirt, only to find that the Sergeant wasn't there again, and his own momentum threw him off balance and down onto one knee on the grass again.

Poul had stepped in to help, but Alard had other ideas and leapt at him, growling and snapping. Cursing, Poul tried to drive the animal off. Alard sank his teeth into the same calf muscle he'd found the previous night and held on. Poul tried thumping the dog on the head and when that failed to shake him loose, he drew a knife and thrust down.

Only to find that a hand had captured his wrist and was holding it, immobile. To Poul's relief, the dog let go of his calf, but the hand still held his wrist. He looked up into the blue eyes of the pale-skinned Mother worshipper. Who had still not worked up a sweat.

"Let it go," Cadogan told him, gently but firmly. He let go.

"Gutless bastard, stand still!"

Leenan nearly called out a warning as Bez grabbed Cadogan's sword from the grass and rushed at the Sergeant. But in a moment, Cadogan had moved, forward, under and up . . . she thought she recognised the sequence from his morning routine—and suddenly he was the only one standing, Poul's knife in one hand, his own sword in the other. He was looking extremely annoyed.

Bez had crashed into Poul and both were sprawled on the grass with Alard standing over them, teeth bared. Cadogan strode up to them and held the tip of his sword against Bez's breast.

"Go. Away."

Bez and Poul went away. Quickly.

Cadogan sighed and watched them leave as he rubbed Alard's head. Alard, transformed abruptly from vicious guard dog to soppy pet, licked eagerly at his hands. "Some people really know how to ruin a man's morning, hey Alard?" He grinned suddenly and pulled at the dog's ears. "On the other hand, a workout is never a bad thing."

"Everything okay here? I heard some shouting."

Leenan saw Innkeeper Imber appear around the side of the building.

"A couple of idiot thieves, Thomlin," Cadogan said, shaking his head. "They changed their minds."

Thomlin snorted with laughter. "I'll bet they did."

A knock at the door drew Leenan back from the window. She settled back on the bed as Magda entered, carrying a tray.

"I know it's early," said Magda, "but the others are up already. I thought I'd come and see how you are. I brought some breakfast for you."

Leenan allowed Magda to fuss for a moment, making sure her pillows were propped up behind her and that the tray was steady on her lap. When it looked like Magda might be about to feed her, as she'd done last night, Leenan took the cutlery firmly in hand herself. Magda obediently left her to it and brought a chair to her bedside.

"You look at lot better this morning," she said. Leenan got the feeling that her friend was exercising great restraint in not taking pulses, temperature, and generally giving her a thorough physical.

"I feel a lot better," Leenan replied. She found it easier to speak this morning. "But I ache all down my right side." She sniffed at her breakfast—eggs, sausages, and stewed butterbeans—then realised what she was doing and hastily shoved a forkful of beans into her mouth. They tasted surprisingly good.

"That will be the bruising coming out. Do you remember what happened?"

Leenan nodded, still chewing. She had overcome the initial impulse to pick up the sausage and tear at it with her teeth and was carefully cutting sections of it and chewing thoroughly, getting used to eating like a human again.

"You could have killed yourself, you know. Whatever possessed you to fly into a lightning strike?"

She tried to mind-speak a reply, remembered that she couldn't, and swallowed hastily. "I didn't have much choice. I had to do something before the dragon instinct took over completely."

"The other dragons flew south. We haven't seen them since."

Leenan speared another piece of sausage. "They'll be making or joining a new pack and finding mates."

"Yes." She sighed. "I'm going to miss them." She looked up into her friend's eyes. "I'd have missed you too." Magda's blue eyes were glittering with emotion.

"I really frightened you, didn't I?"

"Yes, you did." Now that Lee was safe, Magda could feel her professional detachment letting go. The need to minister to a patient had kept her fear in check, and now that there was nothing more to fear the relief caught in her throat. Leenan was recovering, behaving less and less like the dragon she had been; more like her human self. Magda rubbed at a leaked tear with the heel of her hand. "It was lucky you fell into the river. Luckier still that Sergeant Ho was there to drag you out again before you drowned."

She blinked back more tears as she felt Leenan's hand close around her own and squeeze it. "It's okay, Maggie. I'm all right now," she said gently.

"I know," Magda's tears fell unrestrained now. "I'm being stupid, I know. You're all right and I don't need to worry about you now, so of course I start to cry my heart out when I don't need to anymore. Thank you." She accepted the napkin Leenan offered and wiped her face. She sniffed and smiled sheepishly.

"I'm sorry I scared you," Leenan said contritely.

"Just don't do it again."

"I won't."

They both smiled and laughed a little and that restored

Magda to her usual self. "Well. How was breakfast?"

"Good." Leenan was busy mopping up the last of the egg yolk with some bread.

"I'll find some clothes for you shortly. I think it would be a good idea if you got out into the sunshine and walked a little. You'll be sore for a day or two still."

"Where are my own clothes?"

"Oh, someone found them on the field after the battle. We couldn't stitch them up—they were too torn from your change."

Leenan frowned, then realised what Magda was referring to. "No, I meant when I . . ." She trailed off. Of course. She hadn't been wearing clothes as a dragon, and so when she changed back to a human she hadn't been wearing anything then either. And Sergeant Ho had dragged her out of the river . . .

"Don't be embarrassed Lee . . . it's only me here."

Leenan swallowed, feeling her face radiating her shame and horror. "Cadogan . . ." she said in a strangled whisper.

Magda patted her arm. "Cadogan was a perfect gentleman. Besides which, you were badly burnt and half drowned. He'd wrapped you up in his leather tunic to keep you warm."

"Oh Lords." Leenan covered her face with her hands and shook her head, but when she looked up her high colour had abated. "I made a complete idiot of myself." She sounded annoyed now.

"Lee, you didn't have much choice, as you said. I'd rather have you here with us now, a little bruised and your dignity a little dented, than wonder what was happening to you with the dragon pack during mating season."

"Yeah. Well." Other comment was reduced to mumbling.

"I'll just go find something for you to wear, all right? We're bound to have something between the three of us that will fit you until we can buy some things."

Magda moved the breakfast tray to a side table, smoothed

down the bedding and kissed Leenan's brow in a motherly fashion before leaving. Leenan slid down under the blankets, groaning, and pulled a pillow over her face.

The bedroom door opened a crack and Sylvia glanced up from her lotus position on the floor. Tephee blinked back. Pywych, still sleeping on the bed, yawned, and folded his head back down to complete the furry circle he made on the covers.

"Sorry," said Tephee, "I'll come back later if you . . ."

"No, no, that's all right." Sylvia sighed and unfolded herself. "I can't focus anyway. Or unfocus, really. And my head aches."

"Poor Sylvia." Tephee entered and closed the door behind her. "Maybe you shouldn't have tried to dry yesterday's clothes."

"It was such small magic." Sylvia frowned and rubbed the bridge of her nose. Even the smallest magic gave her headaches or nosebleeds these days; perhaps it was just as well she couldn't concentrate enough for the bigger magic. Magda kept telling her to rest, but it was an itch in her blood, all the time. It wasn't just the headaches, either. She had grown . . . vague. She had risen with Tephee this morning, saw the clothes were still damp and waved a hand to dry them. Instead of then meditating and going down to join Tephee for breakfast and a walk she had sat on the floor in a half dream, thoughts wandering from a memory of her husband when they were first married to counting the tiny golden teardrops sewn into the decorative bedspread. She felt like a faded picture of herself.

"Madam Imber said she'd brew up some mistglow tea for you—good for headaches, she says." Tephee suddenly smiled, a little sheepish. "She keeps calling me Witch Tephee. So do the kids."

"It's a very real title of respect, for them. I'm not really comfortable with it myself."

"I don't know," replied Tephee wistfully, "I sort of like it."

A smile spread across Sylvia's face and her eyes regained their old sparkle. "Welcome back!"

Tephee looked puzzled and her lips forming enquiry as Sylvia straightened up onto her feet. "You've been so meek and mild these last few weeks, I was beginning to wonder where you'd gone."

"Oh. Well." Tephee frowned again and sat on the bed to look out the window. "I'm . . . I didn't mean to be . . ." She was blushing and stammering and looked up guiltily at the older woman as she came to sit beside her. "I'm sorry."

"Now there you go, running back into hiding again. Come back out here, where I can see you."

Tephee only blushed and looked away.

"You used to be so confident," Sylvia said gently.

"I used to be so selfish and stupid, you mean. I was self-centred and pushy and thoroughly horrible."

"You were hurting." She had been thrown out of her home at fifteen when her mother couldn't cope with her witchly child. Magda, unaware at that stage that magic was real, had taken her in, only to react with shock and fear when Tephee had conjured the dragons as a gift. Rejected, the girl had run away and found Sylvia living a hermit's life by the sea. Magda had found them there, found her own magic, and after Leenan had joined them, they'd returned to Tunston for the winter, where Tephee's mother had first invited her daughter back home again, only to refuse her again later. No wonder her time with them as they tracked down the King and sought to defeat Zuleika had been so filled with her need to protect herself from that kind of pain.

"That's no excuse," Tephee retorted miserably. "I've learned my lesson. I'll be a good, meek little girl now."

"Is that what you think the lesson was?"

That finally brought Tephee's head around, so that their gazes met. "I . . ." She tried to decipher Sylvia's look, but it was only mildly expectant. "No. No, I suppose it wasn't. It was about . . ." She thought back on that journey from Tunston through the mountains and the plains to Tyne Castle. She thought especially about that last, terrible day as the battle for the kingdom threatened to overwhelm the King, his army, and the witches. "It was about earning trust. And keeping faith. And . . . and being humble."

"Ah." Sylvia's dark, exotically elfin features quirked wryly. "There's a word."

"Why? What . . ."

"Do you think I'm humble?"

Tephee nodded slowly. "I guess."

"Do you think I'm meek?"

"No. I . . ." Tephee flung her hands wide in exasperation. "I was awful, Sylvia! I was miserable. I had to change who I was."

"Who you are is constant. But you can change how you think and what you do."

Tephee looked dubious.

"Be yourself, love," Sylvia said, wrapping an arm around the girl for a hug. "Just remember you're not a goddess."

Tephee hugged her back, with a strained laugh. "Tell that to the Imbers."

"I have tried."

After a pause, Tephee said: "The respect is nice."

"So it is. Maybe you'll find you are respected more as you get older."

Tephee drew back and plucked at her skirt with a sigh. "Do you know . . . I'm nearly seventeen now?"

Sylvia raised an eyebrow. Wasn't Tephee only fifteen still? Or was that when she'd first met her? Why were there so many small, insignificant things she couldn't remember? She looked into the young girl's face and realised that the childish roundness had given away in recent months to subtle planes and angles. Beneath the mop of light-brown hair, her hazel eyes were large and clear, her lightly tanned skin smooth and unblemished, her jaw strong and nose straight. She was turning into a very beautiful young woman.

"I've been wearing the same kind of clothes since I was twelve." Cast offs. Long, layered skirts not quite reaching her ankles, feet unshod or pushed into flat sandals or shoes, high-necked long-sleeved blouses that effectively hid the changes in her body.

No wonder she still looks so young, Sylvia thought.

"Do we have any money?"

Sylvia knew what was coming and smiled. "Yes. The King gave us quite a lot before we left."

"Do you think . . . ? I'd like to buy some new clothes."

"Would you like me to come with you?"

Tephee smiled. "Would you? I don't really know what to get."

The door opened and Magda walked in, suppressing a small grin. It widened in greeting for her friends. "Are you going shopping today? We need to get some things for Lee as well. Have you got something she can wear in the meantime?"

They fell to, searching through their luggage for items that were neither too long, too large, too short, or too tight while they planned their day out.

CHAPTER NINE

They made an odd-looking group as they walked from the Half Moon Inn through the small square and down a cobblestoned arcade into the main square of Jubilee. There was Magda, tall and dark haired, whose blue eyes regarded everything with the curiosity of a tourist; Tephee in her layers of outgrown skirts; Sylvia, alternately looking over everything with interest and wandering distractedly along, gazing into space; Leenan, still pale and her bruised side aching, walking with her arms folded and eyes downcast, trying unsuccessfully to be inconspicuous in her ill-fitting borrowed clothes while Alard trotted at her heels; and finally Cadogan, dressed smartly in his uniform. He was polite, distant, leaving the women to talk. If he noticed that Leenan was, not so subtly, keeping her distance, he seemed neither to notice or mind. Watchful, but not tense, he followed and waited as they inspected different stores in passing. The only time he broke his soldierly posture was when he idly patted Alard's head when the dog was not allowed to follow his mistress into a store.

One narrow doorway led to a seamstress. It reminded Cadogan of Lyria and Kynwyn, and he stood to attention outside, lost in thought for a while thinking how much the two of them would have enjoyed the market. He would have to bring them here one day. When the witches emerged some time later, Leenan and Tephee were both dressed in simple lace-tied dresses which they had bought ready-made. The simplicity of style suited them both, though Leenan felt vulnerable in a skirt rather than the trousers she had usually worn last time she was human. Tephee was smiling self-consciously, aware that she looked more grown-up now. Cadogan's gaze flickered several times in Leenan's direction, but he did not venture an opinion until Tephee cajoled him. Even then he confined himself to a gentlemanly "Very becoming."

"One of us will have to come back tomorrow," Tephee said with a pleased grin, "to pick up the rest. We've been measured up . . . do you think the green really suits me?" This to Leenan, who had stopped to study her feet, it appeared.

"Oh—shoes!" realised Magda. "Where can we get some shoes, Cad?" She hesitated at the look on his face. ". . . ogan."

"Madam Imber recommended a place on the corner . . ." He led them. Leenan waited until the dizziness had passed, then followed them.

While they were inside the cobbler's workshop, choosing styles and leathers, Cadogan noticed two figures sliding past, following a well-to-do traveler as he sauntered towards the local pub. Cadogan cleared his throat noisily and the two looked up.

Poul blanched. Bez scowled. Then they both swallowed.

"You're . . . you . . ."

Cadogan arched an eyebrow.

"You're the King's Man," Poul gasped out.

"So I am."

Bez's scowl deepened, though it was tinged with fear of what might have happened. Poul had the grace to look ashamed of himself. "Sorry," he mumbled.

Cadogan's lips merely compressed in a forbidding line. "Keep out of trouble," he told them sternly, "and this won't be taken up in court." It would, Cadogan reflected, be a monumental waste of time and money to try these two for treason—which is what assault of the King's own guardsman amounted to—

mostly because he had not been wearing his uniform at the time and a treason charge would be impossible to uphold. It was the assault upon the uniform and who that uniform symbolised, and not the man, which was condemned by law. He didn't expect, however, that this pair would know of the distinction. The would-be thieves held themselves stiffly and when given a dismissive nod, they fled. Cadogan sighed.

The women emerged, Tephee now shod with elegant summer shoes and Leenan with her feet in more practical soft boots—more ready-mades, which were becoming more popular these days, while the special order was being made up.

Sylvia emerged, her small hands twisting at the ends of her long hair—occasionally she lipped a dark tip into her mouth and chewed on the ends until she realised and hastily pushed her hair away. She glanced at Cadogan's expression and brought her attention back. "Trouble, Sergeant?"

"Not anymore, Wi . . ."—he swallowed down hard on the honorific—"ma'am."

Leenan was staring hard at the point where the two men had disappeared into the crowd. Her nose was wrinkling slightly, as though she could smell them. "They're the ones who attacked you in the yard this morning," she said, anger lacing her voice.

Cadogan remembered the sensation of being watched. "They were hardly a threat, Witch Leenan."

She met his gaze then turned sharply away, embarrassment heating her face again—but the sudden movement disoriented her. A wave of giddiness swept away her balance and she stumbled slightly. A strong hand grasped her by the arm, righting her and she wiped her hands over her eyes.

"Lee!" Magda's hands were on her next, checking her temperature, pulse. "Damn. I shouldn't have let you get out of that bed . . ."

"I'm okay," she protested irritably, "just tired. I'm a witch, damnit. Moved too fast . . ." She leaned on the strong hand for support, then opened her eyes to realise whose hand she was relying on. She pulled roughly away from the Sergeant, unbalancing herself again in her dismay, and found herself surrounded by witches holding her up from all sides.

"Oh, for the First King's sake, leave me alone!" she protested, but the exhaustion had caught up with her in one swift blow and her legs were shaking. "Stop fussing!"

"Here . . ." Tephee found a chair and helping hands lowered her onto the stool.

"I'm all right."

"If you were all right you wouldn't be white as a sheet," Magda reasoned. "Hell, she's shivering. Tephee, can you find a cup of water . . . I need a blanket . . ." Sylvia went off in search of a blanket and Magda shooed away curious passersby with a stern glare.

Leenan stifled a groan, horribly aware of all the attention. She was all right, damnit, just tired. And embarrassed. Lords, fainting in public, how *humiliating*. And with the Sergeant right behind her, witnessing all her frailty once more. She could have cried with the shame and anger of it all. A blanket was draped over her shoulders and a cup pushed into her hands.

"Sip it slowly," Magda advised, guiding her shaking hands.

"I'm all *right*."

"You will be. Here, can you stand?"

"Of course I can . . ." Only her knees wouldn't lock and she sagged back down onto the stool. "Give me a second," she breathed through gritted teeth. She would not be carried back to the inn. Absolutely and without question *not*.

"Let me help," Sergeant Ho offered quietly, his arm extended before her.

I'd rather crawl back. But her body, betrayer that it was, wouldn't be called back under control. Her hands were shaking and her feet were made of stone, cold and heavy. She opened her eyes to a world that shifted unsteadily and blurrily. A crowd of people watching her disappeared from view as a man in black and red moved between them. He crouched down and his blue eyes met her uncertain gaze.

"You should get back to the inn, Witch Leenan."

She frowned stubbornly. She'd get back under her own power, damnit.

"Please, My Lady," he continued gently. His expression and tone were devoid of either unwanted pity or mockery of any kind. His hand was still held out in offer.

"Don't you bloody carry me," she gritted, closing her eyes.

"We'll walk together, ma'am."

Leenan rose unsteadily, with Cadogan to support her on one side and Magda on the other.

"We'll take care of her," she heard Magda say. "You finish the shopping."

"Are you sure you don't need us?"

"No, really. It isn't far."

Leenan was muttering deeply annoyed imprecations for them to go *finish* the damn shopping and not complete her sense of foolishness and being a nuisance by letting her interfere with the whole day, instead of the little piece of it she'd managed to mess up. She was relieved when Tephee and Sylvia went on their way and she could start walking, slowly, back to the inn. By the time they reached the stairs she actually felt a little better, but had to suffer being half carried to the third floor and put into bed. The Sergeant then withdrew, quietly and discreetly as before. She fell asleep before Magda had even left the room.

Magda joined Cadogan, the Imbers, and several others she didn't know in the front bar. It was a little early for the lunch crowd to have arrived so Magda assumed the young man and his wife were friends of the innkeepers. At their enquiring looks she sat down.

"She just needs more rest. I let her push herself too hard—witches heal much more quickly than other people do." She pulled a face, angry for allowing herself to become complacent.

"She'll be all right," Madam Imber assured her. "The Mother looks after Her own."

"I'm sure the Mother would find that easier to do if we took a little care ourselves," she replied, the acerbity of her tone softened by weariness. Madam Imber patted her arm and poured a cup of fragrant herbal tea for her. Magda sniffed at it.

"Mistglow tea," her hostess explained.

Magda sipped—it tasted a little like chamomile tea—and relaxed a little. She was introduced to the strangers at the table—Kieran and Aylene Tamson—who regarded her respectfully.

A pretty woman entered through the kitchen doors, her fine blonde hair tied back under a scarf, drying her hands on her already damp apron. "Is that all, Lina?"

"All for today, Tessa. Why don't you come in for a cup of tea?"

Tessa smiled and sat with the group, gratefully taking a cup into her water-worn hands. She addressed Cadogan. "I hear two of Dallas' boys gave you a hard time this morning."

Thomlin Imber snorted with humour. "They wish."

"Who's Dallas?" Cadogan wanted to know.

"He runs the feed store on Cloppers Row over the back," Thomlin supplied. "Doesn't pay his workers nearly enough then wonders why he gets such bad work out of them."

Tessa sipped her tea thoughtfully. "These two were hard at work a little while ago. Didn't even cheek me while I was hanging out the laundry."

"I . . . ah . . . gave them a little fright this afternoon," Cadogan said, not quite suppressing a smile.

"Oh," said Tessa, and her eyes danced with humour. "Good."

Kieran's mouth twisted wryly. He had pale skin, like Cadogan's, but he was taller and more angular. His accent was filled with the musical lilt that only existed in remnants in the Sergeant's voice. "Are these the same two who . . . ?"

The door opened and Sebastian walked in, looking cheerful and satisfied.

"Sebastian!" Magda waved a hello. "Where have you been? We were going to ask you to join us at the square but you'd left already."

"There's an Arc Hold here," he told her. "I thought I'd stop by. It's a beautiful building—white stone and marbletree pillars. They are carved all around with the story of the First King's arrival and the Journeys of the Lords . . . just magnificent!"

Magda translated a Hold as a church, roughly. There hadn't been a Hold in Tunston, though a public shrine was set at the east end of that town's square.

"Was there a service today?"

"Just the usual prayers from the Holders studying there," Sebastian waved his hand airily.

"Dallas' father is a Holder, isn't he?" asked Kieran.

Thomlin nodded and Lina grimaced. "I don't believe they have a very friendly relationship these days," she said.

Tessa reached across to pat Lina's hand. "See—not everyone in Jubilee is against you. It's just those idiot boys, and that's just because Dallas is such a pig about you."

Lina met her gaze. "You honestly don't care about being washerwoman to Leylites?"

"I'm washerwoman to a lot of people," Tessa told her earnestly, "but I won't work for Dallas."

Aylene's eyebrows rose. "He offered you a job, did he?"

Tessa shrugged. "He asked what mornings I was free, Ay, and

103

I told him I was busy from now until the First King's Return as far as he was concerned." She sniffed haughtily. "I'm not so desperate for money that I need his coppers."

Sebastian was looking thoughtful. "Do you get a lot of . . . trouble . . . in Jubilee?"

"A little." Thomlin's reserve said enough.

Magda shook her head slightly. Humanity was so predictable. Sometimes she liked to think that her race had matured on this world, but clearly not. The same old stupid fears and anxieties bred the same old stupid intolerance and childishness.

Something else occurred to her then, and she sighed. She felt eyes on her and looked up to see Sebastian, the Imbers, and the Tamsons all watching her intently. She found a small smile for them. "I'm just thinking about Lee." They made reassuring noises, but mostly she was thinking: *If there's prejudice here in Tyne, this far away, what do we have to look forward to in Marin Kuta?* She did not want to think about the answer.

CHAPTER TEN

The Arc Hold was as elegant as Sebastian had said. A small building made of white stone, it shone in the summer sun. Tall windows allowed plenty of light inside, so that the interior glowed as well. Magda could imagine the white walls flushed orange with the colours of sunset that would pour through the western window there. Now, in the early afternoon, it spilled around the marbletree pillars that were set three abreast down the length of the main room, illuminating the carvings Sebastian had spoken of.

Although the art style was different, the events depicted were similar to those she had seen months ago at the Arc Temple where she had met Sebastian. The first panel depicted the arrival of the First King and His followers in a gleaming burst of light. Following panels depicted various major events in early history—or myth—a line of men and women, animals and plants emerging from the light, various splits and departures with focus on each of the six Lords. One panel was devoted to a seventh man, highlighted in scarlet, who on the left of the image was depicted as leading a group of women into battle against the First King. In the centre he was leading them to exile, and by the right he had been turned out by the crowd of women, some of whom were seen kneeling and making offerings to the First King. The much-maligned Red Lord, Magda supposed. She would have loved to know what really happened a thousand years ago.

Magda turned to explore further. Along the sides of the room under the windows were tables bearing old books and parchments. Some were thick paper, others were fine ink on lizardskin. One was a bound collection of marbletree tablets. Magda walked around the tables, running her fingers lightly over the books there. She still couldn't read well on this world. It had taken her long enough to learn to speak the local dialect of Earth Standard—mutated and grown in one thousand years of independent development—and she had never needed to learn how to read and write in that language until recently. Peering closely, she thought she recognised some forms of the English alphabet, though parts looked vaguely Cyrillic. Tyne court documents had borne a different script again.

She sighed, turning back to the pillars. The story inscribed on them, of the arrival of the First King and His Lords and following the tale as they separated and established their own kingdoms, noting the sporadic loss of technology through wars and lack of resources, was fairly clear to her. Perhaps not so clear to the Holders who studied here, but then, she had inside knowledge.

She could see how this had become a creation myth. There were potent elements to the story, and certainly the Captain of that colony ship had brought humanity to this planet. Humanity, horses, wheat, corn . . . a whole variety of plant and animal life that colonists might have needed for their new homeworld. Like a god, he'd brought them here and sent them forth to be fruitful and multiply. Except that Magda, of all people, knew he had been no higher power. Just a man who had found his ship going through a tear in space, who had managed to bring the ship to a decent landing. The early pictures were stylised, but she had recognised the first colony fleet's uniform with its distinctive sunburst design on the shoulder—a pattern echoed on Sebastian's Temple robes.

Sergeant Ho's Earth Mother is more like a real religion than this. Should I tell Sebastian he worships a lie? Does it matter? Her fingers traced the outline of the Arc vessel depicted with the First King's arrival, and the people and animals leaving it, two by two. *The Ark in reverse.* Maybe it was more real than she suspected. Places on Earth had worshipped their own ancestors, who were real enough. Sebastian appeared quite clear that the First King had been a real human being. Did his humanity preclude his divinity? Magda pulled at the tip of her nose, frowning. *Theology was never my strong point.*

Two people entered from the back room, talking quietly. Sebastian smiled when he saw her. "You decided to have a look yourself, Magda?" He put the heavy volumes he was carrying on a desk and made an introduction. "This is Holder Ingham Dallas."

Magda nodded greeting to the Holder, apparently the father of the Imbers' troublesome neighbour. Ingham Dallas was a solid man in his sixties, his weathered brown skin and wiry grey curls giving him a harsh look which was softened by intense brown eyes. He returned the greeting. A Holder, she gathered from her talk with Sebastian at lunch, was something like a city councilor or tribal elder, a combination of spiritual guide and civic leader. There were twelve Holders in Jubilee, though anyone was welcome to study here, or pray at the shrine in the small paved courtyard at the rear of the building.

"Did you come to look at our books, Witch Magda?" asked Holder Dallas politely. Magda heard the difference in the way he stressed the honorific. It was manners, only, not religious deference that inspired its use.

"I was just interested in looking around. Sebastian told me how beautiful your Hold was."

"Our Temple brother flatters our study hall." Nevertheless, he was pleased with the praise.

"It is very beautiful," Magda said. "I was thinking how stunning it would be here at sunset."

Ingham smiled. "It is like sitting in the palm of the sun."

Sebastian was looking especially pleased with himself, delighted that Magda had come to see the Hold and was appreciating it. "Perhaps Magda would be kind enough to examine your new book with us," he said to Ingham.

The Holder pursed his lips, ever so slightly. "I do not know what Witch Magda could bring to its interpretation that we Holders cannot."

Sebastian either missed or ignored the tone of disapproval. "Witch Magda may have more insights than you would give her credit for."

"So you believe."

"Is there any harm in it? If I'm wrong there's nothing to be lost, and if I'm right . . ."

"And if we don't, Temple Brother, you will nag me until I'm dead of it." Ingham raised an eyebrow at him.

Sebastian paused, then smiled benignly. "Indeed."

"Sebastian," Magda started towards the door, "there's no need to nag Holder Dallas to death over me, honestly. I really just wanted to see the carvings . . ."

"Oh, please, Witch Magda," Ingham interrupted, "do stay. It won't take a moment." His smile was cool and faintly challenging.

"I don't want to be a bother to you," she replied firmly. "I don't expect I'll be able to bring much insight to your studies . . ." *I probably can't read the language for a start.*

"So I've told Brother Sebastian, but he does insist so. There . . ." Ingham had returned to the table and opened the large book which Sebastian had deposited there. The Temple priest took her elbow and guided her towards the table and, given the choice of either flight or submission, Magda sighed and joined them.

She nearly snatched the page out of Ingham's hand, only restraining herself at his sharp, angry look. Instead she let her hand fall on the page, tracing the words with hovering fingertips.

"Where did you get this?" It came out a whisper.

"This copy, from the Arc Temple at Besgarth. The original is held at the Great Library in Marin Kuta, though that hasn't been seen by anyone from the mainland for nearly fifty years." Ingham glanced at her, puzzled. "The Besgarth copy was made four hundred years ago by Brother Iko who made a pilgrimage to Kuta for the task. He had to smuggle it out, each page rolled tightly and stuffed into a sheep's intestine, which he swallowed and retrieved once he had returned to the mainland." Ingham was filled with admiration for the priest.

Magda gagged at the mental picture, but it explained a few things. Duplicated in haste and then rewritten at leisure from those notes and memory. Brother Iko must have had a didactic memory to have reproduced it so nearly correctly. She shook her head and turned the page, running her finger down another section. It was a more archaic form of the language she had learned herself at school, but near enough to be mostly legible. It had the added advantage of not requiring verb forms, adjectives, or most other parts of speech. Mostly, it consisted of decipherable nouns.

"What is it?" Sebastian was close by her, speaking softly, his voice pregnant with anticipation.

"A manifest," she told him, still amazed. "It's the ship's hard copy. This is the livestock." She turned pages one after the other. "Poultry here—chickens, ducks, geese, pigeons. Cattle. Pigs. Sheep. Horses. Even dogs and cats. Vegetables . . . cotton . . . hemp . . . Just a summary of the computer logs, a rough inventory . . ." At the last page there was a scrawl—perhaps it had been a signature on the original—and under that a list of names. Her fingers brushed the page lightly as she read the first name on the list. Captain S. D. King. "I could have guessed . . ." She trailed off, wondering why Sebastian was staring at her, then realised that she had fallen back into Earth Standard. She shrugged. "It's a list," she said clearly.

Holder Dallas was staring at her as well. "And so the First King came, with two of each beast His people would need; and seeds of the plants for their nourishment and comfort, and He wrote these down, so that the people would know what He had given to them, and His Lords wrote their names for their share to distribute to those for whom He had made them responsible . . ."

This is ridiculous! she thought wildly, horrified at the awed look on their faces. *They've made a religion out of a cargo manifest.* She turned again to the front of the book. As she'd thought, the manifest was headed with fourteen pages of letters and codes which were otherwise unclarified. She had studied her cryonics history, however, as a compulsory subject for her colonial doctorate. Six pages for the cryogenically suspended adults in the cargo. Eight for the further gene banks held in storage, to ensure adequate variation of the gene pool on arrival. Plus the live crew. Standard on the first colony ships. *Wherever you are, Captain S. D. King, I hope you don't think this is funny. Because I certainly don't.*

She snapped the book shut and backed away. Sebastian and Ingham did not try to stop her, or to touch her at all.

"I really have to get back. To see how Leenan is doing." Then she fled.

Sebastian and Ingham were both very quiet for a time. Finally, Ingham said: "I see what you mean."

"I thought you might."

"She's really from the True World?"

"Others have been sent in the past."

"Not for centuries. And never a witch."

"She must be needed."

"This Arc vessel that is said to have come to Marin Kuta . . ."

"Yes . . ."

"Where the First King brought life to this world. That is significant."

"Perhaps she will be our interpreter."

"But she's a witch. That will make things difficult. The Kutans won't stand for it."

"It must mean something." Sebastian placed his hand on the closed book. "I just don't know what." He sighed. "Perhaps when we've caught up with the others it will be clearer."

"Do they know you are bringing her?"

"Oh yes, we agreed that I should go by Tyne to see if she would come. Although . . ."—here Sebastian laughed—"I suspect they might have agreed because I was nagging them so hard."

Holder Dallas' eyes sparkled in reply. "A nagger isn't necessarily wrong. I will tell my wife. I'm sure she will find it a comfort."

Leenan woke up to the sound of muffled laughter in the hallway. She blinked, wondering for a moment why she was lying in bed in the middle of the day, fully dressed, before she remembered. With a small sigh, she got up and went to the door to peek outside. Tephee and Sylvia were just emerging from their room again, trying to be quiet, but when Sylvia saw her she waved hello. Tephee grinned and hurried over to her.

"Hey, Lee. How are you feeling? You look a lot better."

"Mmmph."

"That's a very dragonesque reply," Sylvia remarked dryly.

"I'm fine. I just feel . . . silly."

Tephee rolled her eyes. "Honestly, Lee," then she grinned again. She looked different somehow. Then Leenan realised that the girl's long brown hair, instead of hanging untidily loose, had been washed, combed, and scented and was pinned up on her head with a simple, elegant wooden comb. Her eyes were clear and shining, as though she'd discovered a happy secret.

"You look great," Leenan said, with just a hint of surprise.

Tephee beamed and danced around in a little circle to show off her new self.

"The comb is a nice touch."

"That was Sylvia's idea . . . oh, hang on . . ." Tephee darted into her room then reappeared with a small paper-wrapped parcel. "We got this for you."

Leenan took the parcel, suddenly aware of how much longer her hair had grown. Not quite long enough to tie back yet. She hoped it wasn't a hair comb. She opened the paper and stood gazing at the gift within. A dragon-shaped brooch, carved from old wood and polished to pale bronze, its head raised high and wings outstretched. Unexpectedly, Leenan found herself wanting to cry.

"It reminded us of you," Tephee said softly.

Leenan nodded, not trusting her voice. *Idiot*, she thought. *What's to cry about?*

"We wanted you to know," Sylvia added, "that we're glad we didn't lose you."

She wasn't sure if she started crying before or after they descended on her for a hug, but the tears turned to laughter so quickly it hardly mattered. The three of them ended up in the apple room while Leenan tidied up her hair and pinned the brooch on her dress, chatting about the day's shopping, before they went downstairs together.

Gilly was working in the kitchen, preparing vegetables to add to the meat her mother was braising in a pot over the fire. Madam Imber stopped to fuss over them with tea and honey cakes as she admired their new decorations—Tephee's comb, Leenan's brooch, and a rainbow crystal pendant Sylvia had bought. Pywych made an unexpected appearance, having come down to look for his witches, and was equally fussed over with cream and chicken giblets. Tyler had already been out with a treat for Alard, they were assured. As Tephee and Sylvia talked about their long and fruitful expedition into the shopping square, Leenan sat back and enjoyed being human once again. Now that she was feeling less embarrassed, she thought she might thank Sergeant Ho when she next saw him.

The rear door opened and Magda rejoined them. She exclaimed over Tephee's new look and was delighted to receive a coastal-style hair-braiding loop—a polished wooden ring with long colourful thongs of leather attached. It reminded her of Tamalan, but gently for a change, without that familiar pang of regret. Madam Imber helped her to wind her hair through the leather and attach the beads to the ends so a long, dark plait hung heavily over her shoulder.

"It suits you," Leenan told her, nodding.

"You think so?" While Tephee assured her that, indeed, it brought out the red highlights in her hair, Sylvia studied her for a moment then shook her head and poured more tea, poking a spoon into the elegant pot and swirling the water and herbs in floating patterns.

"You haven't seen Sergeant Ho, have you?" Leenan asked in the following brief silence.

"Oh, he's gone with Thom to collect some supplies from Belvedere across town. He thought you wouldn't mind. We've had news there are more travelers arriving tonight."

"Oh," Sylvia ceased her restless stirring of the teapot, "you must be needing our rooms soon."

Madam Imber patted the air in a calming motion. "Not at all, Witch Sylvia. No one can afford those rooms anyway."

"Goodness!" Tephee's eyebrows rose in surprise. "How much is Cadogan paying for them?" Then she bit her lip, belatedly realising that it was somehow not very social of her to have asked.

Madam Imber only smiled. "If no one can afford to stay in them, it's best if only my personal guests take them, eh?"

"A whole floor for your own visitors," said Sylvia mildly. "That is exceedingly generous."

A burst of appreciative laughter escaped the woman's lips. "Well," she conceded, "when we don't have visitors, we use them ourselves, except for the apple room. That was my mother's room till winter before last." She shrugged slightly at the quick looks of sympathy she received. "Oma lived well, and the Mother took her kindly. It's more than she'd expected. Now . . ."—she set about the kitchen briskly, masking a fleeting expression of pain—"you must excuse me. I need to get things ready for tonight."

They took the hint and departed, liberating a plate of cakes and the teapot as they went out to sit on the grass under the apple tree. Near the stables were more trees—two old apple trees and a few catfruit trees, the latter bare of its tangy, whiskered fruit.

Tephee ate a cake and spent a few moments sucking honey from her fingertips in a most unladylike fashion before grinning. "This is fun. It's like it was before."

Magda sighed. "*Just* like it was before."

Tephee looked surprised, but Sylvia understood. "She means when we left Tunston," she clarified.

"How so?"

"We're all just . . ."—Magda waved her hand in a frustrated gesture—"just following along. I'm following Sebastian, and you're all following me. Last time we did this it turned out to be not such a good idea." She grimaced.

"Things turned out pretty well, I thought," said Tephee.

Magda shook her head. *Three of us have nearly died since we left Tunston. It must be my turn soon.* That was a horrible thought.

"So . . . why are you following?" Leenan's tone held gentle challenge as well as curiosity.

"I'm going because . . ."—Magda took a breath—"because I'm hoping that this Arc vessel might have the medical facilities to help Sylvia."

"And I'm going because if something there can help me," Sylvia said with sudden force, "I want to be healed. I want to be whole again."

"You, Tephee?" Leenan asked.

Tephee thought about it for a long moment before replying carefully: "Things were too . . . ambiguous, at the court. All the people we know at court knew I might have gone either way before the battle. Only Armand ever accepted that I'd chosen his side by the end. I . . . needed to grow beyond what I was, and I need to be away from my past to do it." She looked at her feet in her new sandals. "And I didn't want to be left with strangers."

"I know what you mean," Leenan said. "People never felt very comfortable with me when I was human. Being a dragon was worse. I couldn't stay among strangers."

"You're human now," Magda pointed out. "You could go back. Take Tephee with you." At their sharp looks she clasped her hands into a fierce knot in her lap. "You don't understand. This isn't a holiday. I have a feeling this is going to get very nasty."

"Nastier than Zuleika?" Tephee grimaced. "I doubt it."

"Zuleika was just one selfish woman. This is different. We're talking about religious purism now."

Tephee shook her head. "I don't understand."

"Sebastian came for me because he's under the impression that I'm some kind of . . . of prophet, or angel, sent from the True World. No doubt he thinks that I'll be able to communicate with this vessel . . ."

"Aren't you?" asked Sylvia in her gentlest tone. "Won't you?"

"For Christ's sake, Sylvia, *no!*" She shook her hands, clenched now into fists. "I'm no more holy than you are!"

"According to the Leylites, we are the Mother Incarnate," Tephee said.

Magda and Leenan both snorted derisively at that, and Sylvia smiled wryly. "I see."

"The point is that we are walking into an unknown situation, completely unprepared. This Arc vessel, if it's really there, is already bringing pilgrims. It's in the middle of a country so filled with religious fundamentalism that as little as six years ago, witches were being murdered in the name of the First King. The Imbers have regular problems with prejudice this far away from the action—things will be far worse in Marin Kuta."

"Why insist on going, then?" Leenan demanded. "If it's so dangerous, why do you need to follow Sebastian at all?"

"Because if there's a way to treat Sylvia on that ship, I want it. And besides . . ." Magda sighed again. "This Arc vessel may come from . . . the same place I came from. I want to see if it's real. Sometimes I think my old life was a dream." *Or that this life is.*

"So . . . you insist on going, despite the danger you think is out there."

"Yes."

"I'm going with you." Sylvia was firm. "I can't keep living like this."

Tephee started forward in sudden panic. "Don't make me go back. Not with the way they look at me there."

"And I won't let you go into danger alone," Leenan asserted.

"Looks like I'll be anything but *alone.*" Magda looked helplessly at Sylvia. "Now I know how you felt."

"Frustrating, isn't it?"

A horse and cart wheeled into the stableyard and Thomlin Imber jumped to the ground where he was joined by Sergeant Ho. They began to unload the barrels of beer and wine along with sacks of grain and vegetables. They were clearly expecting a veritable army of travelers to be eating at the inn. The pilgrims would be coming through in earnest from here on.

CHAPTER ELEVEN

That night they had a conference in the witches' room. Tephee remembered not to sprawl on a bed in her usual fashion and sat self-consciously lady-like on the edge of the bed. Magda and Leenan claimed two of the room's chairs and Sebastian another. Sylvia sat easily on the floor, absently dragging a twig of apple blossom beside her for Pywych to chase while she listened. Sergeant Ho stood hitched against the unused fireplace, conspiring to look both at ease and on alert.

"We need to talk about this journey," Magda began without preamble. "The overland route will take weeks, and as the news spreads more people are deciding to head west to see it for themselves. Frankly, the idea of having to elbow through throngs of the devout to reach our target horrifies me. Especially considering the kind of prejudice most of us will be dealing with."

Sebastian was nodding at Magda's comments. "I agree, I would like to get there before the crowds get too thick. The news is spreading very quickly."

"Yes . . ." She gave Sebastian a look before being distracted by Pywych's demanding paws. Sylvia waggled the blossoms and Pywych scored another petal kill.

"Oh," Sebastian shrugged lightly, "those coming through are further east. They may have seen the first envoy travelling this way some weeks ago."

Leenan arched an eyebrow at him. "The first envoy?"

"The Temple has sent others on ahead," Sebastian explained simply. "I backtracked to Tyne to ask Witch Magda to join us."

"You Temple priests don't believe in a quiet entrance, do you?"

"Rumours wash back; then they see us leave. No doubt some are just following for curiosity. Or hoping for a miracle."

An audience for the second coming of the Stores Clerk, thought Magda with a faint air of horror. *God, I hope they're not going to be disappointed. Or that they are. I don't know what would be worse.* "What's important is that we have to get there ahead of them."

Sergeant Ho cleared his throat discreetly. "If you will excuse me, Witch Sylvia . . . Jubilee is on the river route to the coast."

"Yes?"

"I am sure we could purchase passage on a river trawler. It would avoid the more difficult passages through the mountains and it should cut at least a week from our travelling time, particularly if we find one with a night crew. No need to stop, then."

Magda's eyebrows rose. "Do you know how to arrange that, Sergeant?"

He shrugged slightly. "Thomlin knows some people. I can have news for you by midmorning tomorrow."

"We can be ready to leave by midday," Leenan asserted confidently.

"If you are well enough to travel, Witch Leenan."

She pursed her lips in dislike at the honorific and he shrugged again, a little helplessly, at her unspoken admonishment. "I'm fine," she said.

"Very well . . . Leenan." Her nod of satisfaction was greeted with a half smile. "I'll discuss it with Thomlin and arrange for him to board the horses and the carts."

"Ask if they'll look after Py for me," Sylvia asked. The cat was lying on his back and waving his paws in the air while his tail lashed the ground.

"I will, ma'am."

Pywych, aware he was under discussion, stopped to wash himself.

Leenan sat at the window for a while after she woke up the next morning, feeling faintly disappointed that the Sergeant hadn't come out under the apple tree for his exercises. They looked like an unusual but effective meditation technique and she'd been meaning to ask him about it. Suppressing a small sigh, she dressed and went to wake the others.

She woke Magda and Tephee with their usual grumbles, but Sylvia's bed was already made up. They went downstairs for tea and breakfast and while the oats were cooking, Leenan went out to the stables.

Alard wasn't there to bark a greeting. Cautiously, she stepped into the hay-strewn building and heard a muffled gasp.

"Cadogan?"

A gasp again, turned half to sobbing. Leenan tried to walk quietly, skirting the caravan.

She found Sylvia leaning against the rear wheel, her head tilted back while she pinched her bleeding nose. She was trying not to cry.

In a moment Leenan was kneeling beside her, using the hem of her new dress—having nothing else to hand—to mop up the blood. Sylvia protested feebly for a moment before giving herself up to the attention.

"Lords, Sylvia, what happened? Who did this to you?!" Her tone suggested unpleasantness for the culprit.

"No one. Me. Thought I'd come out early. Tidy things up. Pack what we needed for the boat."

Leenan realised that Sylvia's oddly truncated speech was due to a clearly vile headache that accompanied the nosebleed.

"What were you trying to do?"

Sylvia waved a blood-smeared hand. "Move . . . Magda's boxes."

"You should have waited for us."

"I wanted . . . to try. I wanted . . ." Sylvia began to cry.

Leenan, a little awkwardly, enfolded Sylvia in her arms and hugged her. "I know what you want." She patted Sylvia's dark hair and noticed for the first time the threads of grey there.

After a while, Sylvia's breathing returned to normal and she sat up, composed, though her face was pale and drawn. "I'm sorry. I can't help it. Trying to not try magic is like . . . trying not to breathe."

"Maybe meditation would help."

"I can't stay focussed. I can't let go and everything distracts me." Sylvia shook her head and frowned.

"I was thinking of asking Sergeant Ho about his morning routine. It's something different. Perhaps we could both join him."

"Hmm."

They washed their hands and faces at the pump, and Sylvia, with a little cry of dismay at the mess, tried to wash the stains out of Leenan's skirt. Somehow they both ended up soaking wet and giggling. The sight of Tyler peeking uncertainly out of the kitchen door at them encouraged them to adopt solemn faces and they went inside for breakfast. Their entrance was elegant and refined, though the effect was spoiled by their hair—Sylvia's hanging in damp waves and Leenan's stuck out every which way.

Sylvia went into town with Tephee to collect the new clothes from the seamstress while Magda and Leenan sorted through their things and loaded only the essentials onto the cart ready to go down to the river port. There was still too much there. Magda suspected they would have to travel light from here on in, feeling uncomfortably certain that a swift getaway might be required.

Reluctantly, she left her diagnostic and replication equipment in Kayla's old caravan. She had carried those longlife units with her for more than five years, only once leaving them behind her, when she had gone to search for Tephee and found her with Sylvia in that seaside cottage. They were durable and the batteries would last upwards of fifty years without replacement, designed as they were for practical use on the isolated outer colonies. The units were hardly likely to suffer any kind of damage if left here. Still, Magda was unhappy about the necessity to part with them. Later, on a suggestion from Sylvia, Tephee helped her to seal it in by binding the wood along all the caravan's seams so that doors, windows, and even the original paneling were melded into one whole piece.

"I hope you haven't left anything in there," said Sebastian as they finished, which prompted a sudden panicked search for Pywych. Gilly found him upstairs sleeping in the apple room just as Tephee was about to re-create the caravan door. They moved it then, with Sebastian and Thomlin's help, into the corner of the stables and stacked hay around it.

When Sergeant Ho returned, the witches and the priest were eating a robust morning tea to recover from the morning's exertions. Leenan and Sylvia had changed into dry clothes and their luggage now consisted of two small bags containing clothes, combs, and Sylvia's sketch paper and artist tools. Sebastian had a small bag of his own.

"Is that all?" he asked, trying to keep the relief out of his tone. The Sergeant, always a light traveler, had merely emptied his saddlebags, ensured his father's ashes were still secured and wrapped in silk, and bundled it up with his clothes and the King's letters and coin inside a pack made of his leather tunic and some neatly tied leather thongs. He wore his uniform again today, just as Sebastian wore his Temple robes.

"Except for the three trunks upstairs," Leenan told him. Tephee gulped down a laugh at the look of dismay on his face and Leenan grinned wickedly. That surprised a laugh out of him.

A smile suits him, Leenan decided. *I'll have to get him to do it more often.*

It took an hour to say goodbye, Sylvia lingering over Pywych as the cat lay, supremely uninterested, on a feather bed, purring. "Faithless creature," she admonished him. He bit her nose and head-butted her then licked a paw. Dismissal. She went downstairs, feeling apprehensive and melancholic, to find the others waiting for Sergeant Ho. The Sergeant was giving a last-minute list of instructions to Gilly on how to care for his horse, from the way he liked to be groomed to his favourite treats. It made her feel better that the stern Sergeant would miss his horse as much as she'd miss Py. Then she noticed Leenan giving a similar list to Tyler on how to care for Alard. The dog was fretting already, sensing that his mistress was up to something.

Madam Imber hugged them all goodbye, gave them food for the journey. Gilly curtseyed and Tyler bowed solemnly, like his father. Thomlin took them down to the port in their cart, then escorted their meagre luggage on board the shallow-riding, broad-decked *Lady of Grace*. It was, to Magda's immense surprise, a variation on the ancient paddleboat steamer.

The *Lady of Grace* was herself a cargo ship, but there were rooms belowdecks for her owners who sometimes traveled with her. They were much smaller and less well appointed that the rooms they had left at the Half Moon Inn, though fit enough for the owner and his family. Magda and Leenan took one cramped cabin, Tephee and Sylvia the other. Sebastian refrained from commenting on the servant's cabin—which was more like a cupboard, and Sebastian wondered for a mad moment if they stacked several servants in here, like changes of clothes, for the journey—which he was assigned, because he knew that Cadogan had not even that, and had volunteered to sleep on the deck.

Not having to wait for tides, the *Lady of Grace* threw off her moorings and was tugged out into the river by a pair of rowboats manned by two muscular young men, belowdecks the engines were unleashed and the riverboat glided on the calm summer stream, towards the sea. Towards Marin Kuta.

CHAPTER TWELVE

The sun was just rising on the eastern horizon and a cool morning breeze rippled over the broad deck of the *Lady of Grace*. It lifted Leenan's dark-blonde hair from the nape of her neck and forehead as she shifted through the next cycle of movements. Cadogan stepped and dipped beside her, his fluid grace providing the guide for her. They were both dressed in comfortable loose trousers and light shirt, barefoot on the wooden deck, expressions solemn and peaceful.

The crew went about their morning business, having long since recovered from the novelty of seeing the two of them every dawn. To begin with, all four witches had appeared on deck each morning, but Tephee and Magda both enjoyed sleeping in too much. Sylvia was still there most mornings, though increasingly she, too, slept in and when she rose she looked hollow-eyed and unrested.

Sebastian was up—monastic life had instilled early rising habits—and he sat on the pilot's raised deck, watching the land slide by and talking to the Captain and his officers.

Leenan glided through the kata she had learned, enjoying the sun and the breeze, the unintrusive sounds of the great paddle-wheel turning and the river sailors calling out occasionally. She had ceased to be self-conscious at the knowledge they were being watched by the crew. Cadogan was so supremely unconcerned that his surety encompassed them both.

They finished the set in unison and there was a short pause

before Cadogan blew his breath out in an energising huff. "Good. You're improving all the time. Are you ready for the defence class?"

Leenan nodded, pleased at the praise. She took up a position opposite him, mirroring his own stance. The defence class had become a component of their mornings three days ago, after the incident at the Lordale border. After passing from Tyne to their allies' Kingdom of Wij, and thence into Argent with all consideration and favour being given to Cadogan's uniform and the letters he carried from King Armand Bakar-Tyne, entry into Lordale hadn't been so easy.

"Mind if I join you?" Magda emerged on deck, looking both sleepy and grim. Leenan suppressed a sudden pang of disappointment at the intrusion. Cadogan paused a beat before standing back a little to open a space for Magda. "I've done some self-defence before," Magda told him, "but I think it's time I brushed up."

More than time, she thought unhappily. If what had happened at the last border check was anything to go by, her own small magic wasn't going to be of much help if they got into trouble. Even a little self-defence, though better than nothing, was not much more than nothing in the face of the growing suspicion and wariness they had encountered in Nimmorn. She was still appalled at the memory of Lordale garrison troops holding Sergeant Ho for eight hours, despite the King's letters, and threatening to bundle the four witches in after him. She supposed only fear had held the troops back from wholesale arrest. The Captain of the *Lady of Grace* had shrugged helplessly, saying that he'd been forced, on arrival, to declare all witches travelling with them. Magda had imagined in an absurdist moment a planetary customs house with a special queue for having "Witches to Declare" leading to a quarantine cell. As if their witchliness could be irradiated out of them before they were safe to unleash on the unwary population.

Leenan had been seethingly angry and Tephee ready to storm the prison to free the Sergeant. Sylvia had kept them both in check while Magda waited, under guard, at the Portmaster's office and Sebastian spoke for the Leylite foreigner behind bars. A good portion of King Armand's gold changed hands, Sergeant Ho was freed and finally, half a day later, the *Lady of Grace* slipped her moorings and sailed deeper into what they were all now thinking of as Enemy Territory.

On the deck of the ship, Magda listened attentively to the Sergeant's instructions, applied them earnestly in mock attacks with Leenan. The techniques from the university's defence course came back, surprising the Sergeant once or twice, though never enough to actually knock him off his feet. Leenan was getting the hang of it quickly, Magda noticed. Standard moves from her morning kata were now being put to more practical use.

A small crowd gathered around them, watching with equal amounts of amusement, curiosity, and derision. Someone commented that fancy footwork would lose out to good steel any day. Another laughed, correctly observing that most of the fancy footwork was employed to run away from the attack in subtle ways.

"That's the whole point," muttered Leenan, her annoyance distracting her, allowing Cadogan to sweep her feet out from under her. He caught her before she hit the deck too hard.

"Ignore them, Witch Leenan," he murmured, helping her back to her feet. "In any fight, you can't afford to be put off by the non-essentials. Be aware of everything and distracted by nothing."

She took note and went back to work.

Magda drew back, perspiring and panting with exertion. Sergeant Ho, she noticed, was hardly breathing heavily. On the

Captain's Deck, she caught sight of Sebastian leaning on the rails, watching with a concerned expression. Her gaze traveled back to the small group of sailors forming a loose circle around them. Some of their expressions made her stomach contract with dread.

Someone shouted something rude about this "pansy fighting," inviting raucous laughter and further impolite observations regarding Sergeant Ho's masculinity. Nothing perturbed the Sergeant in the slightest and his cool disregard was annoying the more vocal among them. The comments became harsher, more challenging, and the Sergeant was untouched.

"Try fighting this, you white-bellied Leylite!"

Magda began to shout warning and protest, but before a sound emerged Cadogan had turned, stepped aside, wrapped one hand around the mop being jabbed at him and tugged slightly, allowing his attacker's forward momentum to continue unheeded, and with a boost. The sailor concerned found himself flung across the deck. The Sergeant watched until the man stopped sliding then turned to Leenan with a faint nod. "Be aware of everything," he said clearly.

"Be distracted by nothing." Leenan was grinning. "Yes, I see."

He was, Magda saw, suppressing an amused grin of his own. Instead he turned and inclined his head towards the unhappy crewman. "Kind of you to assist with my pupil's training. I hope I didn't hurt you."

The audience laughed and the crewman cursed, glared and, when Cadogan had turned his back, took another chance. He found himself hurtling through the air once more, his crewmates stepping rapidly aside to avoid being hit by his flailing arms. Sergeant Ho's manner remained light and implacably polite.

Magda knew that Sergeant Ho knew he was making a dozen

temporary allies and one enemy. His expression was bland, but for those blue eyes of his gone hard and cold as steel. His enemy, more infuriated with every failure to dent either the Sergeant's defences or his mockery, rose behind him. A broad, serrated blade appeared in one hand and the temporary allies grinned awfully in anticipation.

"That's enough of a demonstration for one day. But thank you for the spectacle." Sebastian materialised between them, as though his Temple robes were a shield. Magda thought she could hear the sigh of disappointment from the crew as their ill-tempered mate sheathed the fishing knife and got his temper under control.

"You've been very good-natured about this demonstration," Sebastian told the man—not so much a lie as an instruction as to his future conduct. "Sergeant Ho, being the King's Man, is peculiarly qualified to defend His Highness and those under his protection."

Reminder of the Sergeant's standing in the royal court of Tyne sobered them all, and the audience dispersed. When the deck was clear, Sebastian allowed his gaze to meet Cadogan's.

"I could have disarmed him." Cadogan was perspiring slightly, and still coldly polite.

"I know," said Sebastian quietly.

After a moment the stiffness in Cadogan's manner subsided and he ran his hands through his short black hair. "Thank you."

"You're welcome." Sebastian's mouth curved into a brief smile, then settled back into serious lines. "We'll be coming into Port Lordale tomorrow morning. We should talk about what we're going to do when we arrive."

"Yes." A small sigh. "Yes, of course."

"The Captain has said we may use his boardroom."

Cadogan nodded and Sebastian returned to the Captain's Deck. The Sergeant then glanced up at the witches. "Perhaps you could fetch Witch Tephee and M'ady Sylvia." The cool, distant humour with which he had absorbed the crewman's attack had dissipated, leaving an embarrassed reserve in its wake.

Magda left to find them. Leenan frowned.

"How can you let that go so easily?" she demanded, nodding towards the crew as they returned to work around the ship.

"Not so easily, M'ady," Cadogan admitted with a grimace. He regretted now his baiting of the sailor. It had made him no lasting friends, one certain enemy, and he had allowed his pride to goad him. He had wanted to flaunt his skill to Witch Leenan. *Slow to learn, Mother, I know.* With a parting salute he left them and climbed the ladder to the Captain's Deck.

Sebastian and Sergeant Ho left the port after several hours of negotiation. Berths for all were secured and down payment made, and the Sergeant wondered if the Captain would set sail tonight without waiting for the rest of the money or decide that the gold coins still due were worth the risk of taking six strangers on a dubious trip to an island state that had closed its borders anyway.

He'd wait, probably, Cadogan decided. Captain Prithkincardi had the look of a man wary of lean times. He was contracted to a merchant in Berrinsland and while the Marin Kuta ports were admitting only a few small ships into their harbours there was less work around than normally available at the height of summer. His ship, a compact, sleek runner called *Aln's Pride*, was built to send perishable goods between ports along the coast. Such a specialised ship naturally had berths available for messengers, who often booked passage for any number of reasons, for all kinds of people. Captain Prithkincardi had never asked a lot of questions, provided passage was paid for in good, gold coin.

If he knew they were witches, no amount of coin could have persuaded him, Cadogan thought. *Witch-hating fever seems to have spread. Even those who don't believe the stories want to distance themselves.*

Cities were claustrophobic, dehumanising places at the best of times. In Port Lordale there was an added pall of tension—undercurrents of suspicion and fear that made it almost unbearable. They had given into the oppressive mood from the start, when they'd lied to the border garrison about who the witches were, and why they were here. Cadogan had been in full uniform, and Sebastian in complete Arc Temple regalia. They had told the border guards half truths—that Sebastian was to join his fellow priests at Marin Kuta to theologically investigate the claims of a miracle there. Sergeant Ho, they said, was the King of Tyne's envoy to ensure the priest's safe passage. Sylvia was cast as Sebastian's wife, and Tephee their daughter, while Leenan was their maid. Magda claimed to be an acolyte priestess and cousin to Sergeant Ho, which leant the man some official legitimacy beyond his uniform and papers, since his pale skin bespoke his Marin Kutan origins so clearly.

Taint of Leylite and witch sympathies apparently removed, the group had been eventually allowed to pass. They hired two carriages to take them to Dale Heights, the well-to-do part of town, and the Tyne Ambassador's home there. There were plenty of signs along the way of the last thirty years of refugees from Marin Kuta—pale faces in the shadows and alleys of the poorest parts of town. They'd skirted the edges of what appeared to be some kind of Kutan Quarter, where shops and houses were crowded together and all the faces were haunted.

Both the priest and the Sergeant had become quiet. Leaving the witches in the King's sanctuary, they'd gone to negotiate passage on a ship to the island and now returned in as much silence as they'd parted. It was only when they had returned to the Ambassador's house and were seated in a small reception room, waiting for Ambassador Linden to arrive, that either spoke.

"You don't have to come with us," Sebastian said quietly.

It was a moment before Cadogan answered. "The King asked that I guide you both to Marin Kuta. He told me I had a choice." A sigh. "I don't."

"Certainly you do," Sebastian countered. "King Armand wouldn't . . ."

"You mistake me. The King could ask me to walk on broken glass, and say I had a choice, but I'm sworn to his crown and his word. I could not go back and tell him I had not protected the witches and yourself with all my power because I was worried about the consequences. I knew the consequences before I came. I accepted them then. I want to go on. Besides . . ." Cadogan rubbed his fingers along the wood grain of his chair, studying the colour and texture of the fine furniture, "I am twice sworn. To the King, and to the Mother." He glanced up at Sebastian's expression and found it less dismissive than he'd expected.

"How does your belief bind you to this? Of course. The witches themselves. Have they asked you to stay?"

"No."

"Then how . . ."

Cadogan shifted in his chair. "They personify the Mother on earth, in all Her aspects. She manifests Herself in the world through those She chooses . . ."

"By the First King, Sergeant Ho, they're not . . . goddesses," Sebastian sounded both scandalised and amused by the idea.

Cadogan gritted his teeth on rising irritation. "Not goddesses, but a manifestation of the Goddess. Mortal women with the blessings of the divine."

"Witch Zuleika was divine, then, by your reckoning."

"Yes," agreed Cadogan stubbornly.

"Despite all the death and destruction she caused."

"The Mother isn't always benign. She is the hurricane and the storm as well as the sun and breeze."

"Yet you took up arms against Her."

"I took up arms against the Usurper Saebert. I . . . withstood Witch Zuleika."

"Wouldn't that be heresy?"

"The Mother does not expect us to stand in a blizzard and curse the sky, or allow ourselves to be torn apart by a hunting ptyka—it is not heresy to seek shelter or protect yourself against Her darker aspects."

"Your Mother seems very unpredictable."

Cadogan grimaced in annoyance and Sebastian shrugged.

"I don't mean to be disparaging," the priest told him, "but I don't understand. We know the First King brought life to this world . . ."

"He brought *new* life," Cadogan corrected him, "human life, and others."

"New life, then. He brought His Lords and conquered the world . . ."

"The Mother brought Him here and made room for His people."

"So He is the Father to your Mother."

"*He is* . . ." Cadogan bit down on harsher replies. "The First King is adopted son to the Mother. She is in each and every one of us."

"But only witches are divine."

"Witches wield Her power."

Sebastian nodded slowly. "How then . . . do you see the Red Lord?"

Cadogan frowned. "Much as you see him, I suspect. For different reasons perhaps."

"He gathered the first witches together and led them to attack Paradise. When he failed to conquer the First King, he and his followers were exiled, and the witches turned on him for his failure." Sebastian shrugged. "That is the popular interpretation. It is a question of great theological debate, in terms of how witches are to be reconciled in the Arc of Entry. My own Temple has a slightly different view. We are considered to be very open-minded in this area."

"I'm sure you are," replied Cadogan with a neutrality he had to work hard to achieve. "The Red Lord was rejected by the witches, but not for his failure to succeed. It was for his attempt to do so."

"Ah, I have heard . . ."

Ambassador Linden arrived then, with a small entourage of clerks and servants. Cadogan took several deep breaths and rose to give respectful welcome to the King's representative. Linden waved him back to his chair and when all were present and comfortable, they began to compile a report to be sent back to the King. All they observed and deduced would be recorded.

"You can complete the report on your return," Linden said, with tactful certainty.

Sergeant Ho, less certain, merely murmured agreement.

CHAPTER THIRTEEN

It should have been better on board *Aln's Pride*. He had his own small cabin just belowdecks, spare but clean, and a narrow bed more comfortable than the deck he'd been sleeping on for weeks. He should have slept more, remembered less.

Instead, Cadogan Ho lay staring at the darkness in a cold sweat. His senses were alive with the tang of salt air, the smells of ocean and ship, the sounds of wind and water and the creaking of rope and sail. Some people thrived on these sensations. They only filled him with dread and an aching sense of loss.

It shouldn't be so hard, after all this time. I'm in a cabin this time, passage paid, not crammed in the hold behind a few moldy sacks.

Dae Ho had paid someone to look elsewhere when he smuggled his family into the cargo hold. Ten-year-old Cadogan had taken his little sister Arika on first; then his mother Mariko, carrying the baby, and finally Dae. A family still numb with shock at being driven from their home, numb with loss for their eldest boy, Rudig. Bright, brave Rudig, cursing the rabble as they cut him down, and then Witch Akiko whom he had tried to protect.

The young Cadogan was numb with that particular horror, having witnessed it all. Five minutes of his life that would always elongate to take in every detail before he broke and ran to tell his father. Amid cries of disbelief and fear, they had taken only what they wore and run, before the mob reached their home. A neighbour, a sane and compassionate man, had helped them,

135

until there they were—five refugees huddled in the damp and cold, praying to the Mother for protection.

They remained silent as the ship left its mooring and headed out to sea. All was well for hours. Until Koto woke, hungry and afraid. It had been Rudig's favourite joke, that Koto's lung power could drive a sailing ship right across the King's Sea in a day.

Shouts, crashing hatchways, and a light spilling from a lantern over the frightened group, and the curse: "Lorddamned Leylites!"

A thump on deck brought Cadogan back to the present with a start. Suddenly claustrophobic, he threw back the light blanket and groped his way to the stairs that led onto the deck.

The summer moon reflected kindly on the sea. A few crewmen on the starboard were coiling up a heavy rope one of them had dropped. Cadogan rubbed perspiration from his brow and crept forward until he stood at the prow, gazing out to the dark horizon.

It wasn't much better up here. His father had fought like a master, but there were too many sailors in too small a space, and as soon as they had grabbed Arika he gave up, meek as a lamb.

They were marched up to the Captain who discussed them with the first mate as though they weren't even there.

"Lorddamn. What am I supposed to do with bloody Leylites?"

"If the Kutans know we harboured heretics, Captain, that'll be the last trade run we do with them."

"No one has to tell them."

"We can't keep every man on the ship silent."

A huff of irritation. "We can't keep them here. Not enough water or supplies on board. The men won't share with Leylites."

"No, sir, they won't."

"Oh well. Overboard then. Maybe they can swim to shore."

And that was how it was. Yelling and fighting and screaming and begging for their children. It took five men to throw Dae overboard, and Cadogan broke one man's arm defending his mother before he too plunged into the icy wet. All of them. Even the baby.

The cargo ship slid away into the night, and they clung together, treading water.

The Tynean ship which found them hours later had been bearing down on a pirate ship which had surged past fifteen minutes before, nearly swamping them. The *Alyce* abandoned the chase to send a lifeboat for them, but by then baby Koto had long been drowned and blue and taken from his mother's arms by the sea. Mariko was inconsolable. She developed pneumonia on the journey back to Henatith port in Tyne and joined her youngest in the Mother's ocean.

Hello Mama. Hello Koto, Cadogan thought, mesmerised by the prow of *Aln's Pride* slicing through the waves. Part of their spirit was there now, in the swell and dip of the water.

For the first time in thirty years, Cadogan shed tears for them. *I'm sorry I wasn't strong enough.* A ten-year-old against a ship's company of sailors. What had he thought to achieve? *I'm sorry.*

He slept on deck that night, propped against coils of rope and bundles of sailcloth. He dreamed his mother's voice, singing him to sleep with an ancient lullaby.

The day passed quietly as the sun rose behind them and traveled with them westward. Sebastian took himself up to the poop deck to get better acquainted with the Captain; Cadogan called off the morning exercises and spent his time aft, watching the waves and a school of water lizards off to starboard. The witches kept to their cabins, or walked on deck, trying to be unobtrusive.

Midmorning found Sylvia and Tephee clambering the netting over the bow of the ship to watch for sea dragons. Sylvia had taken her sketch pad with her and had managed to tangle her limbs up comfortably in the netting so that she could lean back and leave her hands free to capture the mood of the sea in charcoal, away from the salt spray. Leenan and Magda wandered to the port and stood in companionable silence for a while, until Leenan, catching sight of Cadogan's shadow up front, sighed.

Magda followed her friend's gaze and smiled, though she schooled her expression back to polite interest when Leenan turned back to her.

"Cadogan's in a weird mood today."

"He's got a lot on his mind. It must be hard, coming back."

"Hmm." Leenan glanced back towards him, then returned her gaze to the horizon. "He's not as heavy set as he first looks, don't you think?"

Magda tried to suppress a recurrent grin. "Can't say that I'd noticed."

"It's just that he's so self-contained, I think. Makes him seem kind of solid, somehow."

"I thought that was just because he's short."

"He's just shorter than you, Maggie, and everyone we know is shorter than you."

Magda laughed. "All right, I'll give you that. And he is very graceful."

Leenan thought about the word. "Yes, he is, isn't he? It's lovely watching him do his exercises in the morning."

"Is it?"

"He just . . . flows . . . like he's drawing up some kind of power from the ground, and using it in perfect balance."

"He has very nice eyes too," Magda suggested.

Leenan blushed rewardingly. "Really? I hadn't noticed."

Magda spluttered out a choked laugh and Leenan gave her friend a defensive sidelong glance. "It's not like that! It's just . . . he . . . it's . . ." She stumbled into a frustrated growl and finally an acquiescent sigh.

"You're in with a chance," Magda told her with irrepressible mirth. "He does worship the ground you walk on."

"That's not funny."

Magda sobered at the sharp look on Leenan's face. "No, I'm sorry. It isn't."

"He acts like I'm some kind of . . ."

"Divine inspiration?" Magda completed for her, all seriousness. "I know the problem. I feel like a milkmaid who's been mistaken for a saint." She glanced up towards the poop deck, where Sebastian was in conversation with the Captain.

"Hmph." Leenan frowned. "He's so busy being respectful he doesn't notice that I'm here." She pointed to herself emphatically, "Me, Leenan, not the Embodiment of the Mother on Earth. It's very irritating."

"Oh, I'm sure he notices," Magda said.

Leenan gave her another of those sharp looks. "We're friends. That's all."

"Mmm." Magda was saved from further comment by a sudden cry and a thump from above.

A young crewman had lost his footing in the rigging high above and had fallen some feet before hitting the main spar and scrabbling for a hold. He was even now slipping from his precarious hold, unable to maintain a grip with his injured arms and ribcage. If he fell again, either the deck or a long fall into the sea, which would feel as solid as the deck from that height, would be the end of him.

He slipped, shrieked, grabbed the spar and the ropes around it as his nearest crewmates tried to climb to his aid.

He couldn't hold on. With a despairing wail he slipped . . .

. . . and glided to the deck, startled, unharmed.

Tephee stood nearby, her eyes closed and arms outflung as she wrapped her power around him and displaced the momentum and the pull of gravity. Once he was set gently down, she opened her eyes and stumbled.

The sea hissed into the silence.

Cadogan appeared cat-like on the deck, hurrying to Tephee's side as she knelt on the boards. She smiled a little and waved him away. She'd done much harder things than that.

"First King defend us," the sailor said hoarsely, "she's a witch."

Cadogan turned to the stunned crewman and said, slowly, quietly: "She saved your life."

"She's a witch."

"Thank her kindly, and leave her be."

The young man looked up at the Sergeant and was puzzled to meet, not threat, but supplication. He returned his gaze to the pretty young lady kneeling before him on the deck. She looked pale and drained.

"Thank you," he said.

"You're entirely welcome," she replied, with a lovely smile.

Cadogan helped her up then, and took her back to the large cabin she shared with the other three. Sylvia followed wordlessly. Magda glanced up to see Sebastian's worried face, exchanged a glance with Leenan, and they too went belowdecks.

Darkness fell and Magda, sleepless, knocked on Sebastian's door softly. At a murmured sound, she entered.

Sebastian, folding his priestly surcoat, smiled welcome and gestured towards a chair. Magda sat in it, trying not to fidget. The priest said nothing, taking his time to arrange the robe just so and place it on a small table by his bunk. Once that was done he lit another lantern and hung it back on the wall. Finally, he sat and regarded her attentively.

"I was just on deck," Magda said, her voice a curious monotone. "I overheard two of the watch. They say that Tephee made that young man fall. It's ridiculous. She saved his life. They all saw it."

"So they did."

"It's ludicrous. They don't even see the flaws in their logic."

"This isn't about logic, Magda."

"Of course it isn't. It's about religion. Logic has nothing to do with it."

He frowned, but she was far away, a scowl marring her brow.

"Magda," he placed a hand on her shoulder, "there is conflict between the First King and witchkind that simple logic cannot eradicate. Faith has a deeper logic than simple human beings can easily comprehend . . ."

"Bullshit!" She pulled away from him, then sighed and glanced back. "What conflict?"

Sebastian's expression became distant in turn, and his blue eyes as unreadable as stone. "What do you think it was?"

She remembered the carving at the Hold in Jubilee. "Not long after the First King arrived, some people began to develop witch powers. The Red Lord took their part. Sides were taken and the first great split occurred."

Sebastian smiled suddenly, and Magda flinched from the expression.

"You see!" he exalted. "You *know*."

"For heaven's sake, Sebastian, what's to know? It's been the history of every religion from Judaism to Christianity to the Saturn Prism and beyond."

His sudden grip on her wrist was surprisingly strong. She struggled against his hold. "Don't fight it, Magda. You are the First King's emissary and witch in one. The closer we get to our goal, the more I am convinced you have been sent here to heal the breach between the Arc and the witches."

She wrenched herself free at last and stumbled as she rose and headed for the door.

Sebastian was immediately contrite. "I'm sorry. I didn't mean to hurt you . . ."

"I'm no messiah," she snapped, panting with fright and exertion. "And while they," she glanced upwards, "are blaming every frayed rope and wild wave on us, we're all in danger. We were mad to come. If it wasn't for Sylvia I'd have let them rot, ship and all. They're not gods, Sebastian. Just unlucky."

She'd found the door handle and slipped out, slamming the door behind her. She half ran, half stumbled against the pitch and yaw of the deck to her room. She nearly fell, but strong hands caught her and held her steady.

Sergeant Ho tilted his head questioningly. "Are you all right, Witch Magda?"

"I'm . . . no." Magda was crying, and furious with herself for weeping when she was so angry. "And for Christ's sake, just call me *Magda*."

He looked satisfyingly taken aback. "Of course. Magda." His expression was almost comical, except that it made her feel more like screaming than laughing.

"What the hell are we doing here, Cadogan?"

"We're going where the Mother takes us."

A strangled sound escaped her, short, sharp, smothered by her clenched teeth. "You're as bad as he is!" Magda pulled away from his gentle hold and stormed into her cabin. That door slammed behind her, too.

He watched her go, chastened and puzzled. It wasn't unusual for witches from foreign lands not to recognise the Mother's aspect in themselves, or to fight against the divinity within them. Not all the Mother's gifts were welcomed.

An image of Leenan came to his mind's eye then, accepting

of her gift but reluctant to acknowledge the Mother's spirit within her. Yet she studied with him, meditated through movement with him and seemed to understand. It confused him, that the Mother on Earth was also his pupil, but he took to the task with reverence and thoroughness. It was a puzzle too, at how this caused offence. Her green eyes flashed with such animation when she was irritated with him . . . and also when he made her laugh, he was pleased to note.

Witch Akiko used to laugh a lot, he remembered. So had Rudig.

The memory turned him cold. Cadogan felt the walls close around him, dank and claustrophobic and he swallowed against the knot in his chest. He tried to think of his little sister Kynwyn, or Lyria, but his mind skittered from one thing to another, refusing to cleave to kinder memories. The one face he could hold in his mind was Leenan's. Dark-blonde hair, oval face, and uptilted nose. Those eyes as green as the sea that had drowned his brother.

Leenan was surprised to hear a knock at her door and Cadogan's voice. The others had gone up, despite the known antipathy towards them among the crew, because the lookout had sighted land in the distance. Sebastian's presence inhibited negative behaviour to suspicious glances and the occasional warding sign. Leenan had hoped to complete a kata in private to focus herself before joining them.

"Cadogan, hello. Come in . . ." He did, and stood to a very formal attention. He was in his uniform again, as though it could somehow ward off evil. He looked decidedly uncomfortable, Leenan thought. "Is something wrong?"

"Witch Leenan . . ." he said at last, "when we get to Holyshore . . . go back with the ship."

"What?" She was so surprised she forgot to correct his use of the honorific.

"You should go back with the ship," he reiterated firmly. "Back to Port Lordale."

"And why should I do anything like that?"

"It's too dangerous . . ."

"And it's not dangerous for Maggie, or Sylvia, or Tephee? Or you?" She was caught between anger, incredulity, and a peculiar hurt. What made him think she needed looking after? Did he have so little faith in her? "I can look after myself, you know."

"I don't mean you can't," he said, trying to explain himself now, "but you don't know this place. You don't know what they'll do, if they find out you are witches."

"So why aren't you trying to get the others to stay behind?"

"I can't protect all of you. I may not be able to . . ."

"I don't need *protection*," she retorted angrily.

"I . . . no . . . but . . ." Cadogan tried to gather his thoughts, tried to express what he was loathe to admit. "I want to," he finished simply, looking beaten.

"Cadogan . . ."

"I want to protect you. I don't want anything to happen to you."

"You can't do that, Cadogan. I can't let you. I have to be with my friends. I can't run away."

"I'm not asking you to run. Just . . . to not be where I can't . . ."

"Cadogan,"—Leenan placed her hands against his arm—"it's good of you, but I can't let you protect me like that. I have to stand on my own."

He was mesmerised by her proximity. Her green eyes flamed with her emotion. "It's not . . . good of me. I am . . . duty- and honour-bound . . ."

"I am not divine," Leenan told him firmly, and he softened

with regret and longing.

"Oh but you are," he murmured. She was so close . . . he could feel the warmth from her skin, feel her breath, feel her heartbeat almost . . .

The narrow gap between them had all but vanished. She was . . . so . . . close . . . his lips brushed against hers. *I mustn't . . . do this . . .*

He drew back suddenly—flustered, embarrassed, and ashamed. "I'm sorry."

"*Sorry?* Oh, for the Lords' sake, Cadogan!" Her voice caught in her throat, her initial scornful response to his apology giving way almost instantly to frustration and a fierce ache.

He couldn't bring himself to meet her gaze again. "You won't . . . change your mind?"

"Cadogan . . ."

"As . . . you . . ." He was unable to finish and he all but fled from the cabin.

Leenan would have chased after him, ready to grab him and shove him against a wall and shove and shove and shove until he listened to some damned *sense*. But she was shaking too hard to do more than get to the door then lean against it. "Oh, Cadogan, you *idiot*."

It wasn't until she heard the thumping from above that she could bring herself to join the others. Shouting, which until then had blended with the sound of the sea, caught her attention and she cautiously made her way out into the daylight.

The thump had been the sound of feet, all running towards the port side of the ship. The crew stood there now, staring and crying out as they pointed at the thing that kept pace with them as the ship sped west. She followed their uplraised arms and gasped.

It was like a house, or a covered wagon, or a Holder's Temple. All and none of these. It was distant, and at least half the length of *Aln's Pride*. There was fire at its rim and light reflected from it, like a fierce little moon. It was the most terrifying thing she had ever seen.

Someone shook her, hard, and she dragged her eyes away to meet Magda's.

"It's just a shuttle craft," Magda was shouting at her, trying to be heard through shock. "It's not a sign from God, it's just a shuttle. An Arc ship. Like the one I arrived in. It's nothing to be frightened of."

"The one . . . you . . . arrived in?"

"Don't you bloody start!"

The irritation brought Leenan back down, the normality and straightforwardness of it. "Why is it here?"

Magda peered up at it, squinting against the brightness. "I'd guess they've been scouting the area with it. Maybe even trying to break orbit. Doesn't look like it was a good idea."

The term "break orbit" was outside her frame of reference, but it was clear that whatever it meant, it was a bad thing. "Why shouldn't they break it?"

"Something's wrong with the engines. Look." Magda gestured. "The underside is overheating and the port attitude adjusters are on fire . . . oh, shit!"

The shuttle dropped suddenly, plummeting several hundred feet before the pilot regained control and some altitude. The craft lurched westward, striving for the nearest shore, then listed northward, closer to the ship full of terrified sailors.

Some were praying, others cursing, and Sebastian's attempts to keep them calm were not working.

"It's the witches," someone cried out. "The First King is sending a sign."

"No, no! The First King does not hate the witches!" Sebastian's tone lacked conviction. He was staring in terror and awe as well.

"He sends us an omen!"

"An omen!"

"The witches . . ."

The cries rose and became a confused babble, but for all that the message was clear.

Someone screamed and Sebastian cried out; something was lifted high overhead and thrown, thrashing protest, over the side of the ship and into the sea.

"*Sylvia!*"

Tephee erupted from the prow, scrabbling to see where Sylvia had been sucked under the waves by the ship's wake. Waves of magic repelled those who tried to grab her, but there were too many of them. A flash of red and black struggled amongst them, leaving wounded and wailing in its wake, but Cadogan couldn't reach her before two men seized her from behind with a length of rope around her throat.

Magda and Leenan darted forward in the same moment, running towards the melee.

Tephee's eyes bulged and her hands twitched behind her. One man fell. The other took a great wooden holding pin and hit her. As she crumpled, Cadogan appeared, his face set like ice but his eyes burning. His movements were economical and deadly, easily dispatching his opponent and for a moment no one dared fight past the body of Tephee's assailant.

Sebastian reached them through the crowd as Magda dropped beside the girl.

"Get her inside . . ."

"They're maniacs!" Magda dissolved into swearing as she passed her hands over Tephee's bleeding head then tried to drag her away from the hysterical mob. Sebastian stooped to help.

An explosion above and the shuttle dropped again. The heat from the stricken engines blasted over the deck, fierce even at this distance. A moment, a deadly pause and then . . . a collective roar of fear and rage and they surged forward.

Sebastian and Magda carried Tephee clear as Cadogan was swamped by hatred and fists. Then Leenan was caught in the tide.

She hadn't learned enough yet to fight them off. Hands clawed at her and she kicked and bit and cursed them to the Red Lord's Hell and back; she tried to summon her magic to hold them away, or to change her form, but in her terror and fury she couldn't focus, and then she fell, sickeningly fast, into the cold and hungry sea.

Cadogan could only see her falling. Not the mob, or the shuttle, or the blows, or his inevitable fate. Only Leenan, falling, and his father, falling, and his mother and his sister and his baby brother, falling. Falling and drowning . . .

They didn't need to pitch him overboard. Roaring blue murder himself, Cadogan fought to the side of the ship and climbed onto the railings and dived into the sea after them.

A shout of triumph rose from the crew and they turned towards new prey. Sebastian was crying out to Captain Prithkincardi for assistance, who in turn had taken the lash indiscriminately to those nearest, baying for order and obedience to no effect.

The shuttlecraft's engines cracked, and it plummeted like a stone. *Aln's Pride* forged westward, leaving the drowning far behind, until the First King's omen crashed from the sky, directly through the prow of the sailing ship. It splintered, burned, and both ship and shuttle began to sink.

CHAPTER FOURTEEN

Cold, salty water surrounded him, holding him down and he struggled, near panic, towards the surface. His boots, filled with water, dragged him back down, so he kicked them off. He lost a mouthful of air in the effort, but followed the bubbles up to the surface where he broke into the blessed air.

Cadogan gasped, swallowed salt water, spat and gasped again. The water still heaved from the ship's passing, but the waves were settling again and he twisted around, looking for her.

"Leenan!" The twinge of panic returned. *"Leenan!"*

He saw her then, some distance away, and swam rapidly towards her. Her face was pale with shock.

"Are you all right?" he managed. The waves slapped against them, making it difficult to keep from swallowing seawater.

"Yeah . . . I'm . . ."—*splutter, spit*—"okay. Where's Sylvia?"

Cadogan scanned the distance, trying to see the wake left by the ship. He thought he saw a dark head bobbing among the waves. "Stay here."

"No . . ."

"Stay!" Anxiety and frustration produced a parade-ground bark. Leenan was so surprised that she did so.

It felt like a long time before he reached the other witch, but by then Sylvia had seen him coming. She met him halfway, divested of all but one petticoat and a thin shirt. Everything else was on its way to the bottom of the sea as she'd stripped to keep her water-laden clothing from dragging her down.

"Sylvia . . ."

"Lords!" Her voice was a whisper and her dark eyes wide as they stared past his shoulder. Cadogan turned to see what had so horrified her.

Aln's Pride, smashed and heeling over, fire and smoke and the bright Arc vessel now dull and sinking fast. Bodies scattered in the choppy waters. The sounds of destruction and shrieks of fear could occasionally be heard.

Mother take you all, Cadogan thought savagely. *But not for at least a day. See how my brother died, you godless sons of bitches.* He tapped Sylvia's shoulder and she dragged her attention away.

"We have to . . ."—a pause while he breasted a wave—"get back to Leenan."

She nodded awkwardly and they swam back. Some of the strain disappeared from Leenan's face when she saw that Sylvia was unharmed, but she glanced at the wreckage of the sailing ship. They all shared the same grief.

Magda and Tephee.

"Which way to the shore?" Sylvia twisted in the water, trying to orient herself.

"Too far." It had been close enough to see, but not to swim, unless the Mother sent them tides, or better yet a boat. Without one or both, drowning was certain. He glanced towards Leenan and saw that she was in a daze. "Leenan?" Cadogan reached out for her arm.

Leenan broke out of her apparent reverie and began to tread water again. "I might be able to do something. I can feel them out there . . ."

"Feel what?"

"Water dragons,"—she gestured around—"there's a school nearby. Hang on."

She disappeared under the swell and Cadogan nearly grabbed her in alarm. A brief moment of activity and she reemerged, gasping, with her shirt in her hands. "Here. Don't lose it. I'll need it later."

Stunned, he took it and stuffed it inside his own sodden shirt.

"You sure?" Sylvia understood at once what she meant to do.

"No," Leenan admitted, "I'm not even sure I can, but I don't think we have much choice. I have to try."

Cadogan realised what she meant to do as she sank below the surface a second time.

It was hard to concentrate at first, but the imperatives of life or death can be marvelously focussing. Leenan reached out and captured the shape of a water dragon in her mind. They were related to the land dragons but only distantly. The school was close to the surface, where it was warmer, where they could hunt and erupt into the air to seize low-flying birds. Their sinuous bodies were coils of power, their two fins would fan and stiffen to guide their short flight. Bright eyes to see in either element, sharp teeth, strong jaws.

Leenan felt the shape of it, and made her body change to fit. She had so prepared herself to fight for the transformation that it took her by surprise when the power rippled through her, unimpeded. It felt like pushing on a door she thought had been locked, only to find her momentum carrying her through the doorway and well to the other side. Perhaps the lightning strike had left her with more than bruises and a healthy respect for storms. She felt like something had finally been freed inside her.

There was a moment of extraordinary pain which dissipated into disorientation before she blinked and saw the world the way a water dragon does.

Her first action was to dive down to snag her sinking trousers, though her new sandals would have to go. Her limbless new body flexed and she emerged in front of the others. She tried to mind-speak and discovered that this kind of dragon had very limited ability to do so. She had to hiss instead and push the trousers on them. No way was she going to return to human form and not have something to wear, this time.

It was funny and rather sweet, the way Cadogan managed to look embarrassed, even treading water in the middle of the ocean. Then she realised that the man was carrying every shred of clothing she still owned down the front of his shirt, and was grateful that reptiles did not blush. With a massive flex of her whole body she dived, then surfaced and rippled across the surface of the sea towards the sinking ship.

Leenan was not prepared for the disturbing sensation of hearing sounds underwater so clearly. Tearing timbers, air escaping in great bubbles to the surface, ropes snapping, all were distinctive and identifiable, even when she was so unused to listening in this environment. Worst were the last sounds of a man trapped under a fallen mast as he drowned. Leenan tried to find him, willing to free even someone who had tried to kill her rather than let him die like that, but the cries ceased long before she could locate him.

She began to move amongst the wreckage, pieces of wood, cloth, and rope floating past her, along with other items from the ship. Once, a body. She recoiled at the scent of burnt flesh and saw the rising pall of smoke. The collision with the great metal sky ship had set fire to the shattered prow of *Aln's Pride*, and it would burn until she was swallowed by the sea.

Something was floating ahead of the shipwreck, silvery, like a giant soap bubble; shining like the sky ship before it had plummeted into the ship and then the ocean. Leenan's curiosity was not enough to induce her to go nearer to investigate and she turned instead to the more immediate task of helping her friends.

A portion of the ruined deck loomed ahead. She thought it would suffice. She circled it and was startled by a horrible shriek. Growing numb to the horror of it, her first thought was *Lords, what now?* Then she realised that the sailor clinging to the edge of the decking, trying to clamber onto it, was pointing at her and shrieking. Something slapped into the water near her head and she raised herself up, twisting her neck to look behind. Another seaman, in an overcrowded lifeboat, had tried to whip her with a length of rope. She arched up angrily, hissing, and he nearly clambered out the other side of the boat in his efforts to get as far away as possible.

"Holy King, look at the size of it . . ."

Leenan was suddenly aware of how much larger she was than the water dragons she had sensed before. She could change her shape, but not her size—Magda had talked to her once about the distribution of mass and the wisdom of not trying to turn into a mouse because she'd be a mouse about the size of one of the King's hunting dogs.

Magda . . . dead and drowned, now, along with Tephee. Leenan had been unable to sense them among those clinging to the wreckage.

"First King preserve us," one of his crewmates in the same boat muttered, his fingers laying a warding trail against temple, throat, and heart as he prayed, "Lords defend us."

First King damn you all to hell, Leenan thought ferociously. Water dragons could neither blush nor cry, but the anguish escaped her throat in a skin-crawling wail.

The man clinging to the decking jerked back and swam as far from her as he could while the lifeboat took off in the other direction. Leenan hissed after them both.

It was hard work to guide the platform where she needed it to go. The wood was rough against her skin when she pushed it. At last she maneouvred it away from the chaos surrounding the lost *Aln's Pride*. Cadogan and Sylvia swam to meet her and there were a few awkward moments while they pulled themselves onto it. They used their hands as oars initially, until some planks drifted by that were more suitable, and slowly made their way towards the shore, through the splintered remains of ship, cargo, and rigging. Leenan swam around them in agitated circles. When two crewmen swam towards them, she shot out of the water and flew over the top of them, jaws snapping at the air, regardless of their intentions. She hit the water and twisted, reappearing an armspan in front of their faces as she reared up and hissed, just to make herself perfectly clear. Whether meaning to take or share the makeshift raft, they abandoned the idea in a panic.

After that there were some distant shouts—mostly curses flung at them—but no one else tried to approach. Leenan didn't care what they said as long as they did not come within striking distance of any of them. She was prepared to bite off limbs if necessary to protect Sylvia and Cadogan from these murderous lunatics.

The day was growing hot and it was grueling work to keep the raft moving. Cadogan found some floating rope and wound it around a spar of wood so that Leenan could tow them for a while, giving him and Sylvia some respite. Sylvia glanced back at the scene of annihilation they left behind but Cadogan could not do it. Not until she said, very quietly: "Cadogan . . . look."

He turned at her hushed tone and watched with her while a second Arc shuttle grew large out of the distance, descended slowly, pulled the silver bubble floating on the sea to itself like a witch calling a cup to her hand and with the bubble held snug against its belly, it rose and disappeared into the sky once more.

As it vanished, there was an unearthly groan and *Aln's Pride* surrendered finally to the sea. The waters swirled and churned and men clinging to anything that would float struggled to escape the sudden vortex. Some could not and were sucked down with the ship.

Follow my father's ashes down, you bastards. You drowned him in the end. The bitterness in him turned to loss. There was no returning Dae Ho's spirit to the land that bore him. The dust of his remains mingled with the sea—mingled with the spirit of his son Koto, and the spirit of his first wife, always left here with her baby. Mingled too with the offerings of his second wife and little daughter. And his only living son. Who could not even save his father's ashes.

He returned to the task of rowing, despite the sun and the ache in his shoulders. It was better than thinking.

The sun had begun its descent when the raft came in to the shore. Cadogan slid stiffly off and the cool water was a welcome shock to his body. Sylvia climbed off after him and they dragged the raft onto the sand. They had landed in a quiet cove on the rocky shore, having navigated the reefs. Some thick, fleshy plants grew among the rocks that encircled the small stretch of beach and beyond those they could see shrubs and trees. Cadogan helped Sylvia into the shade then turned to see Leenan ripple away back to deeper waters.

"Wait . . . !"

"She'll need to eat," Sylvia pointed out, her own voice hoarse. She protested only briefly when Cadogan made her sit while he pushed the raft onto its side against the rock, making a rough lean-to. After a few moments he crawled under it with her and held out a portion of one of the thick plants.

"Eat some of that," he told her, "it will help the thirst."

Sylvia sucked at the moist centre of the plant. "Oh! It's . . . sharp." She licked at the liquid seeping through her fingers. "Good though."

"I know. My brother and I used to eat these up north, where we lived." Cadogan gnawed at the plant. Rudig had called them joyjuicejugs, because he'd liked the silly sound of it. It felt strange, remembering that. For so long all he had held of his

155

brother was the noble and foolish way he'd died. He'd forgotten Rudig's huge sense of the ridiculous. Cadogan had always been the serious one. Rudig had made him laugh. They'd had a lot of fun together.

Cadogan realised that his silence was being watched. He glanced at Sylvia.

"I'm sorry," she said, not in apology, but sympathy.

He sighed. "I walk a path that was chosen for me."

"Maybe you need to choose another path."

"The Mother guides my steps."

"Unless you believe she intends you to be slaughtered in her name, I suggest you reexamine that one. She might be offering a choice of roads."

"Hmm." Well, perhaps so. This road had not been very auspicious, so far. *Is that what you want, Great Mother? Am I blindly following a path I only think is mine?*

They drifted into exhausted sleep until the sound of someone calling out to them from the beach woke Cadogan. He ducked out into moonlight to see a slender shape in the shallows.

"It's about time!" Leenan's voice was like fresh water to his heart, despite her apparent irritation. "You sleep as soundly as Magda does . . . did . . ." She faltered.

He swallowed. "Your things are dry," he said, gathering the shirt and trousers from the surface of the raft where he'd laid them in the sun. He held them out but turned away discreetly as she stepped out of the water and took them. There was a brief, warm glow as she dried herself with magic and then pulled her clothes on.

Despite himself, he found himself picturing her as she dressed. Her damp hair clinging to her neck . . . shrugging her blouse onto bare shoulders and fastening the buttons . . .

What an interestingly shaped rock. Like a . . . pair of . . . um . . .

no . . . okay . . . what an interesting skyline. Lots of trees. Tall trees. Winged tree lizards in the branches. Good eating, those lizards. Plenty of breast meat . . . oh, Mother . . .

"You can turn around now."

Oh no I can't.

"I . . . should look around. Keep guard. Others may get here, too. You should rest." He gestured towards the lean-to.

When she didn't move, he ventured to face her. She was very still. Tears she had been unable to shed before made shining tracks down her cheeks.

My thoughts shame me. "Leenan?"

"I couldn't find them."

"They may still be alive. The Mother . . ."

"Looks after Her own. You've said. But I can't *sense* them. I've done it before, meditating, but this time . . . nothing. There's no sign of them."

Cadogan began to reach out to touch her. Stopped. "I'm sorry."

She saw the look on his face. "It's not your fault, Cadogan. Magda wanted to come. We all insisted. You can't be responsible for what you didn't cause."

But for what I didn't do? I failed them. I failed you. I failed. Again. But all he said was: "You'd better get some sleep."

Leenan stared at him. "Yes," she said at last, "I suppose so." She walked past him and ducked to join Sylvia under the shelter.

Cadogan waited until she was inside before walking down to the water's edge. The sand was cool against his bare feet. Rough too, the grains individually etched into his soles. He sat, facing the horizon, and wrapped his arms around his shins. He rested his forehead on his updrawn knees and tried to breathe steadily, but his chest was tight. He tried to release the tension, to meditate, to find peace in the sound of the sea and the night.

A sob escaped him, muffled against his drawn-tight body and

he could not let go. Only draw in tighter, trying to contain un-
containable grief.

CHAPTER FIFTEEN

"Leenan! No!" Magda saw her friend lifted up and thrown, crying out, over the side of the ship. Cadogan, fighting to get to her, roared a bloodcurdling curse and as those nearest him flinched away he launched himself into the sea after her.

The Captain of the *Aln's Pride* was cursing the air blue himself, using the lash wildly in an effort to restore order. It was as effective as whipping the ocean into submission. His crew watched the pale foreigner plummet into the foaming wake of their ship then turned with a triumphant roar to send the rest of the Lord-cursed witches after them.

By then, however, Magda had stopped watching them. She'd heard the sound of attitude adjusters squealing into overload and watched, horrified, as the craft tilted and a gout of flame burst from the engines.

Magda was sitting on the deck, cradling Tephee in her lap. Sebastian was crouched by their side, holding a lynch pin awkwardly before him for protection. The crew halted uncertainly at the sight of an Arc priest defending the ungodly but were far from pacified.

All heard the squeal which changed in pitch to a howling whine. They saw the gangling witch go pale and begin to swear and they looked up to see the First King's Omen fall from the sky. Directly onto them.

Panic. They yelled and scattered and cried out for mercy before the great shining thing smashed into the ship, tearing off

159

the prow and setting the rigging on fire.

Magda gathered Tephee into her arms and rolled over, trying to protect the girl from fire and debris. She felt a solid body fling itself over hers, a hand covering her head and Sebastian's feverish prayer.

"First King be with us. Lords protect us. Walk with us in the cold and dark. Lead us to the green field and the running brook. Let Your shadow be the shade that gives us respite. Let Your eyes show us the vision of Your future. Let Your wisdom guide us and in Your compassion forgive us. First King be with us. Lords protect us. Walk with us . . ."

The deck lurched and they slid down the suddenly angled deck towards the turbulent sea.

Magda's feet scrabbled for purchase on the wood until they slammed into a row of wooden barrels that had been lashed to the deck for storage. Tephee was wrenched from her grasp and Magda snatched in panic, seizing the girl's arm and pulling.

"Stop . . . muttering . . . goddamnit . . . help me!"

Sebastian, his expression glazed in shock, gazed at her un-comprehendingly.

Her grip wasn't good. Tephee began to slip away.

"Lords! For Christ's sake, Sebastian, snap out of it. *Help me!*"

He shivered, seized, pulled. The three of them huddled behind the barrels as others fell around them.

"She's sinking." Sebastian was pale but recovering fast.

"I *know* she's sinking!"

"If we get caught in the suction we'll go down with it."

"Terrific. So what do you suggest?" She was hugging Tephee tight, running briskly through the checks. Pulse. Yes. Rapid and fluttery, but there. Breathing. Yes. No obstructions? Good. Bleeding? A little. *Wake up, Tephee, wake up.* Damnitdamnitdamnitdamnit . . .

160

"We'll have to go over the side and swim to safety."

"Safety? Jesus . . ." A sob caught in her throat, then was stifled. There was a moment of visible effort, and then she was very, very calm. "I'll need you to help me with Tephee."

"But she . . . yes, of course. Of course."

Sebastian rose first and looked for the nearest route to the side of the ship. The angle of the deck had reduced to a steep but navigable forty degrees and the crew was abandoning ship with less chaotic frenzy. Where the smashed hull of the ship had sunk below the waterline, bubbles roiled up, tossing wreckage and drowned men onto the surface. The ship was sinking steadily.

"Good," Magda said when he told her. "We won't have as far to jump."

The priest led, staggering from hand hold to hand hold, stopping to assist Magda with Tephee's still unconscious form. The sea was mere feet below them. Sebastian clambered over the side first, gasped as he hit the water.

"Here . . ."

Magda could not be elegant with her friend. She hefted the girl's body over the unnatural angle of the ship's side and watched her hit the water. Sebastian grabbed, pulled the girl to his side and began to move away from the ship while Magda jumped in after them.

"Come on," he pushed away furiously, "she's going down."

Magda hooked a hand under Tephee's chin and towed her, side stroke, away from the drag of *Aln's Pride*. Sebastian did not stop, so neither did she, until the priest seized upon a tar-sealed chest that had floated to the surface. It sank a little as Magda found a grip on it, but held.

"Come on, Teph, come on . . ." She pulled the girl close in and tried to raise her head further out of the water. "Help me . . . hold her . . ." The drill again. Pulse—still there. Breathing

. . . breathing . . . Damnitdamnitdamnitdamnit.

She'd never been taught how to do this while up to your neck in ocean, wreckage, and hostile forces, but there was no time to do anything but improvise. Using her feet to turn Tephee over she shoved her further up onto her shoulder. One hand anchored Magda to the floating chest; with the other she tilted Tephee's head to one side, opened her jaw and stuck a finger in to clear a path. Salt water spilled out.

"Hold her up," Magda said to Sebastian and as he hooked one arm under Tephee's arms and around her chest Magda shifted, tilted the girl's head right back and . . . kissed life into her. That's what Sebastian thought, anyway.

"What are you . . ."

Another kiss—he realised it was a puff of breath she blew into Tephee's mouth. The girl's chest rose and fell. Magda felt her throat, went back to work. Another breath, another . . .

Tephee coughed up seawater and her limbs twitched.

"That's my girl," Magda was murmuring, "that's it. You hang in there. That's my girl . . ."

A great roaring sound took them both by surprise. The ship was still sliding its horrifyingly graceful way into the deep, but the sea ahead of it was foaming and shifting like boiling water. A man caught in it was frantically trying to swim out of the path of whatever appalling thing was rising up toward him.

A silver metal bubble erupted from the depths, smashing straight up into the screaming man and flinging his broken body to one side. Waves swamped them before Magda could turn Tephee's face away. She spluttered, gasped for air, once more did the survival drill . . . heart still beating . . . lungs still breathing . . .

"Come on." She adjusted her hold on Tephee and pushed back out into the water, towing Tephee behind her.

"Magda!"

"She's going to die if we don't get help. That pod is the only help we've got."

The "pod" she referred to was the silver bubble that had burst to the surface. It was a shining ball, the size of two laden wagons. Water steamed from its surface in elegant ribbons.

"Witch Magda, *don't*. It belongs to the First King."

Magda was too busy swimming to effectively swear. ". . . Jes . . . goddamn *shuttle*," were the only words he heard. She would not come back. After a moment, despite the fact that every other able body was swimming away from the thing as fast as they could, Sebastian let go of the chest and followed her.

From a distance the pod had looked smooth, but Magda had taken hold of one of the various indented grips. Incomprehensible symbols were painted in white and black at intervals near the grips. Magda struggled to hold Tephee clear of the shifting sea until Sebastian arrived, then passed the task onto him. He watched her, awestruck and a little frightened, as she ran her hands over the silver surface. He finally noticed the faint seam in it, outlining a narrow square above the waterline.

"We're in luck," she said, "it's surfaced right side up." Magda slotted her hands into more of the indentations and pulled herself up to inspect the square more closely. With a small grunt of satisfaction, she tapped something and a tiny whirring sound ensued. A small dark circle appeared, only as big as her palm, and she tapped on this further, a rhythmic tattoo of three rapid taps, three longer, three rapid again, for several minutes.

First King, she is Your envoy, Sebastian was thinking, between triumph and terror. *She will show us the path.*

A sound emerged from the pod, and he nearly dropped Tephee. Magda tapped her rhythm into the circle again.

Another sound . . . a . . . voice? Indistinct and incomprehensible.

"Open up in there!" Magda shouted, pounding her hand on

the pod in a most irreverent fashion. The Voice spoke again, sounding oddly uncertain if it was meant to be the voice of God, and Magda rolled her eyes.

She shouted something else in a crisp tone, but to Sebastian the words were twisted and strange. Vowels flat and nasal. The Voice again . . . now he listened, it too had that flat, nasal ring to it. Magda knocked on the pod with her fist. In Earth Standard she called out: "This is Doctor Magda Czajkowski of Solfleet Central. I have a seriously injured patient out here and I want in *right now.*"

Sebastian had never seen Magda, normally so quiet and pensive, so animated. Her blue eyes blazed and her voice was like steel. She was *magnificent.* The words she spoke were peculiar . . . alien, yet somehow familiar. It was almost as though he understood this language he had never heard before. Had she said something about the . . . Soul Fleet? The scriptures had never mentioned a Soul Fleet, but it made sense.

He heard the Voice respond and although the words were unknown he thought he understood the meaning from the tone. *Wait. We are coming.* Despite everything, Sebastian smiled. He had heard the voice of the Arc and his heart was full. He was blessed.

The seams in the pod grew wider. There was a slight cracking sound and a hiss of air. Magda swung back to allow the square to swing open.

The face that looked out from the square was perfectly ordinary. It belonged to a man in his mid twenties. He had sandy-brown hair, pale skin, and worried brown eyes. His fine eyebrows rose as he looked at Magda.

Magda wasn't looking. She gestured for Sebastian to tow Tephee closer, and the young man, seeing the pallor of the girl's skin and how raggedly she breathed, leaned out to catch hold of her and pull her inside. Magda followed.

Sebastian stared after them, envious of the honour but knowing himself to be unworthy, and then the young man reached down and beckoned him. So Sebastian stretched out his arm and climbed into God's Chariot.

The Chariot was rather more cramped than Sebastian had expected it would be. Then he realised that he had arrived in a tiny antechamber and that, as the square door closed behind him, another door was opening up. He stepped through it with the young man and his eyes widened.

It was still smaller than he'd expected, but only because every surface was covered with Arc machinery. Another man was inside, standing well out of Magda's way while she examined Tephee on the floor. She held her hands over Tephee's forehead and temples, moved them to hover behind her neck, where she had been hit. She swore.

Sebastian watched her as she shook her head, unable to sense anything, then grimace when one of the young Lords directed her to a compartment on the wall behind her. She retrieved a colourful box from it and with cool efficiency she set to work. One tool she held flashed as she ran it over Tephee's skull; another hummed when she applied it to the bloody patch at the back of her head. Another item she held to the light, set a mark, and held it to Tephee's neck. It hissed and after a moment the girl moaned and her eyelids fluttered.

Magda issued more curt instructions and the sandy-haired man fetched a covering made of light, shining fabric and helped to pull it over the girl. He stood back, looking concerned and embarrassed, while the older man regarded them all with an expression both sour and troubled.

They are not . . . they are just men. They are not . . . the First King. Perhaps . . . I thought they might be envoys. Yes. Even Witch Magda is only human . . . as well as witch . . . This is not what I imagined it would be like. A wave of sudden giddiness and Sebastian sagged to his knees.

"Sebastian!"

"I'm . . . all right." He was staring at them, at the room, with a kind of glazed joy.

He waved Magda away with one hand, held the other to his forehead. "I think . . . it's just the shock wearing off." His weak laugh turned into a cough. "Or setting in. Oh dear. I feel rather odd."

The younger man reached him first and caught him before the priest fell face first into the deck. With a helpless look at Magda, he held Sebastian in his arms to see if he was still breathing. Magda looked over him, feeling his forehead and pulse.

"He only fainted," she assured them. "Give him a minute to come round."

"Will she be all right?" The young man nodded towards Tephee.

"She needs better equipment than this, but I think so. There's a hairline fracture back there and she's concussed, but I can keep an eye on her. Thanks."

"You're welcome. Ah . . . what about him?" He glanced down at Sebastian, who was beginning to stir.

Magda frowned. "He'll be okay. He just thinks you're God."

The older man snorted. "He's not God. He's just Second Pilot Mayhew. He's got a couple of engineering degrees to go before godhood."

Mayhew shrugged. "For someone slightly closer to God than me, First Pilot Benedict, you can still ditch a shuttle in a huge expanse of water and still hit the only ship in bloody sight." He raised an eyebrow in sardonic response to Benedict's black look.

"I didn't aim for the goddamn thing!"

"Christ, we should have had you out shooting for us in the

Centauri Wars. Scores like that without even trying could have ended the war in a week."

"Oh, very funny, Mayhew. I didn't see you waving your magic wand and getting those thrusters to come back on line."

"*Stop it!* Don't you know there are people *dying* out there?" Magda's voice whipped out, disgusted and angry. She caught her breath then, realising at last. *Leenan. Sylvia. Cadogan.* She closed her eyes and reached out with her senses, as Sylvia had taught her to do. Nothing. No one. *No . . .*

Mayhew sobered at once. "We know. We couldn't get the shuttle to come around. We'd have gone right through the middle of the ship if Benny hadn't pulled her as far as he did." He frowned. "We hit someone when the pod came up, didn't we?"

Magda wiped her hands across her eyes, found that she was shaking. "Yes."

"Shit."

"Did it damage the pod?" Benedict wanted to know.

"Jesus, Benny, didn't you hear? We killed someone on the ascent . . ."

"I heard, Mayhew, and there's nothing I can do about it now. But this thing was built for ejection in space, or over land—not from twenty metres underwater." Benedict's tone was strained but even. "If the transmitters have been smashed, we've been sending out a distress beacon for the last fifteen minutes to the fish, for all I know. If we've been holed we'll sink, and we can feel sorry for those poor bastards out there while we go down with them."

Mayhew turned away but did not argue further.

"Shit," he said again.

Then they heard the hum and a voice from the comlink. "You in there Benedict? Mayhew?"

Benedict hit the respond key. "We're in here! We've got three passengers so allow for that in the tractor."

"Passengers? Jesus, you guys know how to screw up big time, you know that?"

"Yeah, Docker, we know it. Now get us the hell out of here." He keyed the comlink off and glared at Mayhew. "I'll tell them you're the one who insisted on taking them on board."

"Thanks buddy. You're a prince, you know that?"

There was a metallic thud and a sensation of pins and needles.

"I hate this tractor shit," Mayhew muttered. The priest in his arms groaned and began to move. "The Captain's going to kill us," said Mayhew despairingly.

"Which is nothing compared to what First Officer Redmonde is going to do." Benedict actually looked worried.

Magda, intent on checking Tephee's condition, figured that she had faced much worse in her life than Solfleet Command. Damn if she didn't intend to raise a little hell herself.

Chapter Sixteen

Cadogan returned from his foraging to find Sylvia kneeling on the beach. She held a fistful of trickling sand which she moved in sweeping circles with an attitude of deep concentration. Her usual demeanor of appearing somehow carelessly tidy had vanished—her blouse and underskirt were wrinkled and limp and her long black hair was matted with dried salt and knots. He couldn't see her face, but her whole body expressed both weariness and tension. The eastern horizon behind her was pale, just losing the coloured flush of dawn. It would be another hot day.

He adjusted the folds of his uniform shirt, now being used as a sack to carry wood and pieces of moist plant, and walked down to join her. His bare feet on the sand made a slight crunching sound. The surf whispered onto the shore, hissing slightly as it wrapped around pieces of wreckage that had washed ashore overnight. No bodies had yet been pushed out of the sea, thankfully. He was still angry with the ship's crew, even when they were dead and given up to the Mother, and he was afraid to look for anyone else.

As he approached he saw that Sylvia was making patterns on the beach with the trickling sand. She did not look up, but said a quiet "good morning" to him. Her voice was subdued, only just audible above the susurration of the surf.

Cadogan crouched beside her and opened his shirt to pass her some of the water-plant. The sand pattern, he noticed, was a simple, elegant whorl, like the knot that symbolised the royal house of Tyne.

"Where's Leenan?" asked Cadogan. His own voice sounded unnaturally loud.

"Still asleep," said Sylvia. "She's exhausted herself changing shape like that. Whatever she ate last night gave her enough to change back to her own form, but she'll need to eat again when she wakes up." She brushed sand from her fingers then clasped her hands around her knees. "It's strange. For months she has been unable to change, and yesterday . . . twice. Perhaps being struck by lightning wasn't such a bad thing."

Cadogan, remembering acutely how fragile Leenan had felt in his arms as he carried her from the river, pale and burned, did not comment.

"You'll have to start a fire yourself," said Sylvia after a moment. "I can't even conjure a ball of witchfire without getting a headache." Her tone was peculiarly flat.

"All right," he replied.

"I never thought I used magic for much," she continued, still studiously neutral, "but now I find I used it all the time. To light a fire. To untangle my hair. To make pictures . . ." She glanced at the sand pattern she had made. "I made sea sculptures with shells and water . . ." She sighed and rubbed the back of her hand against her forehead.

"Your powers will return," said Cadogan gently.

She shook her head. "No. I don't think so. Magda thought that perhaps the Arc vessel might offer a chance . . ." Cadogan heard the pain that closed up her throat, that made her back and shoulders stiff with the effort to hold it in. "But my friends are dead," she said at last, "and we'll be lucky if we make it home alive."

"No harm will come to you. Not this time." He said it calmly enough, but the intensity of it was unshakable.

Sylvia turned her head to regard him with a speculative eye. "This is not your fault, Cadogan."

"I have to start the fire. Do you know how to find seamoons?"

Sylvia let it go and pushed herself to her feet. "I lived by the sea for nearly twenty years. I'll find us some seamoons and a couple of water-melons."

Cadogan made a fire on the leeward side of the shelter where Leenan still slept and made a careful mound out of the dried grass and driftwood he'd collected. He still had his knife, and used this to whittle a drilling stick and a base. By the time Sylvia returned with the small, half-moon shaped mussels dug up from the wet sand and three of the round, fleshy sea plants that grew in the shallows, he was feeding twigs into the lick of flame he had started. "It will take a while," he warned.

"I'm not in any hurry," she said.

Leenan woke when the scent of food reached her. The mussels and sea plants had been shoved into the flames, among the coals, wrapped in the large leaves of a nearby tree. Cadogan brought her some of the moist plant to relieve her thirst, then split the meal among them. She insisted they divide the portions equally, but Cadogan and Sylvia both managed to give her extra, claiming they weren't hungry. Leenan was, of course, ravenous.

Over their makeshift meal it was agreed that they would try to make it to the nearest port. They might convince a fisherman or coastal trader to take them back to Port Lordale, or Berrinsland. Anywhere, as long as it was away from here. No one spoke of the previous day at all, not even to say aloud the names of their lost friends. Their grief was bound up with their fear of what Marin Kuta might do to them, and to let go of one was to succumb to the other.

Barefoot, disheveled, weary and apprehensive they left the

beach, and walked southward under the shade of the trees in silence.

Mid morning they came to a stream flowing eastward, to the ocean, and gratefully they stopped to finally quench their thirst. Sylvia splashed water over her face and head and tried to untangle some of the knots with her fingers. Leenan sat with her back against a tree. Cadogan stood nearby, watchful and silent.

She scrubbed her hands across her face and sighed. A tremor shook the sound and she left her hands over her face.

"Leenan?" For all his grim expression, Cadogan was hesitant. "Are you all right?"

With her face covered, she shook her head. "No." She dragged in a breath and held it, trying not to cry. "I keep expecting them to walk out of the woods at any moment. I can't believe it's come to this."

Cadogan frowned, distressed by her distress. "I'm sorry, Leenan . . ."

"Don't!"

He took a step backwards, startled by her anger as she rose to glare at him.

"Stop it! It was *not* your fault! We chose to come here—we knew the risks and we chose to come anyway. I'm not stupid and I'm not a child. I don't blame anyone, and I don't expect to be treated like an idiot, not responsible for my own choices." Leenan had stalked towards him, but he stood his ground—not defiant, but immobilised. "What do you think you could have done to stop it?"

"I shouldn't have let you . . ."

"*Let* me? What makes you think you could have told any of us what to do? Do you know how arrogant that sounds? As if you had the power to stop us, or to stop what happened? I *have* power, and I couldn't stop it. I didn't know how." And her rage crumbled into grief and she began to sob.

"Leenan . . . no . . ." Awkwardly he tried to pat her shoulder, but she drew away. "Even as a witch, there wasn't anything you could do. It happened too fast, and there were too many of them. Tephee tried to hold them back, and they killed her for it."

Sylvia appeared, folded her arms around Leenan, who turned and clung to her.

"Think about that," Sylvia said to Cadogan, softly. "Tephee was the most powerful of us, and even she couldn't do anything."

Cadogan shook his head. "I can't think of what I should have done, and I've thought of nothing but what I might have done differently since it happened. In here," he tapped the side of his head, "I know there was nothing I could do. But in here," he tapped over his heart, "reason doesn't count."

"I know all about that," Sylvia told him, rubbing her cheek against Leenan's hair as the sobbing subsided. "It can turn you into a recluse, and make you very lonely. Let it go."

Cadogan's expression darkened. "Marin Kuta has a habit of eating alive the people that I love. Every time I cross that ocean, I lose someone." His blue eyes were like cold steel, and that steel was a hard edge in his voice. "I will not lose any more to this place. Not while there's a breath in my body."

Leenan drew away from Sylvia's embrace and gave him a cool and dignified look. "Shouldn't we be moving on then?"

"Yes, Witch Leenan," he replied stiffly, "we should."

It was hard going, barefoot on a hot summer's day. They had no containers to carry water, so Cadogan led them along the stream further inland. When the stream disappeared underground at some rocks, they took a final long drink and turned south again. They continued, in a strained silence, until they came across a shallow creek. They sought refuge from the mid-afternoon heat under cover of the sparse woods.

After refreshing themselves, Sylvia disappeared into the woods saying that she needed some privacy, leaving Leenan and Cadogan awkwardly alone.

Leenan broke the silence first. "I'm sorry I lost my temper before. I shouldn't have . . ."

"It's all right," he interrupted, his voice low. "You were right. I just . . . I keep thinking there was more I could have done. Wishing I could change it."

A pause, and then: "What did you mean, that you lost someone whenever you crossed the sea?"

After a long moment he told her. "My family were found as stowaways when we were escaping. They threw us overboard. My baby brother drowned."

"Oh . . ."

"My mother died indirectly as a result. Now Magda and Tephee are gone. But . . ."—he looked up to meet her gaze— "not you."

"Cadogan . . ."

He dragged his eyes away from hers and stepped back.

"For the Lords' sake, Cadogan. Stop running away from me."

"I apologise, Witch Leenan . . ."

"*Stop that.* Why do you do that all the time? Call me 'Witch Leenan' whenever you feel uncomfortable? It's really annoying, you know that?"

"I'm sorry . . ."

"*And stop apologising.*" Frustration was making her temper boil again, as did the expression of regret and meekness on his face. "Aren't witches supposed to care for anyone? Aren't they meant to fall in love and have families?"

"It's not that . . ."

"Then what is it?" The anger drained and she held her hands out to him, beseeching understanding.

"I'm not worthy."

"*Horseshit!*" Fury again. "Cadogan, I am not a goddess. You are not my acolyte. Stop using it as an excuse."

His own temper flared unexpectedly, mixed with despair and disgust. "Leenan, I'm a soldier. I'm forty and still a Sergeant. I own nothing. I have nothing to offer you."

"I don't *want* anything! Not *anything* you can't give."

So they stood facing each other, flushed with emotion, poised on the edge of anger and frustration. Or something else. Each waiting for the other to give, just a little.

Something in his stance flickered, and Leenan thought he was about to walk away from her again. Idiot bastard. Lord-damned stiff-necked, noble, gorgeous fool.

She took two steps towards him, seized his shirt front and pulled him to meet her; his chest against hers, their mouths meeting for one brief, intense moment before she dropped back in a mixture of shock, satisfaction, and anticipation. If he called her "Witch Leenan" after that she'd . . . she'd . . .

His arms went around her, pulling her back into the embrace, and he kissed her, without apology or hesitation, for a long time. His hands stroked her hair, her face, held her to him while her own hands were trapped between them, flat against his chest where she could feel his heartbeat thudding. She curled her fingers into the cloth of his shirt, unwilling to let go. His two-day beard was rough, but she reveled in that sensation as well as all the others. His arms were strong around her, his mouth was warm. He smelled good.

They parted, eventually, but Cadogan left a trail of kisses from her chin to her temple. Leenan sighed contentedly and laid her head against his chest.

"We'll settle this," he murmured into her hair, "if we get out of here alive."

Before she could ask what he meant by that, they heard the

sound of someone approaching and sprang guiltily apart. It was Sylvia, returning from her ablutions.

"There's someone coming," she reported breathlessly. "They've got horses, and dogs."

Cadogan cursed and urged them both down to the creek. "Hurry." They splashed into the water. "What way? Where . . ."

A dog bayed and shouts followed, and "where" was soon obvious. Five horsemen crashed through the woods, a dozen dogs surging around them and down towards the creek.

"Uncle Ensho! Here!" A young voice, shrill with excitement. As his horse came into view they could see he was dressed in robes with the starburst on one shoulder. Another rider, older and in more colourful robes, thundered into view behind him, the other three hard on his heels. Arc priests. Warrior priests, every one.

"Witches!" came a triumphant voice. "The ones that sank the *Aln!*" It was as though they were branded with the deed. In a sense, they had been, with dried salt spray, weariness, and their foreign looks. Who else could they be, but the witches those few survivors had described?

Leenan drew down into a crouch, one hand flung forward to help her to focus. *Fear. Danger. Run, run, run. . . .*

The lead dog yelped and balked, the others collided with him then stopped, whining.

Danger. Panic. Run, run, runrunrun . . .

The dogs tucked their tails between their legs and fled, yelping and howling.

The head rider cursed and kicked his mount to a gallop towards them. The other four came after, dust and leaves flying behind their horses' hooves, swords brandished and yelling revenge and murder.

They were nearly on top of them before Leenan could send her magic. A horse reared above her, threatened to trample her, but Sylvia pulled her out of the way as the hooves came crashing down. The young rider shouted, startled, and fell from the saddle and the horse galloped into the woods, its eyes rolling.

A mounted attacker swung at Cadogan, a deadly, arcing blow aimed to sever limbs. Cadogan stepped under it, seized the wrist behind the sword, felt the horse's muscles a finger breadth away as it pounded past him. The rider shrieked as he was pulled from his mount, over Cadogan's shoulder and completed the curve by tumbling underneath the horse's flashing hooves. Cadogan had stepped away as both horse and man streaked past. Now, he had a sword.

The young acolyte who had fallen first staggered upright, cursing them to the Red Lord and back.

Cadogan blew out a slow breath. Instead of running, as the assailants expected, he waited while two riders bore down on him. A sidestep . . . he was at one horse's flanks, shielded from the other, older rider. Cadogan's hands were moving and lifting, hooking a foot out of the stirrups, slapping the flat of his blade against the animal's rump. It screamed and reared and the rider fell. He began to rise, snarling, and Cadogan shifted, kicked. As his heel connected with jaw, there was the crack of breaking bone and then silence. The second rider swept on, calling his last mounted companion to his side, and to the young one to: "Use your sword, Willem! Get up!"

The acolyte was advancing on Leenan and Sylvia with a look between terror and exultation. Sylvia flung a handful of mud and pebbles from the creek bottom into his face, hitting him with pleasing accuracy in the eye. He swung his sword wildly and Leenan took the simple expedient of ducking. He overbalanced and she charged up, headbutting him in the stomach. He landed in the creek with a grunt and she kicked him in the ribs three or four times for good measure before retrieving the sword and turning to face the next attacker.

Lord*damn,* she was angry. Red-and-white furious, about Magda and Tephee; about all the fear and despair of the last day; about the interruption with Cadogan.

The remaining two riders were bearing down on Cadogan, who was armed now but trapped between them. Leenan sent a jolt of power which literally pushed the leader of the two from his galloping horse and he crashed into a tree, as though thrown there by a giant hand, before falling in a stunned and bloodied heap. She heard the boy in the river behind cry out, "Uncle En-sho!" but spared no time for either of them. She turned to find the second rider reigning in, sword raised. Before she could move he grunted and the sword fell from his grip. He slithered from his horse, blood and intestines spilling down his clothes.

"Call the horses to you," Cadogan ordered gruffly, wiping the gore from his sword onto the grass. He caught the reins of the nearest animal and led it down to Sylvia while Leenan reached out to calm the remaining horses and bring them to the creek. The young man Leenan had disarmed staggered out of the water with a dagger, but Cadogan merely grabbed and twisted his wrist, and with a second shift broke both wrist and forearm. The youth collapsed, whimpering.

Cadogan, too, was in a cold rage. "The survivors have made it to shore and raised the alarm. They'll be looking for us now."

"Where do we go?" Leenan threw herself into the saddle, refusing to relinquish the sword she held. It was heavy and she laid it across the pommel.

"South," Cadogan said. "There are fishing villages all down the coast. We'll steal a boat if we have to."

Sylvia alighted in the saddle, staring around at the dead and wounded. It made her feel slightly ill, but she couldn't be sure if it was because of the carnage or because she couldn't feel sorry for them. She saw them there and thought only of Magda and

178

Tephee. Had Sebastian fought for them, or had he simply let it happen?

She caught Cadogan's eye.

"We all go back to the Mother," he said grimly. "Even Her poisoned children."

"To the Red Lord with them," Leenan said, and they turned their horses south.

CHAPTER SEVENTEEN

Sebastian sat quietly on the small stool provided, but there was a quality to his stillness that betrayed both tension and fragility. He was watching Magda as she paced back and forth in the confined space. She talked out loud to herself and sometimes she would stop and try to breathe deeply and calmly. Usually her breathing would betray a tremor so before the despair could set in she would storm to the door and pound on it, shouting things to the First King's people. Sebastian didn't understand most of it, though he heard Tephee's name several times and some of the odd curses that Magda sometimes used.

"They had to lock us up in a storeroom," Magda was muttering. She had switched back to the language Sebastian understood, desperate perhaps for someone to hear and acknowledge her, even though some of the words she used were still unknown to him. "A survey ship like this should have had a brig. Something with a bathroom, at least. A bloody stores cupboard. I'll have strips off that bastard Captain for breaking regulations." She stopped and took another shaky breath, glancing towards him. "Stop looking at me like that!"

Sebastian, who had been frowning at the way she spoke of the First King's people, regarded her blankly. "Like what?"

"All that disapproval. You make me want to scream." Her teeth clenched convulsively and she covered her face with her hands. "I'm sorry. I'm . . . tense. I don't know where they've taken Tephee. I can't sense her out there anywhere. I can't tap into my magic at all . . ."

He raised an eyebrow at this, but Magda had returned to her pacing. She caught him watching her again, and glared, so he dragged his attention away from her to examine the walls of their prison.

He'd been watching her to avoid doing that, but now that she had made him look again he felt that same awful tremor within. She had called it a storeroom, and he supposed it looked a little like one. The comparison was appallingly prosaic, when the walls were made from wondrous material he had only ever seen on Arc relics. When there was a soft light issuing from neither sun, nor lamp, nor candle. When the prison was within the great silver castle, bigger than the Arc Monastery in which he'd spent most of his life, into which the First King's terrifying sky ship had taken them.

It had been amazing enough in the silver bubble they had, in their audacity, entered to escape the sea. There he had been confused, overwhelmed, by the almost ordinary men in such extraordinary surroundings. Some great hand had lifted them from the ocean, then, and their bubble had risen to join another great sky ship. They had flown, like birds, these commonplace gods, over the waters and down the coast which he could see displayed on the walls. Images sent by the other ship, Magda had said. Sebastian had been too busy staring at them to listen much. The ragged coast and tiny fishing villages commanded all his thought. *This is how the Lords see us,* he had thought. *We're so tiny.*

Then he had seen the great furrow in the earth which they followed. It had started as a blackened line of burnt trees and became a broad band of ash and earth through the summer fields of wheat, rye, and corn until it stopped where the sky castle was resting. One side of it was blackened too, like it had been under siege, but the rest of it . . . oh, the rest of it! It shone

181

so much in the sunlight that it hurt his eyes. They had swooped then, like dragons onto rabbits, down into the maw of it.

In a daze he had let the others guide him into . . . he didn't know what to call it. A great Arc cavern, in which the sky ship and the bubble rested side by side. The First King's Lords had gathered up Tephee and taken her away, but had refused Magda permission to follow. She had shouted at them, but it was all incomprehensible to Sebastian. He wished Magda wouldn't speak in this tone to the Lords of the True World, even if she was their emissary. A large bearded man, tall and broad shouldered with a deep booming voice had spoken over the top of her, without shouting, and Magda had been appeased by his words. Sebastian wasn't sure what had happened next, except that he was swept along by gentle and firm hands.

And here he was, in an Arc ship storeroom, locked up without water or a bed, or a word to help him to understand what had gone wrong.

Magda was shouting at the door again, Tephee's name once more the focus of her angry complaints. An answering voice surprised her into silence and the door opened to admit a woman carrying a tray. Food and water at last. Behind her was the large bearded man, looking stern and grand. Sebastian rose to his feet respectfully while the tray was placed on Magda's unused stool. Words were exchanged and Magda took a hopeful step towards the door. She turned briefly. "They're taking me to Tephee," she told him. "I'll find out what's going on."

She left and the door closed, leaving him alone to wonder why the First King's Lords had taken the witch with them and left their loyal priest without comfort.

First Officer Redmonde had a grim and unwelcoming expression on his face, but Magda didn't particularly care as long as she got what she wanted. What she wanted, first of all, was to see Tephee. And then the Captain of this ship. She had a barrage of questions she wanted answered as well. For a moment she hesitated, feeling dwarfed by this giant of a man . . . almost everyone she knew was shorter than she was, a few, like King Armand, a shade taller. This Redmonde was half a head taller and so broad across the shoulders that the impression of size was doubled. He filled up the space on either side of him with his presence.

Well, damn his presence, Magda thought. He's just a Solfleet officer, not a bloody True World god. The very thought made the anger in her swell again.

"Have you found them yet?"

"Found who?" He did not break stride as they moved through the corridor.

"There were two other women on that ship, and a man in a red and black uniform." Her voice shook a little. *Please, tell me you found them.* "I told Second Pilot Mayhew about them. Surely you've gone back . . ."

First Officer Redmonde stopped abruptly and turned to face her. His expression changed when he saw the look on her face—a painful mix of hope and fear.

"I'm sorry," he said gently. "We haven't been able to go back to look."

"You haven't . . ." She took a sharp breath. "Your bloody shuttle pilots are responsible for that wreck and every life lost on her!"

His expression hardened. "My shuttle pilots are painfully aware of the fact. They've given me a full report, and what they haven't explained yet is who the hell you are and how the hell you got here."

She refused to be cowed, standing straight and glaring him in the eye she responded crisply: "Doctor Magda Czajkowski, Solfleet Medical Auxiliary Service."

"A colony doctor, eh? Benedict and Mayhew said you knew the emergency code. Is that where this lot are from?"

"Sort of." At his look she expanded: "I was answering a mayday beacon when my shuttle got into trouble. Next thing I knew we'd crashed here. This place has been settled for nearly eight hundred years, as far as I can work out. By an old-time colony ship—cryogenics and gene banks. They've made a religion out of it."

Redmonde suppressed a sigh. "So we gather." He looked down to meet her gaze. "How long have you been here?"

"About five years."

"What happened to your shuttle pilot?"

She had a sudden mental image of Jared Heineger, too cocksure of his skill to fasten his safety straps. He'd handled the crash landing in the coast of northern Berrinsland, but the jarring stop which had forced the air from her lungs had flung him from his seat. Poor Jared, smashed and broken . . .

"He died," she said shortly, closing off the memory.

"You couldn't help him?"

"Nothing left to help."

He nodded in solemn understanding. "We have some injured here who could use you. The field we passed through screwed our instrumentation and we had a bad landing, as you may have seen. Our own medic is one of the seriously injured."

"Is that the only reason you've come to get me?" she asked, her tone waspish.

He raised an eyebrow at her. "No. The Captain also asked for you. He wouldn't let me come for you until now."

It was suddenly too much effort to argue about it any further. "Can I see Tephee now?"

"Of course." They walked in silence towards the medical bays.

Magda noticed the artificial lighting as they walked and tilted her head inquiringly. From time to time the light flickered faintly. "You still have power?"

"For the time being. We can't power the engines, though," Redmonde said with a grimace. "But since hull integrity is extremely suspect, I don't suppose it would help. We sent that shuttle up to send a beacon back through the disturbance, before it scrambled their engines as well. We don't know if it got through, but we're not sending another up after it. We only have one shuttle left. Here we are . . ." He gestured her through the entry to a medical bay where a harried young man was moving between the six beds. Four of them held patients. Magda could see that most of them were suffering radiation and other burns. One of them had an immobiliser set over a serious upper torso injury. Redmonde frowned worriedly.

"How are things, Christov?"

The expression on Christov's face answered before his dispirited: "Not well, sir," came out.

The First Officer looked momentarily lost. He swallowed, took a deep breath, and faced the young nurse again. "Christov, this is Doctor Czajkowski. She's here to see that native girl we brought in. How is she doing?"

"She's doing fine, sir," reported Christov with energy, pleased to have some good news for someone. "The fracture is healing well and her motor control is returning to good order . . ."

"Where is she?" Magda's demand sounded more like a plea. With a glance at the First Officer for confirmation, Christov showed her into the private room that led off the main medical bay.

Tephee sat bolt upright when she saw Magda, then flung herself into her friend's arms. Magda wrapped her arms tightly around her and for a long time they clung to each other, both weeping with relief.

"Tephee . . . thank God . . . I didn't know what they'd done

. . . thank God you're all right."

"I woke up and didn't know where you all were, Maggie. How did you stop them? Where are the others?"

Magda drew away a little. "How much can you remember?"

Tephee shrugged slightly. "Those Lorddamned sailors threw Sylvia over the side of the ship, and I tried to find her . . . I think someone hit me." A long, horrified pause. "Where are the others?"

"I don't know." Tears escaped unchecked this time. "After they hit you, they threw Leenan over the side. Then Cadogan went over. Then the shuttle crashed into us and the ship sank. I think they're dead."

"Oh . . . no . . . Maggie . . ." Tephee breathed a bewildered denial. "The ship . . . sank? Where are we then?"

Magda tried to explain, slowly and carefully, about where they were. It was harder than she'd thought, and left Tephee in dazed silence.

"Tephee?" she asked timidly when she'd finished. "They're not gods . . ."

"I know. They're too . . ." Tephee shook her head, the action making her dizzy. Magda steadied her and examined her with anxious attention.

"I meant to tell you . . ." She was looking pale and shaken as Magda helped her back onto the bed. "It's happened again. Like last time."

"Like last time?"

"My magic's gone. I can't . . . summon anything." She swallowed. "I thought . . . that was why I couldn't find anyone. Why I couldn't sense any of you." Her hazel eyes, bright with tears, gazed searchingly at her. "Are you sure they're dead?"

"I . . . no. But I don't think it's likely they survived."

"When . . . when my magic comes back," Tephee told her, "I'll search for them. Then we'll know for sure."

Magda could only nod. The door behind them opened and Tephee looked up in a sudden start of surprise. Magda glanced around to see Redmonde waiting for her.

"I have to go, Tephee."

"But . . ."

"I need you to rest and get well. I'll be back with you soon, I promise."

"Okay." A suspicious glance towards the bearded giant at the doorway. "Are you sure . . . ?" Meaning, are you safe?

"Yes, love. I'll be okay." She managed a small laugh. "He's just very . . . tall."

Magda made sure Tephee was comfortable in the bed, tucking her in, adjusting the pillow, fussing like a mother hen. With a final kiss on her brow, Magda left Tephee to rest further and joined Redmonde in the main clinic.

"Thanks."

"My pleasure. Is she all right?"

"Yes. The head injury has caused some temporary damage, but I'm sure it'll heal itself in time. Do you want me to give these people a checkup now?"

With Christov she went over each of the remaining patients' diagnostics. There wasn't much she could do for any of them immediately—treatment would take time and patience. She could see that the nurse had already begun to grow skin for grafting in the incubators and that, within the limits of his skills, he had done all that was possible. She suggested minor adjustments to treatment, which Christov gratefully accepted. With that done, First Officer Redmonde took her to the bridge.

Captain Delouise was sitting at one of the science stations when they arrived, studying the information that scrolled past. He was a slight figure next to his First Officer; where Redmonde was tall, broad, and expansive, Delouise was small and wiry. Mentally, Magda was already seeing Redmonde as a bear and the instant suggestion for his Captain was somehow of a watchful and highly intelligent weasel. Redmonde waited until Delouise looked up before introducing her in brisk military fashion.

Delouise eyed her appraisingly before saying, "Welcome aboard the *Albert Einstein,* Solfleet Science and Exploration." He smiled as though he had just told a joke. "I have never been sure if it was meant as a tribute or irony, given his theories on the nature of space and time. No doubt the headquarters hacks just picked the first name they recognised." No response to his acid humour. He grimaced and started again. "How is your young friend? I trust Nurse Ivolich has taken all care with her."

"Christov has taken all care with all of his patients," she answered cautiously. There was a calculated distance in this man's manner which made her wary.

"He has had the best Solfleet training," the Captain said, "as have you, apparently."

"I spent ten years as a nurse on CentOrbit Station, then trained on SolOrbit for my colony doctorate."

Delouise smiled at her. "So . . . our noble among the savages . . ."

She didn't much care for his phrasing.

". . . I was wondering what you could tell me about them." He keyed in a command code and the observation wall displayed an external view. Some distance from the crippled exploration ship a small tent village was growing. "It gets bigger every day," he explained, "and their presence provides a complication."

Magda gazed at the gathering of pilgrims. "As I was telling your First Officer," she said, "I believe that one of the Earth's first colony ships met with the same kind of accident that brought you and I here. It happened so long ago, it's become a creation myth. I saw a copy of the ship's cargo manifest recently, signed by a Captain King. He's become the First King in their mythology. It's like some kind of deified ancestor worship." She regarded him coolly. "I suspect they think your ship is the Second Coming."

"Ah." The Captain's gaze shifted briefly to Redmonde. "It's worse than I thought."

"Much worse," Redmonde agreed.

"So tell me, Doctor Czajkowski,"—Delouise's bright rodent eyes went back to Magda—"have you any suggestions as to how this may be used to our advantage?"

Magda stared at him in horror. "Your . . . ? There is no advantage to this! Your presence here is bringing a volatile situation to flashpoint!"

Delouise only raised an eyebrow at her passionate response. "How so?"

"There is an old disagreement between the First King and the witches . . ."

"Good Lord," the Captain interjected, his voice light and infused with sarcasm. "They believe in witches. Things just get better and better."

"Yes, they believe in witches," Magda replied tartly, "*I'm* a witch."

"No doubt you'd seem so," Redmonde said, nodding, as though that was what she meant.

"So how is this mix of superstitions meant to be so volatile?"

"Captain Delouise, on this island, a woman can be burned alive for being a witch. When your presence here ignites religious fervour, I doubt there'll be anywhere from here to Berrinsland to the Southern Kingdoms where we'll be safe."

"You mean, where *they'll* be safe, I'm sure," said the Captain, still in that light voice of his.

"I mean," said Magda forcefully, "there'll be pogroms and the murder of innocent people. I've seen it already."

He looked at her then. Really looked at her, and he frowned at the expression on her face. "You're quite serious, aren't you?"

"You can't think there is any way this can be turned to *advantage*. These people took one look at one of your shuttles and now three of my friends are *dead*."

That dismissive lightness vanished, replaced by a troubled frown. "The man who is with you," he said at last, "didn't Mayhew say he was a priest?"

"An Arc priest, yes."

"Noah's Ark? How appropriate."

"I think it's meant more like . . . an Entry Arc," Magda clarified, remembering her talks with Sebastian, the first time they'd met at the high Monastery on her way to the Battle of Tyne.

"Well, I'd like to talk to him, see if he has any suggestions. I'll need you as a translator. Go back and have a word with him. I'll send for you later." He waved a hand, dismissing them both.

Redmonde saluted and guided Magda from the bridge.

Magda was speechless with horrified fury. "Any suggestions"? *Christ.* She turned on Redmonde. "Are you just going to let him do this? He's not just dealing with that crowd out there— this is a whole society we are talking about. Whole cultures! Any witch, any Leylite who protects one, is going to be a target! Don't you know anything about history?"

"Actually," said Redmonde, deliberately cool, "I know quite a lot about it. History was my first major. For the record, I think the Captain is playing with fire and I've told him so, several times. Encouraging superstitious claptrap isn't going to help any of us." He paused to regard her steadily. "He hasn't made any decisions. He's just trying to protect his crew. Captain Delouise is a scientist, like the rest of us—he won't be making a decision until he has more data."

"I'm sure that will be a great comfort to all those who die as a result of your mere presence," she said acidly.

"We didn't exactly plan on being here," he replied, growing annoyed.

Magda's own irritation flagged. No one had ever exactly planned on being here. Not Captain King or his crew and cargo of colonists, not herself, and not the weasel-like Captain Delouise. "I know. I'm sorry. It's been . . . a bad day." The understatement of it deflated her further. Even all the fear and grief that had been held at bay by her anger had no power now. She felt hollow, numb.

She fell so suddenly silent, her expression becoming so drawn and sombre, that First Officer Redmonde felt sorry for her. "I'll talk to the Captain about getting some more suitable accommodation for you," he offered, "and some fresh clothes."

"Thanks."

"No trouble."

They walked on in silence for a while until finally she asked, "What's your field then?"

"Sorry?"

"You said your first major was history. What's your other field?"

"Oh. Comparative linguistics. I speak three languages, plus six dialects of Earth Standard. I study the developmental variations in language between all the different colonies, from the early settlements to the Centauri wave." He grimaced. "This place will make my career, if I can get the findings back home." He didn't sound at all convinced it were possible. He tugged at his beard and said: "Would you like me to take a message to your young friend?"

"Could you?"

"If you teach me, sure."

"Tell her . . . it'll be okay."

"Do you think I should?" His tone was gentle, compassionate despite the meaning implied.

Magda fought back sudden tears again. "No. I suppose not. Just tell her I'll see her soon." She said it for him in Tephee's own language, and he repeated it carefully and nearly flawlessly. They went over it a few times until he was completely accurate.

"Sorry about this. The brig area was damaged on landing, along with half the starboard hull," Redmonde told her as they reached the storeroom. A man and a woman, looking uncomfortable with their regulation weapons, stood guard outside. They parted to allow their First Officer at the door. "I'll make arrangements for you to get back to the medical bay soon."

"All right. Thank you."

Sebastian looked up as the door opened and Magda was returned to the prison. As the door closed again behind her, she turned to face him, momentarily lost and drained of her earlier defiance.

"How is young Tephee?" he asked.

"She's fine," Magda replied tiredly, "though she's lost her powers again. I expect it's just a short-term effect of the head wound. They hit her bloody hard."

"The First King is infinite in His forgiveness."

"Sorry?"

"I understand why we are here now," he told her patiently. "I imagine that the First King's emissary would like to see me soon."

"As a matter of fact . . ."

Sebastian nodded, a glimmer of anxiety in his blue eyes. "I will repent, as no doubt you have done."

"What are you talking about Sebastian? Repent what?"

"My sins, of course," he said, looking up at her. "I know my sins are great, or My Lords would not have imprisoned me here. They are right, and I deserve greater punishment than this time of reflection. The First King and His Lords are indeed great and merciful." Magda continued to stare at him, and he smiled benignly at her mystification. "You must feel better, now that you have been cleansed."

Magda was reluctant to continue merely repeating his words, but nothing in them yet made sense to her. "You'll have to be clearer than that, Sebastian. What sins have you committed and how have I been cleansed?"

"I have been too lenient with the witches," he explained, that beatific smile still on his lips. "The First King is unhappy that I have shown kindness to His enemies. And you, His own emissary, becoming one of the tainted instead of representing Him as you ought. But in His wisdom and love He has cleansed you of your witching ways and brought you back to the Arc." His smile widened, to that sunny, beautiful expression that had so impressed her when they'd first met. This time, it made her neck prickle. "He has even cleansed the Witch Tephee to bring her back to the fold."

"For God's sake, Sebastian, she's had her skull fractured by some thug. In fact, I'm starting to suspect it has something to do with the energy fields on this ship. Your precious bloody First King has got nothing to do with it."

Sebastian's smile fell away and his eyes became cold. "How can you stand in His own stronghold, converse with His emissaries, and speak of the First King in this way?"

Her patience snapped. "This is just a survey ship, Sebastian. The people here are just scientists, and your First King was just a Captain of a glorified freight ship who . . ."

Sebastian, eyes blazing, swept to his feet and struck her. His open hand crashed into her face and she staggered back into the closed door. He stood over her, pale with outrage and she instinctively drew back from him. Her eyes, round and transfixed with shock, locked with his.

The fury bled out of him suddenly. "I'm sorry . . ." He reached out to help her and winced when she flinched at the movement. "I didn't mean to hurt you," he said gently. "But you shouldn't speak of the First King like that."

"Get away from me," she gasped.

He moved away, his expression distressed and contrite, to sit back on his stool. "I am sorry, Magda. I shouldn't have hit you. But you must see, we have been sinful and now is our opportunity to recognise that and mend our past wrongs."

He kept talking to her, gently and reasonably, determined that in the end, she would see it and understand.

Chapter Eighteen

The sun was long set and the moon already past its zenith as Cadogan paused to listen. Behind him, Leenan and Sylvia also paused, waiting for a signal to continue. The horses had been abandoned hours before, driven off inland in the hopes of distracting the search for them, although Leenan still clutched the sword she had claimed. She wondered how Cadogan managed to carry a weapon so easily on his hip, as though the weight of it were nothing. Hers was bloody heavy. If it came down to using it, she'd have to just drop it on someone's foot and hoped it slowed them down.

Of course, Leenan reasoned, under normal circumstances it wouldn't have been so difficult. She wouldn't have been so tired, and Lords, she was so bone weary she felt she could lie down on the stones at her feet and sleep for a week. She was hungry and weary, worn out by the energy she had expended since yesterday morning on magic and fear.

Cadogan looked back at them. He nodded towards Sylvia, bringing her attention to the smaller woman, who had dropped to a crouch and was gazing absently into the darkness.

"Sylvia?" Leenan whispered.

"Hmm?" Sylvia blinked. "Oh. Sorry."

Cadogan gestured towards her, a muted offer of assistance. "We can rest a while . . ."

"No . . . I was just . . . thinking about Py." She recognised the quizzical look in his eyes. "I've had him since he was a kitten.

Twelve years." How to explain that she'd always found Py-wych's wise blue eyes and lean, furred body a comfort? How she wanted nothing more than to curl up with Py in her lap in front of a warm fire and fall asleep, safe in her own cottage by the sea. She wasn't used to having only her own two hands for protection.

She wasn't used to being afraid.

But he seemed to understand. "We'll find a boat," he assured her. "I'll get you home soon."

Sylvia wasn't used to having to be reassured either. She muttered something brusquely, embarrassed and angry with herself. As he withdrew his hand, becoming at once very soldierly, she regretted her abruptness, but Cadogan stepped further into the darkness before she could say anything.

The fishing village they were skirting was silent. Smoke curled from chimneys and the only sounds were a distant birdcry and the gentle slap of the sea against the side of the boats moored in the shallows. Cadogan led them down past a row of small stone structures that smelled strongly of smoked fish. Leenan's nose wrinkled and she held her breath on a sneeze. At the same time her stomach rumbled loudly. She blushed scarlet, grateful that she couldn't see the expressions on her companions' faces, nor they hers.

Cadogan gave the all clear to continue and they crept around a grove of trees, strung with woven vines and the skins of the previous day's bluejacket catch. The tanning sheds were on the other side of the village and just now their unpleasant odour drifted over, mingling with the tantalising smell of smoked blue-jacket, and Leenan's stomach clenched spasmodically on another rumble. She hoped fervently she was not going to be sick.

Down to the sea and around the rocks, they crept by moonlight towards the nearest fishing boat.

That birdcall sounded again, uncannily close, and then a soft voice spoke.

"Hush, Carli, hush. There, there."

Cadogan froze and motioned the others abruptly to silence.

Not a bird cry. A *baby's* cry.

He could hear now the mother's murmuring voice, melded with the sound of the sea but obviously human. *Damn.* He strained to pinpoint a direction, distance, but sound carried oddly across the hushed shore.

"Hush, sweetheart, that's my girl. Settle down and mummy can get back to sleep."

She sat up, the baby cradled against her bosom. Not ten strides ahead, seated among the rocks and tufts of long grass, the woman, brown hair gilded silver by the moonlight, was rocking the child and gazing out to sea, talking softly in a pleasant, melodious tone.

Then she fell silent and turned her head, slowly, slowly, and her gaze met his, and her eyes widened in alarm. She did not say a word, but instinctively her arms tightened around her little girl and the baby began to cry.

"We only want a boat," said Cadogan, in measured tones. His hand hovered over the hilt of his sword but he did not draw.

Behind him, Sylvia and Leenan, hearts hammering, waited for someone to act, or react.

The woman tried to soothe the infant, watching them warily. "You're the ones the priests are looking for," she concluded after a moment.

"We just want to go home," Sylvia told her, gently, persuasively, masking the sudden surge of panic that rose in her throat.

The baby hiccuped into small grizzling noises. Her mother regarded them thoughtfully, strangely unafraid of the witches and armed man before her.

"The green boat is fastest and Tobi left a water skin in it for the morning. You'll have to go quickly. The priests are here."

The utter stillness in Cadogan's stance shifted slightly at the news. A shimmer of apprehension and urgency. He waved Leenan and Sylvia ahead.

"Mother protect you, Lady," he said.

"The Mother go with *you*," she replied, the faintest of smiles in her tone.

A voice boomed out of the darkness: "Suri? What's wrong? I heard the baby . . . Who the hell is . . . ? Oh, M . . ."

Light blazed from one of the other huts. Several men appeared, shadows behind the flame. One of them limped and in one hand Cadogan could make out a loaded crossbow.

Two cries mingled in the night.

"Those Lorddamned *witches!*"

"Leenan, *run!*"

There was the faint hiss of Cadogan's sword being drawn as the men behind the torches surged forward. The man with the crossbow raised it as he limped down with the others.

Above all this noise, Cadogan recognised the thin whistle of an arrow slicing through the air. He peered into the night, heard the splash of feet in the water, trying to reach the boats. Heard a muted thud and a shriek of pain and the ungainly slosh of a body falling. He ran.

Leenan was there, and Sylvia, both in the water. It was Sylvia who sagged under the surf, clutching her leg, sucking in air through clenched teeth. Leenan was trying to help her up. The mixture of horror and relief that set his heart beating would distress him later, but now he glanced back at the men descending upon them.

The limping man wore priestly robes, the fire from the torches dancing across his face. It was the man Leenan had thrown from his horse with her magic, injured but mobile. Beside him was the acolyte, his young face drawn with pain and anger, his right arm bound in a sling. In his left he carried a long dagger. Others were with them—servants, villagers. Flame danced across their faces, ordinary men become demons by their hatred. Cadogan saw the limping priest had stopped and reloaded and was taking aim at the women in the water. At the woman standing, a precise outline against the silvered sea.

He saw the crossbow rise up and the short, vicious bolt fly from the string, and he saw the path it took and the speed with which it flew and knew that he could not stop it. And with no more thought than that he turned about all he had ever learned about his craft. His philosophy had always been to simply not be where the blow fell . . . now he took three steps and turned to face the blow he had chosen to meet.

The shaft buried itself in his chest with a soft thud. Cadogan grunted slightly with the impact, rocked back on his heels, but held, determined to give no ground, before his knees sagged and he folded to the sand. His sword fell, unblooded, beside him.

There was no pain. Only a bubbling sensation when he next inhaled followed by the metallic tang of blood in his mouth.

We all go to the Mother . . .

He wasn't afraid. Lyria and Kynwyn would be cared for. Kiedrych had promised. As his vision blurred and darkened, his mind's eye captured the memory of a pair of clear green eyes and his main emotion was one of regret.

I wish . . .

Then darkness.

The sky is clear, a vivid blue that hurts his eyes to look at. A bird flies past, crowing joyously and he reaches out to touch its bright, mirrored plumes. Its feathers make a sound like shattering crystal as it swoops by and he sees himself reflected in them. A small, pale, serious boy with a mop of dark hair and bright blue eyes, a soldier's uniform hanging loosely on his youthful frame.

He follows the bird. The sand under his feet is glutinous and pulls like mud at his bare feet.

Then, shod in heavy boots that make him feel both anchored and powerful, he strides through the hall made of trees that grow trunk to trunk. Light dapples through the green canopy above. He can't see the bird any longer, but he knows where he is going.

In her chamber, the vivid blue sky comes down to meet them. She stands before him, and although he is only ten and knows that he is shorter than she, he looks down into her eyes. She is as beautiful as he remembers her, before Rudig and Koto died. Her blue almond-shaped eyes are the same blue as the sky that fills the room and his lungs and makes him feel like he is drowning in the thickness of that blue . . . He tries to inhale and can't, and a flicker of panic is an ache in his chest.

Smiling, she gives him a goblet. A dragon is carved into it and it is so highly polished that he can see his face in the dark grained wood. He knows he is only ten, but his face looks back at him with grey hairs salted at his temples.

"Drink," she says, her voice light and musical. He drinks. The liquid tastes like purest water and it spreads through his body like light. The thick blueness of the sky leaves his lungs, though his chest still aches.

"Not yet, my dear boy," she says, touching his cheek. He wants to hold her hand and tell her he wants to stay, but the goblet opens its green eyes and then a burnished bronze dragon unfurls from it, flying away.

He follows.

Cadogan opened his eyes slowly and the sight of Leenan's face and those eyes of hers made him want to smile. Except that she looked unwell, hollow cheeked and with dark smudges under her eyes. His first words were: "Are you all right?" said in a faint voice.

Her eyebrows rose and a harsh gasp of laughter greeted him. "I'm not the one who got shot . . ." The rest was choked into silence as she fought for control. Carefully, Cadogan reached out to close a hand over one of her clenched fists.

"I'm so glad to see you," he said.

She gave a little gasp and brought his hand up to her cheek, closing her other hand over his fingers and paused there, unable to speak. Cadogan felt the brush of her lips against his knuckles and the warmth of her faint breath and felt the most bizarre combination of contentment and concern. Leenan held his hand clasped in hers against her chest, where he could feel the racing beat of her heart and realised at last that her skin was cold and that she was shivering.

"Leenan . . ."

"It's all right," she told him, and her voice was as faint as his own, "I'm just tired."

Cadogan considered his surroundings. He was lying on a hard earthen floor. Everything smelled pungently of fish and tanning hides. His chest ached but he was breathing without that painful, appalling rattle of blood filling his lungs.

Leenan had used her power to heal him.

He looked at her again. Leenan's cheeks were gaunt and sunken. Her eyes were bruised and staring as though she had neither slept nor eaten in a week, or as though some image haunted them.

It did. The image of a man falling in the darkness, of blood trickling from his mouth and leaking around the bolt in his body, matting the hair of his chest in cloying pools. Blood trickling into the sand beneath him. Her gaze kept drawing back to the wound, now merely a small dark hollow in his skin.

"I didn't know you were a healer," he said.

She returned her gaze to his face. "Magda taught me some things . . . before the last Tyne Battle." She looked so distraught that the least thing might shatter her. She still held his hand tight against her.

"Where's Sylvia?"

Leenan shuddered slightly. "She's here. Sleeping. She's hurt. I can't . . . I . . ."

"How badly?" He tried to sit up, but a sharp jab of pain immobilised him. She had healed the fatal wound but he was far from well.

"The shaft snapped off. It stopped bleeding . . . eventually. I wrapped it up." She drew a shuddering breath. "I tried to pull it out, but I haven't the strength."

Cadogan drew her hands down to kiss her fingers this time. Her whole body was trembling with fatigue and distress. He smoothed his free hand across her cheek, pushing her dark-blonde hair away behind her ears. "You need to rest."

"I can't," she shook her head feebly, "I need to . . ."

"Nothing will happen. Not till morning. Rest."

Leenan remained fretful, unconvinced.

"We'll need your strength later," he coaxed. He was relieved when she finally allowed herself to be drawn down beside him. Mindful of his injuries, Leenan pillowed her head on his shoulder and he drew an arm around her. Her own was wrapped around his waist.

Despite everything, she was asleep in moments. Cadogan kissed her brow and marveled how, even with the ache of his injury and the prospect of their murders looming, the weight of her against his side was reassuring.

The door opened and a rectangle of early dawn light fell over them briefly. A dark-haired woman, a little older than he'd realised from seeing her by moonlight, appeared quickly, quietly, placing a jug of water by the door. She was, he guessed, in her mid thirties. Brown hair framed a lovely face and round grey eyes. Her figure was still full from recent pregnancy.

"How is your daughter?"

Suri gasped, surprised. "You're awake." She hesitated, aware of the foolishness of her observation. "She's sleeping." A beat. "I have to go."

"Wait . . ."

Suri stopped and glanced back at him. "I can't. They think I've gone to the privy. I told the priest Ensho I would only be a moment."

"What are they waiting for?" *To kill us together, burned at a communal stake?* Once Leenan had refused to leave him, refused to take Sylvia and run for the mainland, it was inevitable. Cadogan's arm tightened around Leenan, and she murmured and burrowed closer into his side.

"Ensho's nephew Willem wanted to . . . to burn you. He is angry about the men you killed, and his broken arm."

"They attacked us," Cadogan told her, uneasy with the confirmation of his worst imagining.

"That is not what he says." She met his gaze steadily. "I don't believe him." She glanced anxiously over her shoulder. "Ensho is less hot-headed. My husband is the headman. He gathered our people to take you prisoner before Willem could act. He and I have been talking to Ensho since then. We've convinced him that it is more fitting you be taken to the First King's sky temple . . ."

"How did you manage that?"

She smiled wryly. "I'm the Storyteller. People listen when I tell them things."

Her voice, gentle and mellow, had a Storyteller's timbre, he realised.

"I think . . . I'm sorry, but I think Ensho liked the idea too well. He thinks it will give him power among his people, and favour with his gods." She looked away, ashamed. "I'm sorry," she said again, her grey eyes troubled. "It was all we could think of. We have five children. We have the village to protect."

"It's all right," he said, weariness robbing his voice of strength and expression.

"There isn't anyone guarding the back of the tannery," she offered, after a pause.

Cadogan frowned. Sylvia seriously wounded. Leenan exhausted to the point of collapse. Himself injured and weak from loss of blood. They would never make it to the tannery wall, let alone force a way through.

Suri saw this too. Her shame increased along with her anxiety. "I really have to go."

"Yes. Be careful. Thank you."

She shook her head, unwilling to accept thanks when she was able to offer so little. "I'll bring food if I can," she promised. In a moment she was gone, leaving Cadogan to stare sleeplessly at rafters draped with skins.

CHAPTER NINETEEN

The meeting with the Captain had not gone well. For a start, Sebastian had been so impressed by Redmonde's sheer physical presence he'd clearly found it difficult to pay attention at first to the small, weasely man with the cold voice. He would insist on answering all questions with a respectful bow of his head. He kept calling them "My Gracious Lords," which Magda refused to translate until Delouise had asked her to, and which he had found rudely amusing once she did. Magda had snapped angrily at the Captain, who had responded acidly. Sebastian had berated her for her insolence to the New Lords and raised a hand to jab a finger at her, and she'd backed away so suddenly that she'd collided with Redmonde.

Now Sebastian was being held, benignly but firmly, in a quiet part of the medical bay while Witch Magda was allowed to tend to the injured Lords and issue orders to their attendants and the young Witch Tephee, grown surprisingly womanly, smiled and flirted experimentally with the Lord Christov. Sebastian gritted his teeth and tried not to wonder why the New Lords allowed them both to act in this insolent manner.

Their Lordly apparel didn't help matters much. Sebastian had felt at a loss when his ruined robes were taken from him, and then proud when the Lords had given him something like their own clothing—black trousers and shirt, made of strange material which had neither buttons nor ribbons to fasten and merely stretched over his body and sat snugly in place. He had been disappointed to find the witches dressed similarly. The fact that the fabric clung immodestly to their natural curves was an added insult to the Lords they flouted. They were not at all properly pious in the presence of the First King's emissaries. His New Lords, sent to bring His word a thousand years after He and the First Lords had passed on to the True World. Theologically, he'd decided, this was who they must be. Not merely agents, as Witch Magda should have been, but a new stage in the Arc of Entry. New Lords for a new world.

Magda took a break from her work and accepted a glass of water from Third Technician Schmidt. She watched Tephee smile at Christov, an expression that mingled shyness with a pleased awareness that Christov liked her. The ship's blacks suited her, Magda thought with some surprise. The childishness had melted away from her in recent weeks. Tephee's face had lost its roundness, becoming lovely with elegant planes and wide, clear eyes. The trousers emphasised her shapely legs and the T-shirt emphasised more obvious womanly attributes. Tephee had been a little shocked by the clothes to begin with, but she'd adapted quickly. Especially when Magda relayed Christov's compliments of how well she looked in them.

It was charming to see how the two of them communicated without a single common word between them. Smiles, gestures, and gazes meeting at every lull in activity. Magda could see that the flirting scandalised Sebastian no end, but found less humour in that than she thought she might. She could just imagine Sylvia, watching in her quiet way, or Leenan, rolling her eyes with some sardonic comment. Or perhaps not, the way she and Cadogan were . . . had been . . .

Magda put the cup down with a loud clack and returned to her patients. Three of the burn victims were stable with some slow progress since she'd first seen them yesterday. The skin grafts were growing steadily and would soon be ready to use and the three men awaiting them were being treated with anaesthetic gel, drugs, and anti-pressure fields. She was more concerned with the fourth patient. Doctor El Hady, burned and crushed by falling containers as he'd gone to the assistance of those injured in the engine room after the crash landing, had been slowly, steadily deteriorating. The immobiliser unit held the doctor's body utterly still but contributed little else towards his unlikely recovery.

Reflexively, Magda tried to reach into him, but of course she couldn't. It felt like shouting in a soundproofed room. The weak pulse of her power was trapped in her head and fingertips and couldn't get out. Tephee had shown no signs of recovering her power yet, although all the readings showed that she was now in perfect health. There was another factor here, Magda was certain. Something external was interfering with their gift. Frowning, she turned to Schmidt.

"Could you get First Officer Redmonde for me, Lucy? There's something I'd like to try."

It was cramped in the makeshift prison wagon and it smelled of fish. They had been seized, wrenched out of exhausted sleep and bundled through an opening in a shell made of sapling strips tethered with lengths of nearly unbreakable fishgut rope. Sylvia had turned white and almost passed out with the pain as the arrowhead and splintered shaft moved in the wound. Cadogan, dressed now only in crumpled and bloodstained trousers, had reached out to help only to be clubbed between the shoulder blades with a beefy fist by one of the priest's servants. Leenan, pale and weak with exhaustion, had been pushed in behind them, too tired and confused to struggle.

The opening was then sealed with fishgut rope and the wagon pulled out of the village immediately after. The limping priest, Ensho, rode on a fine bay horse while his resentful nephew

Willem sat with the big-fisted fellow at the reins of the prison wagon. Two more servants followed behind on horseback along with a third man who exchanged fretful farewells with Suri and kept glancing at the prisoners with an expression filled with shame and anxiety.

Cadogan noted the potential ally, along with the fact that, as the only villager who was accompanying them, there was precious little he would be able to do.

He half-closed his eyes for a moment, taking stock, and his gaze came to rest on Sylvia's ashen face. She periodically shivered, despite a sheen of perspiration on her upper lip and brow.

"Here," said Cadogan quietly, moving to crouch by her. Very carefully and gently he helped her to pull her bloodied petticoat away from the wound and then unwrap the dressing—his own torn short, he noticed. She winced. He swore.

"I need to get that out," he said. The broken part of the crossbow bolt had eased slightly out of the wound in the few hours that they'd slept. The skin around it was red and puckered and fresh blood, mixed with pus, was oozing from the edges. "It's going to hurt."

"Already hurts," she hissed out.

He wished he had a knife. Great Mother, he wished he had a field surgery kit and a military doctor and a bottle of potent alcohol to administer both internally and externally to the patient. This was going to be particularly horrible.

"Let me help." Leenan had finally stirred and angled to see what was going on. The wagon bumped over a rock in the road and she lost her balance.

"Leenan, you're too weak . . ."

The glare she gave him refused any argument. Cadogan pursed his lips, preparatory to arguing anyway, but the rough movement had brought a strangled whimper from Sylvia and he acquiesced. He and Sylvia would both be glad of the help.

"Hold onto the bars," he advised, "and scream if you want to." He wrapped his fingers around the too-short piece of wood protruding from her thigh.

"Wouldn't . . . give them . . ." The sentence dissolved into a startled cry, quickly repressed. Cadogan muttered an apology and tried again. It had moved fractionally out of the wound, giving him a better hold this time. He glanced up to see Leenan watching him, half accusingly, but then she shook her head and reached out to press her hand down above the wound.

"On three," she said.

"Lee," gasped Sylvia, "don't."

Cadogan met the steel in her gaze, acknowledged the determination, and the necessity.

On three, as he pulled, Leenan reached down . . .

. . . and snatched her hand back, gasping. Cadogan shoved the gory bolt aside and reached out a hand to steady her as she nearly fell, speechless with the pain. Leenan opened her eyes at his touch, but the first thing she saw was the open wound and pus and blood and would have been sick if she'd had anything in her stomach. Instead, she reached out to place her hands around the damage.

"No . . ." Sylvia tried to brush Leenan's hands away, but her own were shaking too badly.

Leenan ignored her. Cadogan, knowing that the infection was already bad, did not try to stop her. He caught her, though, as she crumpled, shaking with fatigue. The wound, though unhealed, was at least clean. Cadogan gathered Leenan into his arms and drew her away with him, so that when his back was against the cage she was curled within the cradle of his body, braced between his legs and pillowed against his bare chest and shoulder. She was shivering. Her skin was clammy, despite the rising summer heat, and her breaths were fast and shallow. Worriedly, he held her close to keep her warm, stroking her hair until she stopped trembling.

The wagon rocked and jolted down the road. Sylvia gritted her teeth against the sharp jabs of pain this induced. Cadogan barely noticed the steady ache of his own injury. It was a small thing now, hardly worth thinking on. Not when Leenan was grey and waxen and looking like death . . .

He dragged himself away from that line of thought. Sylvia, he saw, looked better. She tilted her head back against the sapling bars and some of the tension eased from around her eyes and shoulders. The wagon swayed as it creaked down the dirt roads and around them the sound of hooves was like a drum.

"How do you feel now?" Cadogan asked her.

"It still hurts," Sylvia admitted, "but it feels a lot better. Thank you." A pause while the wagon rattled over an uneven stretch and then: "You shouldn't have let her do this."

He grunted slightly and looked down at Leenan with a wan but affectionate smile. "I have noticed," he said, "that she usually gets her own way, regardless. The Mother is strong in Witch Leenan." The honorific was at odds with the tender way he held her.

"She doesn't give up easily," Sylvia conceded. She watched him for a moment before saying: "Do you?"

"Why do you ask?" His eyes narrowed as he returned her steady gaze.

"You think they're going to kill us, don't you?"

"Don't you?"

Sylvia frowned a little. "I expect that's their intention. It remains to be seen whether they'll succeed."

He only shrugged mildly with one shoulder.

"The Mother looks after Her own, you said," Sylvia commented, fishing for reassurance, or truth. She wasn't sure which.

"The Mother," he replied, softly, "is there, whether we believe or not. She's there, whether we worship Her or not." His tone was milder than ever, but behind the casual words there was a faint ring of . . . someone lost.

"If She doesn't care," Sylvia said, her head tilted to one side as she considered this, "then what's the point? Why worship Her?"

"Why die for Her, you mean?"

"If you like."

He only shrugged and looked away. "Not only for Her," he said after a moment, "but to protect what is Hers."

"You stop that this instant!" she snapped.

Cadogan looked into Sylvia's eyes, startled. She looked sternly back at him.

"I recognise that look, Cadogan Ho. Don't you start feeling guilty for things that are not your doing."

It was like a slap in the face, the way she read him. He scowled and she scolded.

"You're only one man and you can't do everything. Even when you haven't got a handful of witches doing whatever the hell they want, regardless of the danger. Might I add that we were amply warned and we chose to go on."

He sighed. "Why not? Everyone else has. Maybe that will count for something, eventually."

Sylvia shook her head. "You're a good-hearted man, Cadogan, but you take too much onto your own shoulders."

"Give me time," he said, his voice light, "I might grow out of it."

A sudden smile quirked Sylvia's lips. "You're as stubborn as she is. Maybe that's why I like you."

"You hardly know me," he demurred.

"I like you too," Leenan mumbled into his neck, shifting slightly. One hand was tucked under her chin; the other skimmed over his belly and into his chest hair, tangling dark curls around her fingertips.

Ridiculously, under the circumstances, he felt a frisson of sexual electricity followed immediately by the withering recognition that in all likelihood they would all be dead before the next sunrise.

The Mother did not seem to take much part in the lives of Her children, those fragmented parts of Herself scattered across the world. Why, then, did he feel so abandoned?

"Absolutely not. I can't believe you're even asking."

Redmonde towered over her and his scorn was formidable.

"How can you call yourself a scientist and not at least be curious to see some empirical evidence?" Magda shot back, cold certainty making her furious.

"How can you call yourself a doctor and risk his life on this . . . this . . ."—one large hand punched the air emphatically— "pathetic fantasy?"

"It's because I am a doctor that I suggested it to you at all." She strode around to stand in his path as he tried to walk away from her. "First Officer Redmonde, that man is dying. With all the technology here keeping him breathing, he will still be dead within days. All I can do in that medical bay is slow it down. If I can get outside the electromagnetic radiation field that I believe is disrupting this gift of mine, and if I can heal all the major structural damage before his system collapses, then he may have a chance."

He glared at her. She stretched her neck and glared back.

"It's a poor chance," she admitted fiercely, "but without it he has none at all."

He shook his head at her conviction. She'd seemed so rational when he'd first met her.

"Red, I can't just let him die." She employed his nickname

and her gentle blue eyes with touching appeal. He shifted uncomfortably.

"Hell, Magda, you're either completely mad, fundamentally delusional, or . . ."

"Or right," she finished firmly.

"You're asking me to put Sam's life at risk."

"His life is already forfeit, Red. If I had the best burns unit and the best surgeon in all of Solfleet it might be different. But I don't. This is the only chance he may have." His expression was still doubtful. "Ask Christov if you don't believe me."

He looked genuinely surprised at the intimation that she might have been lying about Sam El Hady's condition. "Look," he said, "I'll have to ask the Captain . . ."

"Thank you."

Redmonde shook his head. "This doesn't mean I believe a word of it. But if he's going to die anyway . . ."—he frowned—"it might as well be with the sun on his face."

"Thank you anyway. You can tell me you told me so if this doesn't work."

"Don't worry," he muttered darkly, "I will. Jesus." He shook his head again. "Witchcraft. Delouise is going to laugh himself sick." With a sigh, he drew away from her at last and disappeared down the corridor, moving surprisingly quickly for such a large man.

Magda turned to reenter the medical bay, in front of which she had been arguing with Redmonde for the last ten minutes. Walking through the small antechamber and into the medical bay proper. Inside, Christov was showing Tephee some readings on the skin tank, apparently showing her when to push the next button. The demonstration appeared to be mostly an excuse to place his hands over hers while he indicated the readout to which he could just as easily have pointed. Certainly, he could more easily have done it himself. Lucy Schmidt was watching one of the burn patients with more than merely professional interest. Across from her, in front of the private rooms which she and Tephee were using, the two half-hearted guards were lounging on spare chairs, while Sebastian watched unhappily from the back of the room.

Tephee nodded and smiled up at Christov as he finished his demonstration. "Oh-kay," she said carefully to show her comprehension. He beamed back at her, then looked around guiltily as Magda walked up to them.

"Oh, hi, Doctor Czajkowski . . . I was just . . ."

"I could see what you were just doing, Nurse Ivolich," she said, mock-sternly, then turned away before he could see the grin on her face. One of the guards saw it, though, and winked at her.

Tephee, missing this exchange, came up to her. "Well?"

"I think he's going to let me try."

"Do you want me to come with you?"

"I think I'll need you. I won't be strong enough on my own. Do you mind?"

"No . . . that's fine . . ." Though it obviously wasn't.

"What's wrong Teph?"

"It's just . . ."—Tephee threw a glance over her shoulder towards Christov—". . . I don't want Chris to be . . . scared of me."

"Oh, he won't be, love." Magda wrapped one arm around Tephee's shoulders to give her a reassuring squeeze.

"You were," Tephee pointed out reasonably. The first time Magda had ever seen Tephee demonstrate her power, the older woman had gone white with shock and backed away from her as fast as her feet would carry her.

Magda sighed. "I was a bit stir-crazy and very, very stupid. Nurse Christov is neither." She risked a sly grin. "And I didn't have his appreciation for your legs."

Tephee blushed and began to giggle before suddenly clearing her throat and standing a little taller. The girlishness became at once a coltish, self-conscious elegance.

She's getting so beautiful. If only Sylvia and Lee . . . if . . .

"Maggie?"

"Oh." She rubbed at her eyes. "Sorry. I was thinking of the others."

Tephee held her hand in solemn understanding. "When we get outside, I'll look for them."

"Don't expect too much," Magda warned gently.

Tephee patted her arm with a small smile which reminded Magda tearily of Sylvia. "I'll expect what I find. That's what Sylvia would say."

"The First King has destroyed the unrepentant."

Two heads snapped around to stare at the priest. Sebastian's chin twitched up as his gaze met theirs unyieldingly.

"I'm sorry," he said, and even sounded it. "I know they were your friends. But they were witches."

"What's wrong with you, Sebastian?" Tephee demanded. "You used to be nice."

"I used to be a sinner," he said gently. "So were you, until you were cleansed."

She looked to Magda in confusion. Magda frowned. "Just ignore him," she advised and turned away. She found Christov watching them with concern. "Sebastian is having trouble adjusting," she said, switching languages. It was meant to sound light and dismissive, but came out strained.

Further comment was forestalled when the door opened and First Officer Redmonde returned, looking uncomfortable and irritable.

"Well?" Magda demanded.

"Captain Delouise has said you can go ahead."

"He agreed?"

"Actually," said Redmonde with a displeased frown, "what he said was: 'This should be worth seeing. Why not?' " His tone was measured but Magda could see that he was furious. More than furious. And with reason. The callous son of a bitch. Sam El Hady's fate was apparently nothing but potentially diverting. Son of a *bitch*.

"This had better help him," he said meaningfully, casting a glance towards Sam's bed.

"I can't promise to do anything but try," Magda said steadily.

He found her professional caution more reassuring than a passionate promise to succeed. "Okay. What do we need to do to shift him?"

CHAPTER TWENTY

Suri's husband, Hito, had been caught passing them a flask of water. The summer sun was high and hot, the wagon stank of fish and sweat, and its occupants were half dead from dehydration.

Hito's village had been made up of Leylites once. At the end of the Purge nearly thirty years ago, the survivors had renounced their Goddess while the Arc faithful of Holyshore stood by with swords and flaming brands. Now, they burnt their dead and cut their hair as offerings on the Lords' Days. They swore by the First King and had built an Arc shrine in their fishing village. But when the fishing was good, they gave thanks to Leyla; when the storms were wild they prayed in their hearts to the Great Mother to bring their brethren home. So Hito passed his leather flask through the bars to those suffering within, the only kindness available to him.

One of the priest's servants saw him and argument ensued. Hito refused to be condemned for failing to behave like a brute. Priest Ensho refused to tolerate the company of any Kutan who could give succour to the First King's enemies. They took his horse and gear and left him by the side of the road to walk home. The prisoners, who had only had time for a mouthful of water each, were forced to relinquish the flask at swordpoint.

Sylvia wished there was some way to thank Hito—she was touched almost to tears by this small act of kindness. She blinked away the sudden emotion and turned her face to look through the sapling bars. At least her leg hurt less now. She had always been a fast healer, an aspect of her power she had always believed. Perhaps, being powerless now, it was just an aspect of herself. She flexed her foot experimentally and there was the slightest corresponding twinge in the wound.

Sylvia glanced back at her companions. Leenan sat groggily against the other side of the wagon, swaying with its movement. She was still limp with exhaustion but at least some of her colour had returned. Her hand rested in Cadogan's, her fingers elegantly pale against his calloused palm. She saw that he was watching something outside their cage and heard a horse galloping into the distance.

"They're sending someone ahead," she observed.

"To prepare." Cadogan squeezed Leenan's hand briefly. "We'll be there before long."

"Good," mumbled Leenan, "I'm starting to feel sick." Her nose wrinkled expressively. "Never catch me eating fish again. Stinks."

"I'll build you a house made of rosewood," Cadogan said, a painful promise for a future he knew they did not have. "It will smell beautiful, especially in the summer."

Leenan smiled wanly and raised her head to look at him. "You don't have to protect me." It was said gently. Her tone said, *It's all right. Thank you for trying.*

He tried to smile back, and couldn't. Instead, their fingers twined together.

Sylvia wanted to knock their heads together. Their acceptance made her angry. *It's not,* she thought, *that I am afraid of dying. I just don't intend to slide into it, as though I haven't the right to challenge fate. I've tried giving up and I won't do it anymore. They're going to have to fight for my blood.*

Still, her heart lurched when, less than an hour later, the wagon rattled through a rough camp. People pressed in all around them, peering in, jeering; some spat. Men and women with expressions both fearful and triumphant. Priest Ensho had his men urge them back, but only halfheartedly. When the wagon shuddered to a halt near the front line of the ramshackle tent village, someone came up to Sylvia at the bars, grimy and sweating and spitting venom.

"Whoreson witch," he said and through the bars he grabbed her breast, violently and painfully.

Then he shrieked. Sylvia had dug her nails into his wrist, drawing blood, and forced him to let go. At the same time Cadogan's hand snaked through the cage, grabbed him by the shirt and gave one sharp pull, slamming the man's face against the saplings and fishgut. Leenan was there already, her fingers buried in his hair and twisting it while she hissed, dragon-like, into his face. He squealed again, pounding on the bars until all three released him and he staggered back into the dirt.

The shout from the crowd was ugly. Some surged forward while others drew back. Priest Ensho drew his horse around in tight circles while he shouted for order, for obedience, until he saw that their passion was roused beyond defying. His own nephew was standing on the seat of the wagon, crying out that they came with an offering to the Mightiest Lord, the First King. These people had waited before the First King's sky castle for weeks, days, hours, and now His enemies were trapped before them. His enemies still defied Him. His enemies would die to the glory of the First King and His Lords, and then, perhaps, He would step out from the beautiful, terrifying silver castle and bless them for their piety.

Priest Ensho had hoped to make a grander entrance, with all eyes focussed on him and the great prize he had brought. He had hoped to impress these weak foreign priests with his power and initiative. He had especially hoped to control this moment, to make a fine and suitable offering to his gods, with dignity and ritual.

All this he abandoned. The people were wild with religious passion. He gave up trying to stop them and began to direct them, which made it appear as though he were in control of the mob, instead of the other way around.

The fishgut rope was sliced away from the entrance to the cage and Cadogan, being the closest to it, was the first dragged outside.

"Cadogan!" Leenan reached for him, and other hands snagged at her. She pulled away, falling towards the back of the wagon where Sylvia was trying to distance herself from hands reaching in to grab her from the side.

Cadogan was fighting even before his feet were clear of the cage. Not the clean and elegant sweep of the not-being-there, but deadly and cold. One man fell away, clutching a bleeding eye socket. Leenan strained to follow this savage progress. What she saw was a line of people pressing wood, straw, bedding, anything flammable, into a mound. A tall pole rose in the midst of it.

She tried not to retch, understanding fully now what was to happen.

Someone reached in, seized her by the arm and pulled. She fought, terrified, but hadn't enough strength to hold her ground and was pulled inexorably towards the gap.

"Take him out, closer," Captain Delouise ordered. "I want to make sure they see this."

Magda glared at him. He returned the look coolly.

"I had thought," he said thinly, "that this was the object of the exercise."

"What?"

"To have that unruly mob . . ."—he waved his hand at the

tent city of pilgrims—"see the First King's envoy working with those they see as witches."

She stared at him. It was Redmonde who pointed out that the pilgrims had no way of knowing Magda and Tephee were witches. Or that Sebastian was a priest. Delouise pursed his lips unhappily.

"I wouldn't like to think that we have risked Doctor El Hady's life for no purpose at all," he said in his slow, sharp way.

"Don't worry," Magda replied with forced coolness, "I'm sure we have a few surprises for you."

She spoke a few words to Tephee and they walked out ahead of the small group of people who had brought Doctor El Hady's stretcher out into the late morning sunshine. Christov kept looking uncertainly at her in between concerned checks of the field immobiliser. The two medical bay guards had followed with Sebastian, at Delouise's suggestion. Sebastian was quiet and watchful.

Tephee felt the difference almost immediately. She grinned at Magda as they walked away from the ship and the man in the stretcher, then stopped to hold up her hand. A thread of blue fire arced between her fingertips and rose up to form a shimmering ball of witchlight. Magda, less sure of herself, held her hand palm up and concentrated. A similar sphere, though less intense in colour, formed in her hand. They both looked up to see the reaction.

It was, Magda thought, very gratifying to see Captain Delouise with his mouth hanging open. Sebastian was predictably scandalised. Redmonde had his own jaw sensibly shut, the amazement in his eyes shifting quickly to speculation. Christov's eyes were round with astonishment.

Tephee's pleased grin had faded. "He's afraid, Maggie."

Magda closed her hand on her witchfire and met Christov's startled gaze.

"What did she say?" he asked.

"She thinks you're afraid of her."

Christov shook his head slowly, then settled an awed and admiring gaze on Tephee's worried face. "She's . . . incredible."

"He's impressed," Magda translated to Tephee, but the girl had already seen the nurse's expression and had relaxed. "Okay," Magda said in a crisp, businesslike tone, "let's get to work. Chris, I need that immobiliser off him. It's got an EMR field of its own and I can't do anything while it's on."

Christov began to power the unit down.

"Teph, we won't have long . . . Tephee?"

Tephee had glanced over her shoulder at some sound. "There's something going on back there."

Magda glanced back. The inhabitants of the camp, half a kilometre away, were on the move. "We'd better get this done quickly then and get back inside."

"Ready?" Christov asked.

Magda nodded. As the immobiliser was lifted away she and Tephee stepped forward, holding hands. El Hady's breathing rapidly became erratic, strained. She passed her free hand over his chest and, with a gentle boost from Tephee, she reached into him. Tissue mended. Bone knitted. Cell walls held. Ruptures healed.

She drew away and Christov rapidly placed the immobiliser back over El Hady's chest. He grinned up at her. "These readings . . . that's just . . ." He searched for a word. "Wow."

Magda laughed, despite feeling so drained. She caught Redmonde's eye.

"Empirical evidence, huh?" he asked.

"Well," Captain Delouise broke in, "I did say it would be worth seeing."

"Maggie . . . ?"

Magda turned to see Tephee standing apart from them, well

away from the EMR field of the immobiliser unit, squinting at the distant camp. Magda remembered that, among her many talents, Tephee had a way of bringing the distance into close, sharp focus.

"What is it, Teph?"

"They've . . . Oh, Lords, Maggie, they've got Cadogan!" Her voice rose in alarm and indignant anger and she set off, her stride eating up impossible lengths as she used her power to skim across the ground.

"Tephee! Wait! Damnit. Damnit." *Cadogan . . . Leenan and Sylvia too? God, please . . .*

Leenan kicked at the man pulling her from the cage and he lost his grip briefly, only to grab her by the wrist again and twist it. She swore and tried to brace herself, but there was nothing, nothing to hold on to. She felt Sylvia try to hold her from behind, and let go with a cry.

Damn them. Damn if she'd go easily. Damn if she'd go at *all*, if she could help it.

She stopped fighting and wrapped both hands around her assailant's wrists. Then she closed her eyes, felt the pulse of his energy . . . she opened herself up and *pulled* at it. It was like cold water on a hot day. Like fresh meat to a hunting dragon.

She heard a shout and a scream and her eyes flew open to see people clutching at the unconscious man she still clasped, snatching him away. She let go and watched them all fall backwards. She raised a hand and the rope holding the saplings together disintegrated. The crowd surged away from the wagon and she stood, breathing heavily, turning her head to see where they had taken Cadogan. There was a breathless unmoving moment.

Then a stone was thrown, striking her on her chin and drawing blood.

The crowd closed in, like a wild wave to the shore.

Sylvia had seized upon one of the cut saplings, now fallen in disarray and used it, venting her anger at fate, her determination to live, on any who got close enough to make contact. Leenan had leapt into the throng, struggling towards the mound of wood and straw where Cadogan was still fighting like a demon.

Willem had shouted out commands to hold his arms, hold his legs, his feet, hit him, hit him . . . blood streamed from a cut lip and split cheek and he bucked and twisted making it as hard as he could for them. Still, he was losing. Hands grabbed his hair and pulled his head back, hauled his arching body backwards against the stake. Someone punched him in the side of the head to disorient him so that ropes could be tied. Hands behind his back. Arms. Someone let his legs go and he kicked, bare feet breaking a rib, then another stunning blow. Rope around his knees. His thighs.

He heard the fire behind him, eating the straw with a hissing crackle. Smelled smoke.

He saw her, blazing through the madmen with her green eyes alight. For a moment he thought she would make it, but there were too many of them. A stone. A fist. A knife slashed across her path and drew blood along her upper arm. A pike thrust, which she intercepted and a rough piece of wood which she did not. He finally cried out as Leenan crashed to her knees, and then the fire caught on the wood at his feet.

Eyes screwed shut to deny the pain. He heard Sylvia's voice swearing and urging Leenan to get up, get up, look! *Look!*

He looked. Through the smoke and leaping flame he saw Tephee slice like a blade into the crowd.

Delouise tapped his wrist communicator and spoke rapidly to the bridge. He listened intently to the breathless description

Ensign Kyte was giving of the scene on the scanner. With a muttered growl he shook his head and started back to the *Albert Einstein.* "Bloody girl." He glared sharply at Redmonde. "Don't just stand there. Kit up and go."

Grateful for the order, Redmonde left at a run.

Magda began giving curt orders, ensuring that El Hady was secured. "Take him in, Christov. Here, give him a hand . . ." The two guards fell in beside the young nurse to shift the stretcher.

A sound . . . a terrible cheer . . . she looked back to see smoke rising from the distance. She remembered Kayla Brittane telling her how she'd seen witches burnt here, six years ago. *Christ, no* . . . She strained for some glimpse of Tephee, or Cadogan, or one of the others. She saw only a mass of people, gathering around that column of smoke.

Christov and the others had taken the stretcher back to the breach in the hull where they had emerged such a short time before. She started after them . . .

A cry, thin and distant and charged with agony, carried to her and without a second thought she turned to run toward it . . .

. . . and she fell, wrenched from her feet, wondering what had hit her.

Dazed, she stared up at Sebastian. His expression was stern but incongruously he seemed only worried. She thought for a moment she had simply run into him by accident, but when she tried to rise he stood over her.

"She will not be cleansed. Let her burn."

Her astonishment became fury. "Get the hell out of my way." She rose, and he seized her by the shoulders and shoved her down onto the ground again.

"You have corrupted them," Sebastian snarled. She tried to rise again and his hand crushed her wrist, twisted it.

"Don't be a bloody idiot, Sebastian. We were helping them. They wanted us to help . . ."

"You have poisoned the New Lords . . ."

"Let me go."

That cry again . . . or a different one . . . *dear God* . . .

"Let me *go.*"

"First King damn you," he said, his voice perfectly level and calm, but for that hard edge of hysteria making each sound distinct.

"Let me go," Magda breathed, rage making her still and very quiet, "or I will make you do it."

He bent her wrist back further and raised a hand to strike her face.

She was tired from her work with El Hady, but she knew . . . it wasn't how much power you had. It was how you used it.

Sebastian's eyes widened and he choked for breath. He went limp.

Magda shoved him aside and started to run, only to balk at the towering shape of First Officer Redmonde in her path. She raised a hand, prepared to dispose of any opposition.

"Come on," he urged, "we've got the shuttle."

She ran, hearing him shout into his wrist communicator: "Christov, get down to Sebastian. Looks like he's fainted. Keep the sick bay ready. Out."

Magda leapt into the shuttle, Redmonde at her heels, and staggered into the wall as it took off across the grass.

Leenan! Mother, where is she? The fire crackled at his feet, his calves . . . *It hurts . . . I can't . . . Leenan . . . Don't let anything happen to her, please, please* . . . the black trousers caught alight and he couldn't move away or beat it out or do anything but feel it burn, burn, burn . . . *Great Mother . . . where are you?*

Cadogan opened his mouth and let the pain pour out.

Tephee, hands raised to scythe away those who would trample Leenan, jerked her head around. A thrown projectile caught her in the back and she stumbled. A flick of her wrist and three of those closest were tossed into those behind them.

Sylvia couldn't bear it any longer; couldn't help but try. A sharp cutting thought through the smoke and heat and she doubled over with pain and blood streamed from her nose.

Cadogan fell, unsupported, from the pyre as his ropes fell apart at Sylvia's will. Instinct made him roll and beat at the flames with his hands.

Tephee cried out. More missiles—rocks, horseshoes, pans. More than she could prepare herself for. Her focus scattered at all these points of assault. Leenan, blood oozing from a deep split over her eye, tried to sit up.

Ensho, atop the wagon, drew his crossbow and fired. Then again. Then again.

A great roar and a shadow from above, and all became deadly quiet, except for the crackle of the witches' pyre. The crowd stared and stepped away, slowly, transfixed with awe and dread.

The shuttle landed in the clearing that they made and the First King's Lords poured out, dressed in black and shining silver.

"Maggie . . ." Leenan's voice broke with relief.

"Lee . . . oh my . . . Go with them. It's safe." Magda grasped her shoulder briefly, moved on. Because she trusted her friend, Leenan allowed a stranger to help her into the First King's sky ship. Sylvia followed. A bearded giant carried Cadogan.

Magda, muttering oaths and imprecations, held her hands over Tephee as two others carried her black-clad form into the shuttle. Three crossbow bolts protruded from Tephee's chest.

The shuttle rose, leaving silence.

Chapter Twenty-One

Magda had Tephee deposited in the middle of the floor, her concentration solely on the girl. One of the guards helped Sylvia to a chair before calling through the intercom: "Mayhew, get us out of here!" Before the shuttle had risen, he had collected a medkit and had passed her an absorbent pad to mop up her bloody nose while he tended to her reopened leg wound.

Redmonde placed the man he carried gingerly on the floor and hurried to get the burns kit. He turned back to see the younger of the two women had crawled to cradle his head in her lap. Distressed noises escaped her as her hands hovered, wanting to hold him, afraid to hurt him. She stroked his hair, matted with ash, blood, and sweat. She bent low and whispered feverishly to him and Redmonde recognised the name Cadogan.

Cadogan was shivering violently as shock set in. His feet and lower legs were black and blistered, his face and torso bruised and abraded from the subjugating beating he'd had. Redmonde crouched in front of them. The woman cast a shocked stare at him. The side of her face was smeared with blood from her own head wound. She bore a dozen small cuts and bruises that would be easily treated. She was oblivious to a long cut across her right arm which would require cleaning and electro-stitching.

"It's all right," said Redmonde in his gentlest voice, "I'm going to help Cadogan." She reacted to the name by looking down at the man, whose own eyes were glazed with pain. She looked back up with entreaty and said something.

Redmonde took a pressure pack from the kit and aimed it at the soles of Cadogan's feet, pressed, shifted the pack so that the fine spray of gel settled evenly and thoroughly over the burns. Her green eyes watched, hawk-like, while he put the pack down and picked up the dose of painkiller. With his large hands and a surprisingly delicate touch, Redmonde pressed the cylinder to Cadogan's neck and, as the drug took effect and the shivering abated, he patted the woman's hand. She jumped slightly, then relaxed.

"We'll be back at the ship in a minute or so," he told her, aware that she understood nothing, but she smiled weakly at him and nodded.

Then Redmonde heard the hiss of anger from behind.

"Don't argue with me," Magda snapped, "just get the damned CPR unit."

"But she's been clinically dead since we got on board . . ."

Magda actually struck out, hitting Schmidt in the shoulder. "Then get out of my way . . ." She lurched to her feet.

"What's . . . ?" Redmonde began. Magda shoved violently past him to find the CPR unit, a hand-sized lozenge stored with the other medical gear. Schmidt looked to him for help.

He glanced over—saw the older woman staring, her elfin features drawn with sorrow and followed her gaze to the figure lying motionless on the floor. The arrows had been pulled from Tephee's chest and thrown aside, her black T-shirt cut away, leaving her chest and breasts exposed. Three grotesque holes in her body were marked with dark splotches of congealing blood. Her skin was waxy pale. She was not breathing.

Magda swore at him to get out of the way and dropped to her knees beside the girl, placing the lozenge over her heart.

"Doctor," Schmidt tried again, "she has no pulse and she's not breathing . . ."

"It takes five minutes for brain death to set in," Magda

growled. "There's time . . . there's . . ." She swore again as the settings revealed the blood pooled in Tephee's right ventricle, where the arrow had pierced it. "We have to land, get me outside. I just need a minute, that's all. I can do it, I just need . . ." She sounded desperate.

"Her heart and lungs were both perforated," Schmidt insisted, "I'm sorry . . ."

"No!" Magda flung herself to her feet and away, pacing frantically. "I just need some time, to get away from this EMR field, that's all I need, just some time . . ."

Redmonde caught her by her shoulders, forcing her attention to him. "Magda, stop it. Listen to yourself. Tephee's dead."

"You're not a doctor! What do you know?" she spat, struggling against his grip.

"You *are* a doctor," he said, refusing to release her. His voice softened. "Give me your true medical opinion, Doctor Czajkowski."

She froze, staring, and then gasped . . . then again, trying to swallow down the realisation. It forced its way out, a sharp, terrible sob. She stumbled away from Redmonde's loosened grip, her face buried in her hands, shoulders hunched as loud, unbearable cries of loss, denial, spilled from her mouth.

She's dead. Tephee's dead. Dead. Dead. Deaddeaddeaddeaddead . . .

Redmonde exchanged helpless glances with Schmidt, wondering how to deal with her, when the cries stopped suddenly. Magda, ghost white, stared in silence at the body. Then suddenly, hand over her mouth, she ran for the ablutions cubicle. They could hear her retching and sobbing, endlessly.

"Coming in to land, sir," Mayhew's voice announced over the intercom.

"Thank Christ," Redmonde muttered.

Sylvia rose, quiet like a cat, limped to Tephee's body and

knelt by her side. Respectfully, she drew the cut cloth over her ruined, cold chest. Tenderly, she leaned down to kiss the cold, cold cheek. Tears slid down her face.

The shuttle dipped and landed.

The shuttle bay platform had been lowered in readiness for their arrival. Captain Delouise was waiting for them, but the shuttle door opened and he was bypassed in the flush of activity. Mayhew had called for stretchers to meet them and Christov directed the emergency team to and from the lifts.

Cadogan, groggy and verging on delirium, panicked when he was removed from Leenan's presence, only calming again when he heard her voice through the fog of drugs and pain. She held his hand and walked, stumbling slightly, beside his stretcher as he was taken inside, too focussed on him to notice the great sky castle. The image of Tephee's dead body was stark and her grief held in check only by her fear of seeing Cadogan so horribly still. She had tried to reach out to him, to heal him again, but nothing happened.

Sylvia lay quietly on the second stretcher, staring at the ceiling, tears flowing unchecked. Christov was with her, but he kept glancing back, wondering where Tephee had gone.

Magda emerged like a zombie, staring after them, propping herself up on the open hatchway.

"Magda," Redmonde hesitated to touch her, "are you all right?"

There was no response. She stared into space, swallowed up in her own thoughts.

"They'll need you in sick bay." She didn't react. Redmonde took her by the elbow and shook her. "Magda, listen. Christov will need you in the sick bay. He can look after the two women, but Cadogan is badly burned."

At Christov's name she started, then glanced back into the

shuttle where Tephee's body was being put onto the third stretcher. "Oh, God . . . Christov . . ."

"I'll tell him later," said Redmonde. He rubbed her arm reassuringly. "We need him now. You should get after them. Your other friends need you."

That brought her back to herself. She pushed away from the door to follow the others to the lift up to the medical centre.

After she had gone, Schmidt came out with the last stretcher, a thin blanket thrown over it. Captain Delouise shook off his observer status and strode up to her, lifting the corner of the blanket.

"Oh, hell." He frowned, his sharp features drawn into unhappy lines. "Poor bloody kid." He shook his head and flipped the cover back into place. "This has gone too far."

Redmonde didn't trust himself to speak. He found that he was breathing hard, his hands trembling.

Delouise gestured for Schmidt to continue on and watched for a moment until they were out of sight. He turned back to Redmonde with a speculative look. "I'd like to have an autopsy done. Check out her brain . . ."

"I will not ask Doctor Czajkowski to dissect her friend," Redmonde ground out, low and angry. "I will not ask Christov to do it either. With respect, sir, you can go screw yourself."

The Captain's eyebrows shot up in surprise before he grimaced. "Yes, you're right. It's not a good idea." He sighed. "God, people are difficult. I preferred my lab rats on Mars." His eyes narrowed as he looked up at his First Officer. "Don't you ever speak to me like that again, Redmonde, or you'll be reported to Command."

Redmonde stiffened automatically to attention.

"If we ever find a way to get a message through." Delouise's mouth twisted wryly. "Come and see me when you've cleaned up," he added, "I need to discuss this with you."

As the Captain marched away, hands clasped behind his back, Redmonde stared after him.

The medical bay was never designed to hold so many casualties at once. The *Albert Einstein* was a science ship, only quasi-military, designed to work within explored space and never more than a half day from the nearest inhabited planet. Sam El Hady, now breathing without mechanical aid, occupied one bed. The engineers being treated still for radiation burns occupied three others.

Sebastian was lying in the last bed, pale but not obviously harmed. It was only when he tried to move, to free the bed up for those more in need, that it became clear how ill he was. A stroke, she realised, had set the right half of his body in stone, unwieldy and inflexible.

Magda couldn't bring herself to look at him. *I did that.* The thought made her feel sick.

Angus, one of the guards, helped to move Sebastian to one of the stretchers and then to shift Cadogan onto the vacated bed. Christov, murmuring professional reassurances, led Sylvia to a chair. Leenan followed Cadogan, only to stagger. One of the guards caught her and looked around helplessly for another chair; he found one and began to treat all her small injuries. Exhausted and bewildered, she submitted.

Magda issued curt instructions to her helpers, for hypos, equipment, room, for God's sake, a tissue sample to begin skin regeneration, stand aside, hold this, take his temperature, give her this to drink, *move, listen, hurry.*

Christov held the small regenerator unit over Sylvia's injured leg, once the bleeding had stopped. Her eyebrows rose in surprise at the warm, crawling tickle of it. He spoke to her, soft comforting sounds, and smiled when she patted his hand, as though to reassure him that she was all right.

He rose, looking for where he was most needed next.

"Where's Tephee?" he asked.

Magda's back stiffened. The dark-haired woman heard the name and her expression darkened with sorrow.

Christov looked from one to the other. "What happened? Where is she?"

"She's dead." Magda's voice was tight and harsh. She moved in rapid jerks and had to stop, calming herself before proceeding to treat Cadogan's burns.

Slowly, Christov walked across the room to help her with the dressings. His hands shook slightly.

"Do you want to go out for a minute?" Magda said, more gently this time.

He shook his head. "N-no. You need me here. I'll stay."

They worked in near silence for an hour or more. When they had finished, the skin and muscle of Cadogan's feet were regenerating well. Flame burn was easier to treat than radiation burn and already his blistered calves were soothed to pink hairless skin as his cells regenerated quickly in response to the accelerator unit. He slept.

Magda stood in the centre of the room, dazed with exhaustion and horror. She saw Leenan kneeling beside Sylvia, the two of them talking in spasmodic whispers as though simply framing the words tired them. She tried to speak to them but they were right, words were too heavy.

Sylvia extended a hand towards her. Leenan too. She knelt with them and because the words were too heavy to rise up, they wept them out together.

When she first heard their idea, Magda argued fiercely. No more harm could come to Tephee now but she couldn't help the sick ball of fear in her chest that somehow they would find a way. It took Sylvia, once she understood what the Captain and his giant Second were asking, to talk her into letting go of her fear.

"Let them try to give meaning to her death," she said quietly. "If it changes something, it may save other lives. Most people die with no meaning at all. Let her have that."

Both Sylvia and Leenan had adjusted well to the presence of the *Albert Einstein* and its crew. Perhaps they were more Leylite than they'd ever realised. It was certainly obvious to them that these unusual people were not gods, or even the children of gods. They were unexplained, but not divine.

They had certainly been willing to help the Captain. Part of his plan had required a written inscription in both Earth Standard and Tephee's own language. Magda had helped to write and translate the speech he would deliver, but she was otherwise illiterate in local terms. She had found her friends honoured to be asked. It was their farewell.

The shuttle touched down only a few hundred metres from the tent city of pilgrims and priests. The sun had risen a few hours ago but it was still cool under the trees. The pilgrims had been circumspect since yesterday's mad events, unsure what to think, how to interpret the intervention of the First King's men in the eradication of His enemies.

The voice of God, loud and far-reaching, emerged from the First King's smaller sky ship.

"I call upon you all to witness these events," it said. "I don't want there to be any more misunderstandings."

The mass of people ceased to move away. Nervous, anticipatory, awed . . . a thousand people waited and watched.

The side of the sky ship opened and a group of people walked out. Several of them wore uniforms, elegant and formal. One stood at either side of the group carrying weapons of some kind. A short, thin man wore decorations that signified he was of highest rank; he was dwarfed by an impossibly tall, broad-shouldered man. Three women, dressed in simple black shirts and trousers followed. Four more men followed carrying something on a long, broad metal pallet, covered in shining silver material.

The voice boomed out again.

"We come to bury the witch who died here yesterday, saving the lives of her fellow witches. Her friends, and ours."

There was a collective gasp from the mob. Surprise. Shock. Fear.

The pallet was placed gently on the ground. Using an unknown Arc tool that hummed and glowed, two men dug a wide, deep hole under the shade of a grand old marbletree.

"You have been divided too long," said the voice—Redmonde's, with hardly a trace of Standard accent, in a speech recorded earlier and with great care—"We are here to heal the rift between the Arc and witchkind."

The First King's men, the Captain and his giant, lifted a small body from the pallet. She was wrapped in the silver blanket, though her face showed, pale and serene, above the folds. The giant held her in his arms while the Captain climbed carefully into the grave. Then he knelt and passed her down, and the Captain laid her gently on the soil, unfolding the blanket. Those near the front could see the child, dressed in simple black like the witches, laid at the feet of the great tree. No box or binding, Leylite fashion, and her hands had been curled around flowers which twined through her hair and clothes. The Captain reached up and the big man helped him out.

"We bury Tephee Andrieux, and with her we bury the enmity between the Arc and the Leylite."

The three women knelt by the grave. Performing Arc ritual now, in turn they cut a lock of hair and sprinkled it into the darkness below. The Captain and the giant did the same. One of the other uniformed men came forward hesitantly. They moved aside and allowed him room to add a length of his own fair hair.

The two gravediggers returned to push the soil over her body. One of the witches, tall and thin, sobbed and turned away. Her friends closed in on each side, offering support, protection.

Two others joined them now, with the pallet. This they lowered over the grave. They took its long, flat handles with them when they left, and the pallet had become a monument flat on the earth with an inscription in two languages.

"Here sleeps Tephee Andrieux," it said, and Redmonde's rich deep voice spoke it aloud for all to hear. "She gave of herself until her last breath, and so, although she is gone, a part of her lives on. She is a treasured memory and a reminder that our lives are a gift. She sleeps in the arms of the Mother; she is watched over by the First King and His Lords. Remember her kindly."

In dignified sorrow, the mourners gathered together and returned to the sky ship, which rose from the ground with stately grandeur and flew back to the First King's castle.

Cadogan lay back on the bed, his eyes opened but unfocussed. His legs were numb, thankfully, but right now he would have welcomed the pain. That, at least, would have been real.

Nothing else was real. He could see things, but they were all strange and smooth and dead. The sounds he heard were muffled and lifeless. The things he could smell were acid and unnatural.

There was one sound, an awkward shuffling, which came from a real thing. He ignored it, however, until the person making it limped to the bedside, carefully lowered himself into a chair and placed his walking stick to one side. Sebastian poured a glass of water for them both.

"How are you feeling?" he asked.

Cadogan shifted his head slightly to meet Sebastian's gaze. "All right," he replied, although he wasn't. "How about you?"

"Oh, much better, thank you." Sebastian smiled ruefully with one half of his face—the other side was still paralysed. "I haven't been . . . quite myself, lately." He rubbed the side of his nose. "It's difficult, to find your whole notion of the world turned about. You try to make sense of it according to what you know. You can make . . . I made some terrible mistakes."

So how do I make sense of this? How do I know that my life hasn't been a lie . . . ?

"They'll be back soon," said Sebastian, patting Cadogan's shoulder. "I know you wanted to go with them," he continued when there was no response.

Yes . . . and no. How will I make sense of the world if I go out there and I still can't find Her anywhere?

He closed his eyes again, until Sebastian shuffled away, thinking he had gone to sleep. But he was far from sleeping. He was reaching out with all his being, trying to find the Great Mother. Somewhere. Anywhere.

All he could find was . . . the absence of anything real.

CHAPTER TWENTY-TWO

The medical bay was quiet in these early morning hours. Most of the patients had been allowed to go back to their own rooms now, including Lucy Schmidt's young man. Cadogan had been given a cot in the old storage room, which suited him well enough.

Sebastian had found a bed in the regular quarters now. Magda let Christov do the examinations to see what further progress could be made with the paralysis. She had seen from a distance how Sebastian walked with a slight limp, now, his right arm clumsy and stiff. She had heard, from a distance, his gentle voice with its new slur. She knew that one bright blue eye was half shut, and that his charming smile was only half there.

On the whole, she avoided him.

It had been three days since the funeral. Three days of numbness interspersed with sudden and devastating moments of pain which left Magda breathless and awash with tears. She wasn't sleeping well either, and had left the doctor's room she currently shared with Sylvia and Leenan in the middle of the night to tend to Doctor El Hady and an apprentice engineer named Eamon Riley, whose skin graft was not taking as quickly as she would have liked.

Eamon moved restlessly and Magda sat by his side, brushing the hair back from his forehead. No temperature. No sweats or chills. The drugs she had administered to combat the tissue rejection looked to have solved the problem and the graft was now holding firmly and beginning to extend across his chest.

In the quiet night, lit only by the soft glow of the dimmed ceiling light from the work desk, the pain came from nowhere and welled up inside her.

She saw Tephee—on a cot after the Battle of Tyne, barely alive after defeating the Witch Zuleika, so steeped in the act of giving her power away to the King's army that she had not known how to stop; in water roiled by a sinking ship, unconscious because she had launched into the fight to save her friends without thinking; lying on the shuttle floor, her skin pale and cold, her chest pierced gruesomely . . .

Magda saw her own hand on Sebastian's chest, shooting that small command from her fingertips: *Stop.*

A small hand on her arm made her gasp and draw away, hiding her grief and shame, but Sylvia stayed, wrapping her arms around Magda's shoulders and drawing her close. Magda resisted for a moment but then was glad of the arms that encircled her, glad of the warm body she pressed her face against, glad of the sound of Sylvia's voice.

"She wouldn't blame you."

Magda flinched. How did Sylvia do that? "She should."

"Tephee chose her way. She was always too impetuous." Sylvia smiled softly in remembrance. "We never could tell her what to do, or keep her from doing things her own way. Learning things her own way."

"I should have stopped her . . ."

"If you had," Sylvia said, kindly, firmly, "the rest of us might be dead. She held them at bay. She took their attention. She gave us time, and gave you time to reach us. We barely had the strength left to fight . . . if only she could have kept her focus . . ." She shook her head. "I never could convince her she wasn't invincible."

Magda would not be convinced. "I could have been faster. I

should have been there sooner."

"How?"

"I don't know," Magda admitted helplessly, in anger and despair. "Sebastian tried to keep me from going," she said. But she couldn't blame Sebastian now. At the time she thought that she might reach Tephee in time if only he did not slow her down. Only now she knew that even had he helped her on her way, she could never have arrived, on foot, in time to be of use. She looked up at Sylvia, the confession in her eyes before it was on her tongue: "I tried to kill him."

Sylvia continued to gaze down at her, without censure or surprise or approval.

"I was so . . . desperate . . ." Magda's voice dropped to a horrified whisper. "I realised . . . that if I can make a heart begin to beat . . . I could make it stop." She swallowed. "So I made it stop."

"You didn't kill him."

"When you become a doctor," Magda said carefully, "you swear an oath. The guiding principles for your profession. The first, the very first line of that oath is 'Do no harm.' "

"Maggie . . ."

"I did harm, Sylvia. I stopped his heart, for just a moment. I think that must have triggered the stroke. I broke my oath. And I did it for nothing. Tephee died anyway." That was the worse thing of all. She had betrayed dear-held beliefs, with nothing to show for it. To have murdered to save a life would have been terrible enough, but to have murdered for nothing at all? To even have attempted it . . .

"I never knew I could kill," she said, horrified and heartsick.

"You didn't kill anyone," Sylvia insisted, sensibly and gently.

Magda finally met her gaze once more. "But I meant to."

Sylvia understood at last—Magda's grief was not only for

poor Tephee, but for herself. The death of who she thought herself to be.

Leenan woke early, but by then Sylvia and Magda had both risen and gone. She was worried about Magda, who had gone unusually quiet and solemn since Tephee's death and their reunion.

Everything was strange here. The people, their language, the air, the food, the clothes. Magda was moody and evasive. So, for that matter, was Cadogan, but where Magda's troubles made her worry, Cadogan's actions made her feel hurt and angry. Only Sylvia was her usual self, finding equilibrium somehow in the midst of all this loss and alienness.

Leenan rose and made use of the mysterious ablutions cubicle which blasted metallic and flat-tasting water at her from above before blasting her with hot dry air. Then she dressed in the black trousers and shirt she had been given, which were comfortable though embarrassingly form fitting, and made her way down the corridor to Cadogan's room.

He was just leaving. He still walked a little awkwardly, unused to the softness of the new skin on his feet, which were tucked incongruously in a pair of thick cloth slippers. He also wore the ship's regulation blacks, which Leenan on the whole admired more on his form than on her own. She smiled tentatively. He gave her a dark, unreadable look, nodded curtly and stood at attention to let her pass. When Leenan stood in front of him, expression hard except for the hurt in her eyes, he flinched.

"What have I done?" she demanded.

Cadogan's gaze locked with hers for a moment. She was so forthright, so direct. He loved that in her. He wished . . . he wished . . . a thousand things. He could not ease back from his parade-ground stance. "You haven't done anything, My Lady," he replied, distant and formal.

"Then what is it? I've been trying to talk to you for days and you keep disappearing. You keep doing this . . . soldier thing." She jerked her chin up sharply at his posture. "This had better not be more of this witches-as-deities rubbish."

Cadogan had thought he felt as lost as a grown man could do, but now, knowing that she was all he could cling to, and still refusing to drag her down with the weight of his emptiness, he felt so vastly alone it was like . . . like an arrow in the chest. He was drowning in it.

"I . . . I . . ." He couldn't remember any words, let alone form a sentence. Oh, those eyes . . .

She reached past him to open the door and pushed him, unresisting, into his makeshift room.

"What is it Cadogan? Talk to me."

He was shaking his head, denying . . . everything. Leenan caught his arm as he paced past her, restless and unwilling, and forced him to face her. "What's wrong?"

Her green eyes locked on his. Everything he had tried to protect her from rose up.

"She's gone. If She ever was."

It was said out loud now, and though the world had not stopped, still it felt like it had.

"Who's gone?" Leenan wouldn't shift her gaze or let him go until he told her properly.

He stared at her and realised that he was shaking. "I can't find Her. I can't feel Her. She left us . . . in the cage . . . and now . . ." His gaze shifted uneasily to their surroundings. The halting words came more quickly. "An Arc ship. And the Mother is not here. And if She's not here . . . why not? Are they right? The First King is real. I see evidence of it all around me. What have I ever seen of the Mother?" It tumbled out in a rush now, the undercurrent of loss and panic carrying him. "If I've never seen Her, and I can't feel Her . . . was She ever real?" He took a deep breath, shocked by saying aloud the heart of the thing he had been trying to ignore for three days. He shook his head at her expression. "I don't know if it's worse to think that She abandoned us when we had most need, or that She was never there. Have I been lying to myself all my life?" He drew into himself. "If the Mother isn't real . . . what purpose do I have?"

She did not fold him in her arms, as he wished she would. She regarded him thoughtfully and asked him questions. "I thought the Mother gave an explanation for the world, not a purpose. I thought that's what you said. What purpose do you think She gave you?"

"My purpose is to serve," he said, without hesitation.

"Yes." She nodded, annoyed. "You serve the King; you serve the Mother; you serve the witches; you serve me. You serve everyone but yourself." Her gestures were short, sharp with frustration. "Once, just once, I'd like you to do something just for yourself."

"I don't need anything."

"Everyone has something that they want, Cadogan. Think. What is it you want?"

A frozen moment. He brought his gaze up to meet hers and the sudden yearning in his eyes caught her breath.

"I want you," he said, simply.

"Oh . . . Cadogan . . ." All the hardness in her expression was gone.

He tore his gaze from hers. "But that's not my choice. And I can't have . . . anything . . . until I know . . . who I am. Until I know . . . what's true."

Leenan looked like she might cry, or shake him. He turned away, sparing her the choice, but she would not let go of his arm.

"Magda has this theory, about why we can't do magic here," she said. "She says there's a kind of power in this place which interferes with the power of the world. The power we use to make magic. The power you say is the Mother. I think She's still there, in the world . . . but She's also here, with us. You said the Mother is . . . manifest in me. I think She's in here . . ." Tentatively she laid a hand on his diaphragm. "She's within you too. But you need to communicate with Her. To get out of here and find Her again."

His eyes were filled with the one fear he had not been able to face. "And if She isn't there?"

"She'll be there. I'm sure of it. You need to get away from this place and go into the woods for a while . . ."

The fear became pain. "You want me to go."

"I want you to come back again," she clarified, tears brimming at last. "Idiot." She moved to hug him, hesitated at the tension in him until it subsided a fraction. He wound his arms around her and held her close.

"You need to do this. For you," she said.

"I feel . . . amputated . . . from the world. There's never been a time when I couldn't find Her," he whispered, his throat tight. "I thought She would let you die."

"Tephee came," Leenan replied, tears flowing unchecked. "She's as much the Mother's witch as I ever was. Maybe she was meant to."

Maybe she was. He found the thought comforting.

When First Officer Redmonde asked Magda for her assistance in teaching him the local language, she was grateful for the excuse to take a rest from the sick bay. Particularly from Sebastian's frequent presence there. Red had expressed both curiosity and satisfaction to find that some root words were still similar between Earth Standard and the mainland dialect, grinning that if he could only get his thesis back to civilisation he'd be a shoo-in for the New Nobel Award. Until that auspicious day, he worked on compiling a lexicon in phonetic shorthand. She sat by Red's side in the mess, drinking hot chocolate—she did wonder how she'd ever survived for so long without chocolate—and supplying him with material.

"It's more like a long 'ai' sound." Magda demonstrated for Red, who repeated it and made a note on his flatscreen.

The lights in the messroom flickered and Red glanced up worriedly. "Our power is going to fail eventually," he said. "We'd better get hard copies of this."

"Have you got many field units?" Magda finished her drink. "You're going to have to back up your whole ship's library if you want to keep it all."

"The Captain's way ahead of you. Each section is saving manuals, journals, all kinds of data readings, as fast as we can fill them. It's not easy. An entire ship's data was not meant to be carried in a handful of longlife units."

"I guess you'll have to be selective."

"I guess we will. What will happen with Sam?"

Magda pulled at her lip. "He's doing well. I'll keep him on treatment until you actually lose power, then I can use the portable lab equipment. I'll need a longlife for the reference library, if you can arrange it."

"No problem. But . . . why don't you just take Sam outside and do your . . . er . . ."—Red waggled his fingers in a 'spooky' gesture—"magic thing."

It was a surprise to Magda how the very thought made her feel both panicky and unclean. With her lips tightly compressed, she shook her head sharply. Red regarded her with puzzled concern.

The sound of someone entering the large room gave Magda a welcome reason to turn away. It was Sylvia, who turned to thank the young woman who had shown her the way. She grinned at Magda, delighted and excited.

"I went exploring," she said with a laugh, "and got a little lost. Or so I told Captain Delouise. He doesn't like me exploring his sky ship very much."

"Captain Delouise, he is say you?" Redmonde said, with appalling grammar but very clear pronunciation.

"Yes," Sylvia replied, obligingly slowly, "but I did not understand."

Magda began to translate, but he grinned, pleased with himself. "I understand," he said carefully. "The Captain, he is . . ." Red searched for the word in the lexicon he was compiling, couldn't find it and asked Magda. He repeated: "The Captain, he is rude you?"

"No," said Sylvia solemnly, "he was very respectful." Then she grinned. Magda had to translate the last word for Red, who dutifully recorded it.

"You're very cheerful lately," Magda observed with an unexpected hint of disapproval at Sylvia's high spirits. Of course, she knew why Sylvia should be happy, despite everything. The brain scan she had performed on her friend two days ago confirmed what Sylvia had begun to suspect since she had finally tried to use her magic and succeeded in freeing Cadogan from the pyre. Damaged veins and capillaries were being ruptured when she tried to use her powers, but weeks of rest, because she had given up trying, had at last given her body time to heal properly. The bloody nose she had suffered should not happen again, provided she abstained from magic for another month or so and allowed the healing process to finish.

Sylvia gazed at Magda mildly for a moment. "Don't think that I don't miss her."

"I don't think that." Tears again. "I'm sorry. I know Tephee wouldn't want us to be miserable."

"Actually, I think she would, just for a little while." Sylvia's gentle smile was answered with a strangled laugh of agreement.

"Yes, I think you're right. Just enough misery to be sure we cared."

Sylvia held her while she broke down once more, whispered to her and soothed her and let her be miserable.

First Officer Redmonde, feeling awkward and redundant, made more hot chocolate.

Leenan made her way to the mess room at lunch, when it was crowded with crewmen grabbing a quick meal. She joined a queue for a meal dispenser and someone helped her select a bowl of soup and some chocolate. She didn't much care for the food they ate here—it tasted stale and faintly bitter when it tasted of anything at all—with the exception of the chocolate. She would have eaten nothing but the chocolate, actually, but the first time she'd tried that, a kind person in overalls had corrected her "error" and made sure she had plenty of bland vegetables and tasteless meat on her tray.

She made her way towards Magda and Sylvia who were sitting with the First Officer and getting him to repeat things and write them down.

"Hi," she said. "Is there room for one more?"

They shifted to make a space.

"Hello, Leenan. How are you?" he said. The accent and inflection were nearly flawless.

She looked at him in surprise. "I'm fine. Ah . . . how are you?"

"I am very well, thank you." He glanced at her lunch. "The . . . ah . . ." He pointed at her bowl and Sylvia supplied the word. "The soup is not good. The chocolate . . ."—he used his own language, since there was no local word for it—". . . is very good."

"Yes. Right." She could see the others were pleased with his progress and failed to be terribly interested. She looked intently around the large room, instead, trying to find Cadogan.

Red produced a foil-wrapped packet from his pocket and placed it on her tray. "The ration bar is . . . good good? . . . the soup." He listened to Magda's correction and then: "Is better than the soup. You. Ah . . . for you."

Leenan looked at Redmonde and at the ration bar. Unwilling to turn down his gift, she opened it carefully. It was a bar of compressed fruit and nuts. It smelled all right . . . she glanced up when she realised she was sniffing it carefully, and to cover her embarrassment nibbled it. It was actually pretty good. Certainly better than the soup. "Thank you," she said. He smiled.

Chewing on the fruit bar, she looked around again. "Have you seen Cadogan since this morning?" she asked. "We talked earlier today but then I went for breakfast and I haven't seen him since."

"Cadogan?" Red pulled thoughtfully on his beard. "I see Cadogan . . ." He gestured over his shoulder, and Leenan guessed he meant "in the past." She supposed he hadn't had time yet to learn the past tense. "Cadogan go . . . ah . . . he goes out."

"Out?" A sudden surge of fear. Outside? After what they tried to do to him last time? His feet were hardly healed. He had no sword, no knife, nothing for protection. "Out where?"

"To . . . tree. Trees. He has food. He wear . . ." He consulted Magda and let her finish.

"Cadogan asked for some proper shoes—with a fair bit of mime, I understand—took a blanket and some supplies and went out."

"But he didn't say goodbye!" Leenan almost wailed. "What about those maniacs out there?" She started to rise, to find Red trying to gently hold her back. He spoke rapidly to Magda.

"Red says he tried to stop him, but we're not prisoners. Cadogan insisted and there was no way short of locking him up to keep him here. So he went out, in uniform, and walked with him to the tree line . . ." More rapid conversation. "The opposite direction to the camps and Tephee's grave. No one who saw them made trouble. Red says they rather kept their distance, actually."

"He didn't leave a message?"

"Ah . . . he's not sure. Cadogan said something, but Red didn't understand it."

"Does he remember what it was?"

Redmonde shook his head when asked, then thought carefully and tried to piece together a sentence in an unknown foreign tongue from memory. "He say . . . 'I find Her' and 'I come here again.' He say . . ." Red pronounced the unfamiliar word carefully, " 'Promise.' I . . . not . . . understand."

"It's all right," Leenan said, "I do." She settled down to eat the rest of her fruit bar, mollified and thoughtful.

Chapter Twenty-Three

Cadogan would have to thank First Officer Redmonde for finding such a good pair of boots, once he got back. He had been walking for several hours and so far there was only a slight ache in his feet. It would take a while to work up the tough skin he'd developed in forty years, but there was time enough for that.

He had felt some difference when he left the huge sky ship, but he'd been walking for half an hour before he truly felt the residue of its presence fall away. What he felt in its place . . . he wasn't sure. He might have sensed a pulse beyond himself, or it may just have been the relief of leaving that claustrophobic place. In any case, he wanted to find a water hole, or a river, even just a creek if the water was deep enough. He felt very strongly that he had to do this right.

The creek he had been following wasn't deep enough, though it was possible that upstream might offer a more suitable place. The day was typically hot, though under the trees by the water he found it a little cooler. The terrain grew steadily more rocky—mounds of light-brown stone, often overgrown with ground vines, through which the creek threaded on its way to meet a larger stream.

The sound of water over rocks reached him and he quickened his pace. In front of him rose a wall of creamy-brown boulders. Water cascaded in a narrow rivulet, a handspan wide, pooling briefly at the base of the stone formation before pushing on to become the creek he had been following. The pool of water here would be deep enough for his purposes if necessary, but he hoped to find something better still.

The rock formation rose only twice his own length and offered plenty of hand holds. Cadogan climbed.

At the top he stopped, satisfied. The stone mound was shaped like an asymmetric horseshoe, creating a pleasant and secluded hollow where grass and several broad-leafed trees grew. The right side of the horseshoe tapered sharply, the tip of it covered in pliant, pastel-green papervine. The arch of the shape, on which he stood, was thick and even and became wider and more uneven as it swept to the left side. The spring water, source of the creek, bubbled out of the rocks to gather in a deep hollow, the overflow from it spilling over the edge and into the rivulet which led to that bubbling cascade which in turn formed the creek. The pool was not wide—standing in it he would certainly be able to stretch his arms out to touch either side—but he could see that it was deep enough. More perfectly, the place was sheltered, shady and quiet.

Cadogan climbed carefully down into the hollow. He placed the blanket and parcel of ration bars on the grass under a tree. Methodically, he removed his clothing, piece by piece, folding each item carefully and laying it in a pile on top of the blanket. The black shirt. His boots. Trousers. The immodest underwear. These things were made of strange and unnatural materials. Even if it had not been important to enter into this time unclothed, he would not have wanted such First Kingly things between him and the Mother. If she was there.

First, he cleared a space of twigs and small stones, and sat cross-legged on the ground. For some minutes he slowed his breathing, closed his eyes, and tried to empty his mind. For the first time in his life, he found it hard. He feared that the silence and emptiness would not be filled as it always had been with the steady pulse of the world. He thought he felt the trees moving, the water flowing, but perhaps he was only tired. Perhaps his mind was finding meaning where none existed. Perhaps . . .

He sighed and rose to lean against the cool stone behind him, listening to the splash of the spring falling down to the creek. Dappled shade on his face and grass under his feet, he listened to the world move and could not be sure he heard anything else behind it, guiding the spin and sweep of it.

He closed his eyes to concentrate on the shape and texture of the things against his back and feet. His breathing steadied. Slowed.

The stone was hard, cool, smooth—no, not entirely smooth. Bumps and lines made themselves known to his skin. The whorls of earthy colour each had a finely different texture. He pressed his fingers to the compact grains and he could hear water moving through the stone, as an earthworm hears, with its body buried in the heart of the Mother . . . Water pushing upward through the deep, deep buried stone, Her bones . . . water rising . . . moving . . . he followed the water as it rose above, and moved aside, under his feet, finding roots whose thirst it quenched. Mother's milk . . . He could feel it spreading through the blades of grass, feel it moving against the new skin on the soles of his feet. Temperature changed at each point of his nerve endings with the movement of that water.

He could see things differently. Not as individual pieces and parts, but as a whole. The tree and the soil and the wind and the water and the tree lizard and the flock of prit birds wheeling past were all one, and he was one with them. Elements of a greater thing, the way his toes and heart and voice were only elements of his own identity.

Cadogan opened his eyes, squinting at the light. The rock became merely rock, the grass only grass. Had he been wakefully dreaming? Time to be sure. Time to find the truth.

He carefully levered himself up onto the top of the horseshoe, walked gingerly on stone that was hard on his feet, lowered himself into the pool. It was cool and pleasant on his delicate new skin. When he stood in the pool it came to his lower ribs. He slowly crouched until the water reached his chin. He was concentrating all this time, taking deeper and deeper breaths.

We come to the Mother naked, the words came to mind in his father's voice, *with nothing to protect us but Her care. Our fine clothes and our rags are nothing, as are our self-image and lies. She sees us, within and without, as the day we are born. So it is that we go to the Mother, naked, without pretense or protection.*

He took a final, deep breath and immersed himself completely. After a moment, the water stilled, rippling only with the spring water that moved through it. Cadogan did not move, except for his hair which drifted in dark tendrils with the shifting current. He stayed like that for minutes before a thin line of air bubbled from the corner of his mouth and to the surface. Otherwise he remained still . . . like a plant anchored on a river bed; like a sleeping water dragon anchored to the ocean floor.

From stillness . . .

An explosion of water and Cadogan arched his head above the surface, sucking in a great gasp of air and some fine spray which made him cough. Gasping and coughing, he stumbled two steps to lean on the edge of the rockpool, his face buried against his folded arms. For a moment he wept, his tears mingling with the spring.

And then he turned, face to the light, and let his laughter join the birdsong.

Leenan was worried when Cadogan hadn't returned by nightfall. When he was still missing the following morning, she packed some food, borrowed a pair of shoes, and made her determined way down to the exit hatch. She told Magda and Sylvia where she was going, of course—she didn't want them to worry—then found that they had enlisted Red to stop her at the door. She was prepared to argue her way past and was just about to give them an earful when Redmonde gave something to Magda, which was then pressed into her own hands.

"Red says Cadogan wouldn't take one. He asks if you will."

Leenan stared at it. She held a dull-coloured tube of metal.

"It's a communicator," Magda explained. "Push this end . . . see . . . and speak into it. It sends a message to us here at the ship. You'll be able to hear us talk back. Just in case. If you need us, we can be with you quickly."

Leenan nodded, folding her hand around the tube. When she looked at Magda, she could see that her friend was afraid. "I'll be all right, Maggie. I'll find him and call you, and you can come to get us."

"You come back," Magda told her.

Leenan shifted her gaze to Sylvia. Sylvia patted her hand. "I'll have some hot chocolate waiting for you when you get back."

The cargo loading tray opened and hummed down to rest on the grass. It was a short step down into the sunshine, and it was harder to do than Leenan had realised. She could see, under the raised belly of the *Albert Einstein,* the tent city that was still in the distance and for a moment felt sick with fear, her heart pounding at remembered terror. A great bulk, exuding strength and calm, stepped out beside her. First Officer Redmonde, in uniform, stood behind her, making her feel both small and protected. Usually she would have found that annoying, but, right now, she welcomed the shelter.

"I walk you to the trees," he said.

Redmonde had to shorten his long stride so that they could walk side by side. They met a man, collecting water at a shallow, muddy creek.

"This woman," said Redmonde carefully in a speech he had

rehearsed with Magda, "is a friend of the First King."

The man dropped his waterskin, shocked and awed that the First King's people would actually speak with him. "Yes, My Lord," he replied tremulously.

"Tell the others."

"Yes, My Lord. At once, My Lord." He bowed and backed away.

Redmonde watched him go, his mouth pursed, though his eyes were lit with a guilty delight at his effect. He sobered as he looked down at Leenan. "You need me, you call me."

"I will," she promised. She walked into the woods.

Leenan walked for almost half an hour before she felt the . . . otherness . . . in her mind fade completely, though she felt certain she could have used magic before then. She drank from the creek before sitting down in a clear space to close her eyes and meditate the way Sylvia had shown her. She had nothing physical that belonged to Cadogan to guide her, but as she focussed inward, and then sent her mind outward, she took with her the scent of him, the image of his blue eyes below a dark fringe, looking at her with quiet longing.

She found him, hours away, immersed in a pool of water—*drowned?* But she knew he was alive. Her mind spiraled back to her body. Distressed, alarmed, she rose and began to follow the creek.

It was not yet midday when she finally clambered up the rocks that led to the pool, her heart leaping. When she reached the top and looked down, she nearly stopped breathing.

She could see Cadogan lying on the grass within a shaded, shallow basin, his pale body dappled with shadows. He was naked, a fact which both startled and fascinated her. His left arm was flung across his eyes, shielding them from the light. Leenan almost panicked, until she saw his chest rise and fall gently with his breathing as he slept. The dark hair across his chest obscured the faint shadow of a scar where, days ago, an arrow had pierced him, but a longer scar curved across his ribs.

His chest was nice, she thought, muscular, deep. She remembered sleeping against that strong torso while they traveled towards expected death. She remembered wanting to press her hands against those muscles. To trace the line of those old scars and learn his history. Leenan found herself holding her breath as her gaze shifted, wonderingly, down. His stomach lean, pale narrow hips, a line of dark hair arrowing down . . .

She skipped down to his feet. They were small, and unexpectedly elegant. Vulnerable even, with lucent new skin leading to pink and hairless shins. His calves were still beautifully shaped, and his thighs . . . he was a study in compact, graceful lines, even in his sleep. Her gaze traveled the length of him boldly now. She so wanted to . . .

She met his open eyes and, mortified, stepped back, only to lose her footing.

Cadogan had been dreaming of the sound of bronze, leathery wings beating a steady rhythm across the sky; and of a pair of eyes full of humour and intelligence, as green as . . . dragon's eyes.

Then he awoke and there she was. Beautiful. Impossibly desirable in those ship's blacks which clung to every curve and contour. For three days he had avoided her because he was lost, confused, and because wanting her so much had made him feel ashamed. Unworthy. He dreamed he saw the wanting in her eyes.

His dream stepped back, slipped and fell. She would have landed badly, had Cadogan not rolled to his feet and caught her as she slid down the rock face into the secluded hollow.

"Are you all right?" he asked earnestly, as coolly as though he were not holding her against his naked body. Or as though that was the most natural thing in the world. Leenan was real, but still it felt like a dream.

"I . . . yes. Thank you." He could feel her heart hammering, with her chest pressed against his. "You didn't come back. I was worried."

"I meant to come back earlier. It's just so peaceful here. To tell the truth, I've been reluctant to go back to the sky ship." The dreamlike quality was fading, though the encounter remained unreal. Cadogan did not want to let go, and as she did not try to withdraw he was content.

"Oh."

Such a normal-sounding conversation, except that his hands were no longer steadying her. They moved down her back, caressing her spine. She was flesh under his questing fingertips; her breath was warm. She was more real every moment.

"I didn't mean to worry you." His voice was soft. "I've been thinking about you."

"Oh." Leenan's hands were still on his shoulders, where she had steadied herself after her fall, but her fingers were slowly rubbing against his skin. Such a small movement. It felt electric. Leenan made a concerted effort to contribute something more coherent. "Did you . . . have you found . . . ?"

Cadogan beamed at her. "Can't you feel Her?" His hands left her back to gesture expansively around them. "Everywhere. You were right." His smile was just for her, then for their whole surroundings. "I think . . . I understand better than I have ever done before. The Great Mother can't abandon us. We're part of Her. Every tree, every bird, every bug. Every person. It's only when we abandon Her that we hurt each other." *It's only when you don't know your place in the world, when you don't understand that all the individual parts are only elements of the whole, that we try to harm and poison the world, not understanding that we hurt and destroy only ourselves.* He felt that he had always known this, but had forgotten it. He looked into Leenan's green eyes, which were filled with joy at *his* joy.

Leenan. His Leenan. No longer Witch Leenan, the Mother's earthly incarnation, but simply Leenan—warm, human, strong, brave, beautiful Leenan—no longer beyond reach. She bore the Mother's gifts but she was also her own self.

I thought the Mother had abandoned me. I didn't understand. Leenan saved my life. Sylvia saved my life. Tephee saved us all. She has been with me all along and I never saw it.

"You're right," Cadogan said with a small laugh, "I am an idiot."

She began to protest, until he bent to kiss her, and when he tried to draw away to look on her again, wanting to drink her in, she buried her fingers in his hair and held him to her. He discovered he could drink her in just as well with his mouth against hers; against her throat and hands and shoulders . . . When her black shirt curtailed his thirst for her, she helped him to shed the unwanted thing.

She explored the shape of him with her hands instead of her eyes. She felt the knot of an old scar on his shoulder, followed it down to the beautiful musculature of his back, to the curve of his hips, down . . .

He drew her down on the grass beside him and in the dappled shadows under the noon light, they made love for the first time.

It was funny, Leenan thought, how the bare ground could be so comfortable. She snuggled closer to Cadogan's side and he shifted slightly to accommodate her. For the moment she was content to be beside him, skin to skin. He was trailing a finger languidly along her thigh as he hummed an old tune.

"What's that song?" she asked dreamily, noting that she liked it when she ran her fingers through his chest hair.

He smiled, touchingly shy given their recent intimacies. "It's a very old Kutan love song, in an ancient language. It means

. . . uh . . . 'You have a heart of fire. Your . . . singing soul gives imagination wings, my dragon-hearted love.' "

Leenan felt those words melt through her bones. "That's . . . is that what you think?"

"I used to watch you, when you were a dragon, perched on the tower spire. I thought you were magnificent." His hand brushed across her face before he wound a length of her dark-blonde hair around his finger.

An embarrassed and self-deprecating laugh escaped her. "I hope you weren't too disappointed to find I was merely human."

"Oh no," he said earnestly, tracing a line along her jaw with gentle kisses, "that was when I realised you were beautiful as well."

He thinks I'm beautiful . . . She tilted her face so that their lips met, and for a long while she attempted to communicate the fullness of her heart in the way that she kissed him. It still seemed inadequate, so when they parted she shifted to lie across his chest and held his face in her hands. She looked directly into his blue eyes . . . beautiful blue eyes . . . and told him. "I love you."

His smile crinkled his eyes, which were suddenly bright, and she felt both awed and delighted that such a simple sentence could make him so happy. So she said it again, and again, until he kissed her into breathless silence. His mouth trailed to her throat, up her collar bone and tickled her ear, where she heard him whisper: "I love you with every breath in me, my beautiful dragon-hearted lady."

It wasn't until they had bathed in the rockpool the second time—discovering after the first time that it was not possible to bathe together without delicious but departure-delaying results—that they dressed and started back towards the ship. It wasn't until an hour later, when they had stopped to drink from the creek, were distracted by a long kiss and then an intense discussion about Cadogan's "birthing" meditation technique and its revelations, that Leenan remembered the communication tube, which was somewhere under the trees at the rockpool.

Magda, Sylvia, and Red were waiting up for them when they returned, and on seeing them together, arms wrapped around one another's waists, they wordlessly and tactfully withdrew to their own quarters.

"I'm sleeping outside tonight," Cadogan told Leenan as she stepped through the hatch. He smiled at her concern. "It's all right," he said. "It's what you suggested. I'm doing something for me. I don't really like it in there."

"Oh . . . Well. Can I get you something?"

"You can bring me breakfast tomorrow," he suggested with a happy grin.

"It's a deal." Leenan sealed the bargain with a kiss, which led to another, and another.

In the morning, she went back inside to get breakfast for them both.

CHAPTER TWENTY-FOUR

Eamon Riley was finally responding more positively to treatment and he was now talking with Nurse Christov while a fresh coat of gel was applied to his new-growing skin. Christov's responses were short, the young man even quieter than usual.

Magda worked with Sam El Hady, who was now sitting up. He asked questions about his condition and they conferred on the best treatments. Magda had almost forgotten what it was like to talk shop with a medico and found it a welcome distraction.

"That's enough for today," she told the doctor. He was tiring already.

"Yes," Sam agreed, sagging back under the bedcovers, breath becoming wheezy. He frowned. "I get . . . so damned . . . tired."

"It's hardly surprising."

"No. I did . . . smash myself up . . . rather."

"You'll be back on your feet in no time," Magda assured him. He pursed his lips and arched an eyebrow at her, aware that she was talking to him as though he were just like any other patient. She returned his gaze steadily.

"Is that . . . your professional . . . medical opinion, Doctor Czajkowski?"

"It is, Doctor El Hady."

"Hmph." He was already falling asleep. Magda pulled the sheets over his shoulders and checked that his breathing was regular before going through to her office. Sam's office. She supposed she'd have to hand it back to him eventually.

Christov was there, straddling a chair, his arms folded across the back of it. He regarded her pensively. "Will he be all right? Really?"

"In time."

He accepted this piece of medical diplomacy and rested his chin on his arms, a frown creasing his brow.

Magda straightened the disks and notes on the desk. "What is it, Chris?"

"I was . . . thinking of Tephee," he admitted, his voice muffled against his shirt sleeves. He shrugged. "I hardly knew her. Is it stupid that it makes me so sad?"

Tears pricked at her own eyes. "No. Not at all." Magda found it comforting that a near stranger could miss Tephee as much as she did herself.

Christov lifted his chin. "I kissed her once," he confessed. "The night before she died. In the corridor outside the med bay. She didn't seem to mind."

Magda remembered Tephee coming in to bed, grinning with some secret delight. "She liked you," Magda told him, feeling like she had somehow given him absolution.

"How old was she?"

"Not quite seventeen. How old are you?"

"Not quite twenty-two. This was my first intern posting. I was supposed to go back to med school after three months of practical and do my colonial doctorate." He scraped both hands through his hair. "Doesn't look like it's going to happen now."

What was there to say to that? Magda patted his arm.

"Do you think Tephee would have liked it there?" Christov asked after a long pause.

Magda considered for a moment. "I think she would have been intrigued. She would have loved the observation lounge. But in the long run . . . no, I don't think so. I think that the energy sources of technology interfere with these abilities of ours. She would have hated being separated from her power like that."

"Do you mind?"

She had not expected that question. Did she? She had pretended to have witchly power in her first few years here, for survival, for a childhood fantasy. Since she had discovered that there were true witches, with true power—had discovered that she was one of them—her life had been both rich and tumultuous. The best and worst moments of her life had all happened since then. She had saved lives. She had tried to take one. The memory still made her recoil from this power inside her. It wasn't fun anymore. It felt poisoned now, by her own most vicious reflexes.

"No," she said, "I don't mind."

Christov straightened and drummed his fingers briefly on the chair back. "Did Tephee have a religion?"

"I suppose she was a follower of the First King. She sometimes burnt offerings on the feast days."

"I come from a long line of Catholics myself. Do you think she'd mind if I . . ." He faltered, embarrassed, then cleared his throat and continued. "Would anyone mind if I prayed for her? Assuming God is out here too, I'd like to . . . you know . . ." He shrugged.

"Ask him to keep an eye out for her?" She had never been religious herself. It must be comforting, she thought, to have a god to turn to. "No one will mind."

"I'll visit her today, then," Christov decided. "Say a prayer. So He knows where to find her." With a sheepish smile, the young man excused himself.

Magda sighed and walked back into the office that led to the room she shared with Sylvia and Leenan. That made her grin. Leenan had made an early appearance this morning, fetching breakfast for two, and had fled, blushing and smiling smugly in equal amounts at the reaction of her friends. What was that old saw? In the midst of death we are in life. It was good to see that something happy had happened in this whole sorry mess.

"Witch Magda. I was hoping I would find you here."

She froze at Sebastian's voice. Well, she'd known she couldn't avoid him forever, although she'd hoped to. Hands clenched, she turned slowly to face him.

He looked . . . well. Considering. His colour had come back and his blue eyes were bright once more. A trace of the tell-tale stiffness remained in the droop of his left eye and his mouth. She swallowed.

"I've been wanting to tell you," he said, gently and gravely, "that I'm sorry."

Magda blinked. "You're sorry?"

His gaze dropped in shame. "I know what you think of me. I have been behaving like the worst kind of fool. It was wrong of me to keep you from helping Tephee. More wrong still to try to harm you in doing so . . ."

"Sebastian . . ."

"I have been . . ."—he looked up again, meeting her gaze in an attempt to communicate more clearly—"trying to make a changed world fit into my vision of what the world should be like, instead of changing my vision to fit the world." He tapped the side of his head with a rueful twist of his lips. "I think I understand now."

"What . . . what is it you understand?"

"That I was right the first time. The First King wants this schism with the witches to end. Even the Red Lord was one of His Lords once. Something went wrong and you have been sent to put it right at last."

"Is that what you think?"

"You are the First King's emissary and a witch, the personification of the unity which the First King craves."

Magda's lips tightened to a thin line. "You just don't get it, do you?"

He lifted an eyebrow in query and she huffed in disgust. "The First King was just the Captain of a colony ship. Captain King. He got stuck here, like I did, like Captain Delouise did. It was an accident."

Sebastian regarded her placidly. "The First King . . . Captain King . . . He brought colonists here. He brought humanity to this place. If this is true, then all else is still true. He is the Father of our world. He brought his sky vessel through the Arc of Entry and gifted this world with our lives here."

"It's not what you think it is."

He placed his hand gently on her arm. "It can't be easy, being the emissary for the bringing together of two faiths."

"I tried to *kill* you!" The words burst from her, in frustration and horror at the reverence still in his tone. "I did this to you," gesturing sharply at his stiffened features. "Don't you understand?" Her voice broke and the tears began again.

"Yes," Sebastian said. Quietly. Contritely. "I know what happened. I know that I was so confused and afraid that I did selfish and cruel things. I had struck you before and I was prepared to force you to stay, by any means necessary. You did what you must to stop me. This,"—he touched the side of his face—"was not your doing. This was the First King's warning to me, after you let me live, that I had gone too far."

She shook her head mutely, tears falling steadily down her face. She wondered that she still had so many tears in her. Why couldn't she just cry it all out at once, and get on with her life? Why did grief and shame rise up time and again, however often she laid awake at night, her misery leaking from her eyes?

Sebastian placed an arm around her shoulder and squeezed.

"I came to seek forgiveness for my arrogance, for the harm I did you." He captured her chin with his free hand and turned her face towards him. "Magda, I had hurt you in the past and you did nothing that was not in defence of yourself and poor Tephee, but if you need my forgiveness in turn, you have it."

Magda let him fold her in his fatherly embrace and she felt some of that awful tension finally release itself. *He forgives me,* she thought and she was surprised at how relieved she felt. *Now how do I forgive myself?*

It was lunchtime and Leenan was wondering if she dared return to the ship to gather further supplies. Her friends and the ship's crew would no doubt find it very entertaining. She and Cadogan had spent the morning in the shade of the First King's vessel, mostly talking but always touching—sitting side by side, she nestled into his side while his arm encircled her, or holding hands, sometimes simply sitting so that their knees touched. Just now Leenan had her back propped against a tree trunk, some distance from the ship, while Cadogan lay on the grass with his head in her lap. She traced the outline of his cheekbones and jawline with her fingertips, endlessly fascinated by the combined air of strength and gentleness there. Cadogan moved into the touch slightly, like a cat arching into a caress, and breathed a small sigh of contentment.

The silence between them now was companionable, stemming from a mutual enjoyment of the midday warmth rather than a lack of things to discuss. They had already spoken of subjects as far-reaching as their favourite seasons, the flight patterns of tree lizards, whether Sylvia's habit of looking like she knew everything but wasn't telling was some kind of bluff on her part or a genuine spiritual talent of hers, how bad the ship food was, and a studied comparison of the shape and texture of one another's hands. One thing they had talked about was the uneasy mental-pins-and-needles feeling of being so close to the power of the Arc vessel. Cadogan had not exactly refused to return to the ship, but Leenan had a sense that this was another form of his not-being-there. She had no intention of forcing the issue, but on the other hand she really wanted to have one of those wondrous showers and perhaps some chocolate. She also thought it would be delicious to lie next to Cadogan on a soft mattress; to have the warm weight of him pressing her down into something a bit more comfortable than a bed of grass . . .

She found him looking up at her with a quizzical smile. "What are you thinking?" he asked.

I want to do lascivious things with your body. But what she said was: "Do you really see me as a dragon?"

Cadogan caught one of her hands in his and brought it up to kiss her fingertips. "As strong and as beautiful, My Lady," he said. His lips moved on to her palm and wrist before he returned his gaze to her. "How do you see me?" The question was guarded. Almost shy.

How do I see him? His strength and stability. His sense of solidity that was somehow fluid as well. Anchored yet growing beyond himself. His protectiveness that was not cloying.

She looked at him. "You'll think it's silly."

"No I won't," he promised. "Tell me."

"It's just . . . I think I see you as rather . . . tree-like," she finished in a mumble.

To her relief, he grinned with delight. "Really?"

She nodded, puzzled and pleased by his reaction. Something more to talk about later on. For now, he simply settled down in contented silence and made a great deal out of kissing her hand in a slow and sensuous way that was making her blood steam.

"What have you been thinking about?" she stalled for time, wondering if she could convince him to go inside or if she would simply drag him to a secluded place further away into the forest. When the kisses stopped but he didn't respond she glanced down. "You've got that look on," she said sternly.

"What look?"

"That look you get when you've got something on your mind but you won't talk about it."

Instead of protesting, he grimaced. "There's a look, is there?"

"Definitely." She grasped his chin in her fingers and made him meet her gaze. "So spill, Sergeant Ho. I'm not letting you go until you do."

He smiled ruefully, conceding defeat. "I was just thinking," he said, "that I would like to go home."

"Home? Do you mean up north from here?"

"Tyne is my home," Cadogan told her. "Marin Kuta is just where I was born."

"And why should wanting to go home be something that gives you That Look?" She arched an eyebrow at him.

"Because . . . I don't know what you want to do."

"So, my plans will affect yours?"

"Your plans will affect how I feel about going home," he amended.

"Oh, stop doing this, Cadogan!" She swatted him, her annoyance only half feigned. "Just ask me."

Cadogan sat up so that his arm was on one side of her hips, propping him up, and his body hovered close to her. "What are your plans?" he asked steadily.

After I've had my way with you? "Let's go home," she replied.

"But first . . ." His mouth descended on hers in a languorous kiss. Leenan melted into the embrace, her hands sliding up underneath his black shirt. He drew back to drop a kiss on the tip of her nose. "I have an army cot in my room. It's surprisingly comfortable."

Oh. All it took was the prospect of sex. Good. "Then what are we waiting for?"

★ ★ ★ ★ ★

An hour later they were still lying in a tangle of limbs and sated lethargy, the narrow bed making it a happy necessity to remain wrapped up in each other's embrace. Leenan was absently tracing patterns in his chest hair with her fingers, while his own hands caressed circles on her bare back.

"Leenan?"

"Hmmmm?"

"I was thinking . . . I'd prefer to go home sooner, rather than later."

She felt the slight tremor of tension begin in him. She pressed her lips to the base of his throat. "How soon?"

"Tomorrow."

"Fine by me." The tremor subsided. "You know, you've got to stop doing that."

"Doing what?"

"Seeking permission."

Cadogan considered that for a moment. "All right." A long pause while his hands roamed and Leenan willingly succumbed, until: "I'll be going down to Tephee's grave this afternoon."

"What? No! You can't!" Leenan sat up to stare at him, aghast, only to find a "see what happens?" expression on his face. She frowned, guilt mingling with her dismay.

"I want to say goodbye to Tephee," he said.

"It's too near the camp," Leenan insisted. "They'll . . . they'll . . ." She was shocked to find herself crying.

"Hush, love. Shhh." Cadogan folded her in his arms and stroked her, soothingly now. "No they won't."

"How do you know? They're maniacs. Last time . . . last . . ." The horror of it defied words. It was not merely that the mob had nearly killed them. The mob had nearly *burned* them. *Had* burned Cadogan, beaten her, murdered Tephee, and the memory of her terror was fresh.

Yet, here he was, holding her close against his whole and healed body. Murmuring assurances. A solid presence. Her shivering subsided.

"I'm sorry," she said in a small voice, still wrapped in his arms.

"I won't let anything happen."

His confidence was misplaced, she felt, but comforting nonetheless. "Just see you don't," she replied, rallying, "or . . . or else."

"Oh my. We can't let that happen," he said, and she could feel his smile as he kissed her temple, "I'll have to make certain then."

Cadogan had not expected company on this short trip, but he had it anyway. The young healer had caught up with him just as he'd set off, out from the shadow of the sky ship, dressed in a neat uniform complete with a peaked cap and highly polished boots. Cadogan suppressed a sigh. His own uniform, what remained of it, was torn and bloodstained, his sword and meagre worldly goods were at the bottom of the sea with his father's ashes. Captain Evenahn would doubtless find it amusing. Kiedrych's sense of humour tended occasionally to the appalling.

He and Christov exchanged nods and stepped out together into the afternoon. A hundred paces towards the marbletree that marked Tephee's grave, Sebastian ran up to them, a limping gait these days. Christov waited for him and Cadogan, for politeness, also waited.

"Sergeant . . . Ho . . ." Sebastian gasped for breath, waving his fingers at them in a staying motion while he steadied himself. "Are you going to visit Witch Tephee's grave?"

Cadogan nodded, his measured gaze watching the priest carefully.

"I would deem it a great honour," said the priest, "to accompany you."

Cadogan wasn't sure that he deemed it so highly himself, but he was content enough to share the road with him. Christov, only understanding the exchange by inference, inclined his head in solemn greeting to the priest and they continued on their way.

Then he became aware of the pilgrims.

They were walking towards them, hundreds of men and women, walking slowly and solemnly towards them. As though a line marked the way, the First King's faithful stopped and knelt, hand folded at their throats in prayer, heads upraised. A clear path was now defined for the three men, leading down to the tree and the engraved metal slab that served as the Witch Tephee's headstone. Cadogan wondered idly what would happen if he tried to walk through those ranks, or turn back, but since he had no intention of doing either he strode on, unfaltering.

The priest, he noticed, searched the gathering crowd. Dressed still in the ship's blacks, Sebastian was not obviously an Arc priest. It was the healer, Christov, who was made most uncomfortable by this reverent audience. The boy swallowed nervously, wiping his palms surreptitiously on his pants leg. He murmured something and Cadogan caught the name Delouise. So. The sky ship's Captain knew Christov was here, had possibly even sent him. Cadogan cast him a grave look, which the boy acknowledged with a sharp nod.

"Sebastian?"

This from a woman back in the ranks of those lining their human avenue. Her iron-grey hair was plaited and coiled at the back of her head, her brown skin wrinkled and stained with age.

"Elyssa." Sebastian stopped and held a hand out to her. "I was hoping to find one of you."

All around her, the kneeling faithful held the perfect silence of absolute attention. Elyssa's rheumy eyes watered as she squinted over their heads. "Have you been here all along?"

"I brought the Witch Magda, as I said I would."

"What . . . what does it mean?"

"It means," said Sebastian with his half smile, "that a thousand years of enmity is at an end. Our Temple was right these last three hundred years to preach tolerance."

"Good . . ." she breathed. Those around her were still vigilant, their eyes on the three men. Elyssa blinked away tears. "Are the Lords angry with us? After what happened to the little witch?"

Christov felt the force of all those eyes turning to him and he swallowed again. He tried to return the penetrating stares with cool disdain, but only ended up looking like a frightened rabbit. After a long moment, he pulled a coil of strange, clear ribbon from his pocket and read from it.

"I am . . . Ensign Christov." His pronunciation was heavily accented as he read from the ribbon. Cadogan suspected Redmonde had been coaching the young man. "I come from Cap . . . er . . . Lord Delouise, to see the grave of Tephee Andrieux." His head jerked in the direction of the gravesite. He cleared his throat and stood taller, determined to make a better impression.

He needn't have worried. He came from the great sky ship and that was good enough for all concerned. He had spoken to them, and as one they bowed. Christov grimaced.

"Here, you! Down!" A group of men burst out from the lines and a disheveled Arc priest and a boy were forced to their knees before them on the path. The boy was weeping. Cadogan stepped back involuntarily.

Willem did not register his presence, caught up in his own pain and bewilderment. He clutched his broken arm against his chest. Arc Priest Ensho glared up at him, his face, like his nephew's, streaked with dirt and blood. He was held on all sides by men, some in Arc robes, others in rough, plain travelling clothes. Ensho's gaze fell on Christov, then, and the defiance was leeched from his expression. He would not bow, but stared with wide eyes at this young Lord.

Cadogan found himself in battle stance and, with effort, drew a breath and relaxed back to a loose attention. Here were the men who had almost killed Leenan, Sylvia, then himself before finally succeeding in murder, in the name of their First King. He tilted his head to one side, examining them. Willem's arm, which Cadogan himself had broken at their first encounter by the creek, was swollen. Both of them had been beaten, were bruised and bloodied. Willem had turned inward and could not stop sobbing. His uncle's face was lined with fatigue. Shock. Bewilderment. Their own people had taken out the First King's retribution, reacting in panic and dread after the witches' divine rescue.

That was when Cadogan realised he was no longer angry. He knew how it felt to think your gods had abandoned you. He knew that Willem and Ensho, the wild mob, the crew of *Aln's Pride*, had all lost their place in the world so entirely that fear had brought ordinary men to appalling acts. Cadogan's bitterness was now only a distasteful memory. A portion of his father's ashes rested at the bottom of the King's Sea, between two lands, as Dae had always been, and mingled now with the spirits of his first wife and youngest son, as well as with the offerings of his Tynean wife and daughter. In the end, it was more fitting. The Mother had stood by them, had allowed one of Her Chosen to sacrifice herself to protect them. The Mother had revealed Herself to him, in dreams, in waking, in the very soil and sky.

Cadogan crouched before the battered Kutan priest to meet his uncertain gaze.

"We do not always understand our gods," he said, kindly.

Ensho's upper lip tugged into a sneer. "I do not need a Leylite to lecture me on theology." His eyes darted from Cadogan to Christov. When the Lord made no move, the bewilderment was buried under another wave of hostility. "These are no true gods, if they deal with witch-lo . . ." Someone hit him across the back of the head, throwing him to hands and knees. Willem wailed and reached hesitantly to help his uncle before pain and fear drew him back, shivering.

The young Lord stepped forward then, waving his hands in placating motions before dropping to his knees to inspect the damage. The crowd backed obligingly away, eager to do the Lord's bidding. Ensho tried to push him away, was almost struck again except that the Lord shouted an angry command and the crowd drew back further.

Ensho suffered for his wounds to be inspected and to be helped to his feet. Willem screwed his eyes shut, expecting perhaps to be struck dead at the New Lord's touch, only to finally cease sobbing at the gentle hand that was laid on him. Christov held his face and examined his eyes for signs of abnormal dilation. Ensho glared at him.

"We will not submit to the Red Lord's minions," he said through gritted teeth. "Do what you will. I remain loyal to my faith."

Willem whimpered, calming only when the Lord placed his hand against his temple, cupping his head as though he were a child.

Christov glanced to Sebastian for help. Sebastian, honoured to be nominated the Lord's voice, turned to address the listening throng as much as Ensho.

"Even the Red Lord was once of the First King's Council. Whatever the truth of his revolt, the First King never sought this."

"The Red Lord was a traitor and an abomination," snapped Ensho.

"And the Leylites say he used witchkind for his own ends. That they threw him off once they understood how he had used them. How can we mortals pretend to understand the First King's thoughts?" Sebastian raised his hands beseechingly to those around him. "If once there was dissension, now the First King has sent Lords from the True World to bring an end to it. What is past, is no longer. Leylite and Arc are to be united." He glanced back at Christov, who had put out a hand to steady Willem, swaying on his feet.

Christov drew a metal tube from one pocket and spoke rapidly into it. Alien words issued from it until a woman's voice could be heard, hollow-sounding, but distinct. The young Lord spoke to her for some time, before her language changed.

"Cadogan, it's Magda. Find out if the older man has got blurry vision."

Ensho straightened up awkwardly in Cadogan's grip. "The Red Lord visits my sight with strange visions," he said darkly. He saw two or three of everything, all swimming uncertainly in front of his face.

"That is not the Red Lord," Magda told him dryly. "That is dehydration and a blow to the head, from Chris's description. You and your friend have been hurt. You both need medical attention—the boy especially. I would like you to come in for treatment. Do you understand?"

Ensho stumbled, righted himself. "No. I cannot." His voice was a harsh whisper.

"We won't hurt you. I want to help."

Ensho shook his head, an unwise move. He gasped and then: "No."

Christov reported to her in rapid and worried tones. Her tinny voice emerged from the tube once more. "Stop being such an idiot. Nothing bad will happen to you."

"Even though I am the one who killed her?"

The silence was long. Christov asked a question, the woman answered, and he stared at the injured priest in horror. Cadogan and Sebastian exchanged glances, uneasy allies now in this tense scenario.

From the tube, they could hear the drawing of a breath and then: "Where I come from, forgiveness is said to be a virtue. I'm not without sin myself, you know. If I can be forgiven, then it stands to reason that I should make the effort to forgive others. Come back to the ship with Christov. You will be healed with Arc machines, not magic. All right?"

Trembling, Ensho agreed. Christov spoke to the tube again, he and the woman exchanging several comments before the Lord put the tube away in his pocket. He gave Willem a pensive, searching look and with a final, guarded glance at Ensho, he stepped past them all to continue on his way to the grave.

Sebastian put his hand under Ensho's arm to steady him; Cadogan wrapped an arm around the boy who had tried to burn him alive. They helped the unresisting priest and his nephew to sit on the ground in the shade. Willem drew into a ball, watching anxiously, and Ensho placed a protective arm around him.

Christov stood at the foot of the metallic plaque for a long moment, reading its inscription. Then, reverently, he walked to the head of the monument, knelt and drew a knot of beads from another pocket. These he threaded through his fingers, with his eyes closed as he murmured a rhythmic prayer. At the end of it, he reached into his tunic and pulled out a chain that was strung around his neck. Hands shaking, he unfastened it and allowed the silver line to run into his palm. Attached to it was a cross, shining in the sun.

There, in the soft soil, he dug a small hole with his hand and allowed the chain and cross to pour into it.

Christov glanced up when Cadogan came to kneel beside him.

Cadogan held out his palm. Nestled in the hollow there was a seed, collected from the forest with his own hands the previous day. He looked questioningly at the healer, who motioned consent.

Gently, he dropped the seed into the soil with the chain.

"Return to the Mother, Tephee," he said, "and nourish this seed."

When Sebastian joined them, they waited patiently while he cut a lock of hair and sprinkled it over the other offerings.

"First King have mercy," he said. "And Lords protect you."

Christov brushed dirt back into the hole, pressed it down before rising unsteadily to his feet.

In silence still, they collected Ensho and Willem and returned to the sky ship.

Chapter Twenty-Five

Ensho had expected the sky castle to be more ethereal, somehow. It was astonishing, certainly; from the True World, without doubt; but the lights occasionally flickered, as though heaven kept losing its concentration, and the people he saw, although unusual, were hardly divine. Even messengers from the Red Lord should surely have held more divinity in them than this.

The giant man who had so impressed him on first sight turned out to have crumbs from a hastily dropped meal clinging to the fringes of his moustache. The greatest Lord among them was short and awkward, reminding him of a boy he had once known, who had collected insects. The boy who had left his offering of jewelry at the witch's grave was swallowing on emotion as a tear spilled over his cheek. The boy would neither look at him nor touch him.

Now Ensho and Willem were in a room with two Lords who were wounded and recovering—sleeping, now, as fragile as any normal human.

It was the witch who made him feel most uncomfortable. She prepared Arc machines in silence; brought them to his side and applied them to his bruises and abrasions without uttering a word to him. Willem, sitting on another bed with an Arc machine humming over his broken limb, kept touching his healed face in wonder.

Finally, after she placed the last machine away, she stood and stared at him.

"Did it make a difference?" At his questioning look she folded her arms. Her voice was hard. "Killing Tephee. Did it make a difference?"

"It brought the Lords out for us to see," he replied coolly, matching her glare. "They revealed themselves to us at last."

"And that was worth a life?"

"I don't yet know what it was worth. I have to understand who they are."

She looked like she might like to hit him. She held her arms tightly against herself. "She was only trying to save the others." A pause and then she walked out, leaving him with his dumbstruck nephew and the sleeping Lords.

Later, he thought he heard her arguing with someone in an unknown language. Parts of it were almost comprehensible, though the flat sound of it was unpleasant to his ears. The patients on either side of him woke up and the tearful boy came in to give them food and water. Once more, he had only a guarded glare for Ensho and this time he gave young Willem a look of suppressed horror. So, his nephew's part in that day's appalling chain of events had finally come to light. The youthful Lord said something to the others, and now they looked at them with dislike and censure.

When the tall witch returned he was almost glad to see her. She removed the machine from Willem's arm and had him flex his fingers. "Fine. You can go."

Willem bowed nervously and looked to his uncle.

Ensho stood straight and brushed down his soiled clothing. Salvaging pride, he said: "I did what I thought was right."

"How could murder be right?" She sounded angry and close to tears.

"*Aln's Pride* went down with nearly all hands," Ensho said

steadily, "because she carried witches to Marin Kuta."

A shape, small and sly, appeared in the doorway and the witch glanced at it with a sour expression. The sky ship Captain flicked a hand in a sharp, urgent gesture and she turned back.

"Not because they carried us," she said, a touch acidly, "but because they did not give us safe passage." Her nose wrinkled with distaste. She glanced back at the doorway and frowned as the Captain disappeared. Then she sighed. "Ensho, I want to forgive you, but it hurts. Tephee was my friend. Can't you at least try to be sorry you did it?"

He considered this for a long time, until at last he rubbed his thumb along his bristled jaw. "I would not have chosen to act so soon. I had not meant for there to be a burning. My nephew was overcome. The fervour of the faithful became too much. If I had been able to control them, things may have been different."

She waited for something further, but nothing ensued. Willem's face burned with shame but Ensho remained composed. She sighed and led them out of the room where several uniformed Lords took charge. They took the priest and the acolyte down many corridors where the lights were dimmed until a moving room led them to a room, thence to a floor which detached itself and then outside into the late-night air. There they were left.

Ensho tried to take his nephew's arm, but Willem glared at him and drew away.

"We have been forgiven," Willem said, "and still you defy the First King's will."

"We have not been forgiven, Willem. We are an example."

Willem shook his head and backed away. "The Red Lord uses you for his own dark purpose." Refusing to converse further, Willem returned to the crowd, head held proud and high.

With a final look back at the great Lords' castle, Ensho

walked back towards the pilgrim camp.

Leenan had joined Magda for a late supper in the mostly deserted mess hall, wanting to tell her their plans for returning home at the earliest opportunity. She hadn't expected it to turn into a quarrel.

"But . . . but I thought we'd all go together." Leenan extended a hand in entreaty towards her friend. "I don't want to leave you behind."

Magda grasped the hand and squeezed it. "You're not leaving me behind. I'm choosing to stay. There's a difference."

"In intent, maybe," Leenan retorted, her feeling of loss giving way to irrational anger, "but not in effect. You'll be here, we'll be in Tyne. I won't see you anymore." She snatched her hand back and forced a calming breath. She tried the reasonable approach. "There's nothing to stay here *for*, Maggie. You don't belong here."

"Lee, this is where I *come* from. I was born where these people were born. I lived my life on moons and satellites, in . . . in sky castles, bigger than this one. I was travelling on something like this when the accident happened and I came to this world."

"I don't care where you come from! Cadogan comes from this barbaric place, but he knows it's not his home. You belong in Tyne, with us. With your friends."

Magda only shook her head. "I don't belong . . . anywhere, Lee. I thought I did, but everything has changed." *Everything hurts.*

"Come with us . . ."

"I can't. They need me here to look after Sam and Eamon. To teach them your language. They're probably going to be stuck here . . ."

" 'Stuck' here? Is it that bad?" Leenan glared and then began to walk away. Stopped and looked back. "I'm sorry we've been such a burden to you."

"Stop this, Leenan!" Magda seized her arm to stop her from turning away again. "You've been my only friends. You, Sylvia, and Tephee were the only friends I ever made here. You are the best friends I've ever had." Five years of loneliness. In the time since she'd first met Tephee she had discovered her latent witchcraft, witnessed the Battle of Tyne, nearly lost both Tephee and Sylvia to the same appalling conflict, before heading for this hideous island and losing all of them all over again. All the others had come so close to death in the last year—in the last few *weeks*—but she had survived it all unscathed. It wasn't fair that Tephee was dead. It had been her turn.

It had been the most wonderful and the most awful period of her life. She had survived when she should not; she had tried to kill. Penance of some kind was necessary. Only then could she forgive herself.

"But I have to stay," Magda said. "There are things I have to do."

Before Leenan could argue further, a small hand on her shoulder made her look around. Sylvia patted her gently.

"Leave it go, Leenan," she said in her soft, calm voice. "She would return to Tyne if there were not bigger things here that had to be done."

"Bigger things?" Leenan glanced from one to the other in sullen curiosity.

"Magda needs to work with Captain Delouise," Sylvia continued, "to reshape Arc belief. The Captain's ideas are not very subtle, I'm afraid, and they'll need a guide to settle into this world. She is unusually suited to the task."

They were both staring at her now.

"How do you do that?" Magda asked after a stunned pause.

Sylvia smiled her placid, secret smile and said: "There's nothing magical to it. I observe, closely, and then don't report my observations until an opportune moment." The mystic's expression turned suddenly to an impish grin. "It's all in the timing."

It broke the moment. Tension vanished into laughter. When Leenan caught Magda's gaze next she grimaced wryly.

"I still wish you could come with us."

Magda nodded agreement. "Maybe one day."

Leenan turned to Sylvia. "How long would it take you to get ready? Cadogan wants to leave tomorrow, if he can. He really dislikes it here—not many good memories, I suppose."

"Actually . . ." Sylvia drew up straight to reply, "I'm not going back either."

Leenan's jaw snapped on her first response. She felt despairingly like having gained a lover, the world thought she needed to shed a few friends to make up for it. A few steady breaths and then: "Why not?"

"Magda has some plans for treatment which may speed my recovery process."

"Well, that won't take so long. A few weeks . . ."

"And I'm curious."

"You're curious." Leenan arched an eyebrow at her.

"Oh yes," Sylvia replied with a sparkle in her dark eyes. "Everyone here is so unusual. I've no doubt they come from the True World, just as Magda did, and the First King . . ."

Magda looked alarmed. "Sylvia, they're not gods . . ."

"Of course not, Maggie, any more than you and I are. But it's certain that the First King brought human life and many plants and animals here, just as the Arc Scriptures say."

"Well . . ."

"I made a hermit of myself for half my life," Sylvia expanded. "Ever since Tephee and the two of you appeared at my door and made me part of the world again, I have found it endlessly fascinating. It's an interesting place to be, don't you think?"

"Too interesting for me," Leenan admitted with a frown. "I

never meant to have all of this happen. I left Scipp to learn how to use my powers and found myself in a war for a foreign kingdom. Someone has been trying to kill me ever since I left the mainland. I don't want this anymore. It's not fascinating, or interesting. It's vile. I want to live somewhere calm and secluded and live a normal life." She stopped, her own vehemence surprising her.

"Normal?" asked Sylvia with an amused edge. It brought an answering ring of wry humour.

"Well," Leenan said, "normal for a witch and a Leylite living in the court of Tyne, anyway." She grimaced, doubting that life would ever be as uncomplicated as she hoped it would be.

She found Magda and Sylvia regarding her indulgently, Magda breaking first into laughter.

"Stop looking at me like that. I'm just happy for you. He's lovely."

"Yes," Leenan agreed with satisfaction, "he is."

Power had finally failed in the second engine, so now all reserves were directed towards the medical bay, the science stations, and the food dispensers. The mess hall itself was lit with the torches normally used for running hull repairs. Doors all over the crippled ship were jammed open with furniture. It was very dark.

It made Magda feel claustrophobic every time she left her rooms and had to walk down the dim-lit corridors to the mess hall. She wasn't sure what she would do when the last generator packed it in. She wasn't sure that Eamon and Sam would do so well without the technology required to aid their continuing recovery.

She supposed she might have to use magic again, and the thought made her feel . . . scared.

Sebastian found her sitting outside the *Albert Einstein*, leaning against one buckled strut, her face towards the sun.

"Magda?"

"Wh . . . oh. Sebastian. Hello."

"Are you looking for the shuttle?"

"No. No, it won't be back for a while yet."

Captain Delouise had insisted that Cadogan and Leenan return home in the shuttle. In the end they had left a day later than originally planned, giving time for Cadogan to draw a rough map to Jubilee. They would have to go overland from there, after they had collected Alard, Pywych, and Cadogan's horse from the Half Moon Inn. The Captain had also wanted them to make a crowd-drawing landing, though she hoped that Redmonde would show more restraint. Leenan hated fuss.

"Perhaps you should have gone with them," Sebastian said after a long moment regarding her sad expression.

Magda shook her head. "I have things to do here, first."

There was a long silence. Companionable, almost. Magda studied her hands. Sebastian studied the horizon.

"Magda . . ."

"Sebastian . . ."

"You first . . ."

"No, you . . ."

Sebastian smiled his lopsided smile. "Please, Witch Magda, after you."

Magda rose and walked a little way from the ship. "I've been thinking." Not entirely accurate. She had been sweating. Examining. Reasoning. Debating. Remembering.

Choosing.

She turned to face him again. "I could . . . I can fix that, I think." She gestured hesitantly towards his stiffened muscles. "I've looked at the readings Christov took. I'm sure I can do it. It might take a few sessions, but . . ."

"Thank you, Magda, but it's all right."

"It's not all right, Sebastian. I caused it to happen. The least I can do is . . . *un* do it." *I found out I can kill. But I can still heal. I can still choose to be who I want to be.*

"It's very kind of you, Magda, but no. Really. This is the mark the First King gave me. To remind me." He smiled kindly at her. "I may need a little reminding from time to time in my travels."

That was when she noticed the nylon backpack he had slung over his shoulder. He had a pair of sturdy boots on his feet and was dressed in ship's blacks. Someone on board had made a white over-robe for him. No designs were sewn into it yet, but a sunburst had been carefully drawn onto the right shoulder.

"You're . . . you're leaving? When?" Silly question.

"I have my purpose now. I must go forth as a messenger for the First King, to bring His command for reconciliation to all those who were not here. I have taken my leave of the Lord Captain Delouise. He has given me this." Sebastian reached under his robe for a cylinder, thicker than the usual communicator, which he wore on a chain around his neck. Magda recognised the simple recorder. She had helped to compose a message for King Armand on one just like it, though Redmonde had supplied both voice and image. Clearly Delouise and Redmonde had seen fit to put it to wider use.

"I wanted to say goodbye."

"Oh." So many goodbyes in one day. Magda was tired of them. They weighed on her like stone.

"Well." He hesitated before hefting the bag higher on his shoulder. "Goodbye then."

As he stepped away, Magda found herself reaching for him, grasping his arm. "Sebastian! I . . ." He regarded her with something between hesitation and hope. "I'm sorry," she said at last, "for everything."

That lopsided smile again, and for once she could see that

his charm was still in it.

"I'm sorry too, Magda, for all the pain this journey has brought. But I think some good may come of it in the end."

"I hope you're right."

"I'm sure it will."

"Take care, Sebastian."

"And you, Magda." His blue eyes sparkled with their old animation. "First King protect you, and the Mother guide your path."

"Lords be with you, Sebastian." At the last moment she leaned forward to kiss his worn cheek. He held a hand to her cheek for a tender moment and then was gone, limping slightly, heading for the pilgrim camp and thence . . . the world.

The noise from the inn carried distinctly through the walls, which Leenan thought would at least mask the sound of the door closing. She crept quietly out the back into the stableyard and paused for a moment, reveling in the cool air on her flushed skin.

Something leaned against her leg, and she leant down briefly to pat Alard's head. He whuffed contentedly.

The sound grew momentarily louder, indicating someone had gone into the kitchen. Leenan walked swiftly away, into the shadow of the inn, then skirted around it to the apple tree that grew alongside it.

It only took a moment to grasp the lower branches and swing herself up into the tree. Alard whined.

"Hush . . . shh . . . good boy."

She stayed very still and quiet while the someone—Thomlin Imber—peered out the back door for a moment before shaking his head, closing the door, and returning to the party.

It was very kind and flattering, Leenan supposed, that such a large and raucous party was being thrown in their honour, but she'd never much cared for crowds. After recent events she cared for them even less, and although this gathering was more friendly in intent, it was hot and loud and full of strangers and she felt like she would scream if just one more person grinned that knowing grin at her and winked at Cadogan.

It was nicer up here in the apple tree. Cool, dark, sweet smelling. Secluded.

She tilted her head back to glimpse at the night sky through the canopy of leaves. She wondered what Magda and Sylvia were doing. Maybe they were looking at the stars too, there in Marin Kuta. It gave her a sense of kinship that they might be. Saying goodbye had been even harder than she'd thought it would be. Lingering hugs and tears and promises to keep in touch. The communications tube was safely in a small bag in the apple room upstairs, along with a change of clothes and a metal cylinder Cadogan had been asked to deliver to King Armand.

She smiled thinking of Cadogan and the solemn way he'd returned Sylvia's hug goodbye. Magda had frowned sternly at him, her face stained with tears, and said: "You take good care of my friend."

He had smiled and replied: "If she lets me."

They'd laughed and hugged then. Leenan pulled a face. Where did people get this idea that she was so difficult to deal with?

Light spilled out into the back courtyard again and she held very still.

"I don't know where she went, but I wouldn't want her walking about town in the dark. Even being a witch." Thomlin.

"She's probably gone to check on the animals. Get back to your guests, Thom, I'll have a look." Cadogan. The door closed and Leenan watched his shadow move in the darkness towards the stables. He stopped at the door, head cocked as though listening, then turned and walked with a soft tread around the side of the house. He would pass beneath her in a moment . . . Lords, she liked watching him move. Like a shadow, like water, like a cat, flowing through everything.

The flow stopped directly under the apple tree and he glanced up at her.

"It's getting a bit much, isn't it?" he observed. When she sighed glumly and resumed her sky-gazing position, he nimbly levered himself onto a branch next to hers. "They mean it kindly." His own tone held an element of worn patience.

"I'm just tired of them looking at me like I'm . . . I don't know . . . like it's some public delight that we're sleeping together. Who told them that anyway?"

"I gather from young Gilly that it's obvious. She calls it 'making cow's eyes at each other.' "

Leenan snorted. "Charming."

"Well," Cadogan smiled, "I suspect I wouldn't know how to hide it if I wanted to. And I don't want to. Do you mind?"

She returned his smile then, dropping a hand down to him. He reached up and clasped it briefly then brought his feet up onto the branch under his feet. In a moment he had swung onto the upper branch with her, facing her as she leaned back, his feet braced on either side of her against the broad trunk, his hands braced on a branch above.

She laughed, knowing he was showing off, and he grinned. He steadied his balance then brought his hands down to her shoulders. She placed her hands on his thighs and leaned forward for a kiss. He obliged.

"Leenan . . ." His breath murmured hot against her mouth.

"Mmmm . . . ?"

"I know you are the Mother's witch, and I am only a lowly Leylite on a Sergeant's wage . . ."

Leenan pulled back to glare at him—*Lords, not that again!*—

only to find him with an uncertain and expectant look on his face.

". . . but will you marry me?"

The momentary silence was enough to shutter his expression, until Leenan overcame her surprise and took his face in her hands. "You don't have to marry me, Cadogan. I won't run away."

"I know I don't *have* to," he replied, resigned and a little wary.

Leenan leaned forward to rest her forehead against his; their noses touching. "Then of course I'll marry you."

He went to hug her so enthusiastically that his delicate balance was thrown off. Leenan hung onto the branch with a startled cry. Cadogan slipped sideways and had to twist suddenly to convert the near tumble into an acrobatic backflip, landing heavily but neatly on both feet on the grass beneath the tree.

Just like a cat. Leenan scrambled down after him, and after making sure there was nothing more wrong with him than a sheepish grimace, launched herself into his arms. He caught her and spun her around, kissing her as he set her down. It was not very dignified. Leenan was delighted. His self-possession was one of the things she loved, but she took delight in shaking off the layers of reserve. How perfect to find that Sergeant Cadogan Ho could be positively playful.

"We should get to bed early," he told her, resuming some of that stately dependability. "We have some long days' travel ahead of us and I'd like to make an early start."

"Yes. I suppose we should." Her fingers, inching beneath the waistband of his trousers, were making alternative suggestions. Cadogan proved to be easily persuaded.

A cool breeze was blowing from the west, lifting Magda's long hair from her shoulders and across her forehead. She lifted her face into it and for a moment imagined this same breeze having moved across the land and sea to reach her. Perhaps it had blown through Jubilee, where Leenan was tonight, before finding her here.

Magda tilted her head to look at the evening stars coming out in the indigo sky. The stars at least would be the same in Jubilee. She felt as though she could whisper hello to the constellations, and like a satellite beacon they would relay the message to Leenan, so far away.

She heard a footfall but did not need to turn to see who it was. Sylvia walked quietly to her side in the darkness, slipped a hand through the crook of her arm. Together they regarded the night sky.

"She'll be all right." Sylvia's voice hardly lifted above the breeze.

"I know she will. But I miss her already. And I miss Tephee." That pricking in her eyes again. How long would it be before she could think of Tephee without the pain?

"So do I." Sylvia raised a hand to draw Magda's attention to the marbletree in the near distance. "I don't suggest for a minute that Tephee wouldn't rather be alive, but I think she would appreciate the respect she's finally getting."

A fire glinted warmly under the tree. A small group of people were kneeling around it. When she squinted, Magda could vaguely see that they were burning offerings at the grave.

Magda found a smile at last. "Yes. She would."

Tomorrow she would bring Sam and Eamon outside and work her healer's magic for a while. She thought that Tephee, who had always enjoyed her power, would have approved of that as well.

"Sylvia?"

"Yes?"

"Thank you for staying with me."

"There's no need to thank me, Maggie. I'm happy to. I have a feeling it's going to be very interesting. Very interesting indeed."

ABOUT THE AUTHOR

Narrelle M. Harris has been writing ever since she learned how to hold a pencil—short stories, novels, plays, poems and even the occasional song. Periods of time spent living and travelling overseas have found their way into her books, and many of her friends have found themselves with cameo roles in there as well. Some have even inspired whole characters. When she is not cannibalising her life for art, she works for an international aid agency. She lives in Melbourne, Australia, with her husband Tim, a freelance journalist, and their cat Petra, who is aghast at the idea that she might be expected to earn her keep in any way. Her website is: http://www.nmharris.iwriter.com.au/ and you can contact her directly by e-mailing Narrelle at wyrdsis@bigpond.net.au.